COLD FIRE

Matt Hilton

SEVERN
HOUSE

First world edition published in Great Britain and the USA in 2023
by Severn House, an imprint of Canongate Books Ltd,
14 High Street, Edinburgh EH1 1TE.

severnhouse.com

British Library Cataloguing-in-Publication Data
A CIP catalogue record for this title is available from the British Library.

ISBN-13: 978-1-4483-1051-7 (cased)
ISBN-13: 978-1-4483-1068-5 (e-book)

All Severn House titles are printed on acid-free paper.

Typeset by Palimpsest Book Production Ltd., Falkirk, Stirlingshire, Scotland.
Printed and bound in Great Britain by TJ Books, Padstow, Cornwall.

This one is for
Louis Matthew Hilton and Evie Rose Isabella Hilton.

BEFORE . . .

During her first incarceration the finality of a slamming door usually sent a shiver of nausea through Carol Wolsey, but during her second spell it meant security, safety, a night of peace without fear.

This time her cell door didn't slam. It creaked open on steel hinges and admitted four figures, one of whom she'd lived in terror of since that other bitch caught up with her at the family trailer and had her dragged back to the correctional centre on a parole violation charge. Three of them rushed in and held Carol down on her narrow bunk. The fourth approached, a gold tooth at the front winking with each satisfied smirk. She bounced a small canister on the palm of her hand.

Carol wasn't a bad person. She was one that had made bad choices. Case in point there hadn't been a partner decent enough to stick around and help her raise their kids, so she'd turned to petty crime and prostitution to put food on the table and heroin in her veins. She had finally gone to prison for dealing, and had been, she thought, tricked into naming her supplier, on the promise of leniency in sentencing. She had been sent to the Maine Correctional Center out at Windham and, after serving a requisite four months of positive rehabilitation, had been allowed to participate in the women's reentry scheme, where the emphasis was placed on 'reducing the risks of reoffending and the increasing of positive outcomes.' Through the scheme she'd gone to the parole board and was granted early release. It took her only days before she was back to her old tricks – out of necessity, of course, because she wasn't a bad person.

Carol's original testimony had helped reduce her sentence, but it had also helped convict a truly bad woman.

Unlike Carol had, this woman had not been given an easy ride through minimum-security custody or programs designed with gender-responsive principles in mind. She'd gone direct to gen pop and had soon established herself as the apex predator, who even some of the toughest and longest serving cons obeyed. She had put an unfulfilled hit on Carol Wolsey, who after snitching on her, even had the temerity to try and pick up the slack from her drug supply operation while out on parole.

Snitches get stitches was a mantra of criminal types, but this woman preferred another pithy saying: if you play with fire, you'll get burned.

Liquid jetted from the canister, soaking Carol's hair and face. It stank, the fumes searing her nostrils and her mind. The lights went out, making the single flame so bright that Carol screamed in terror before it was brought anywhere near her.

ONE

Even at the busiest of times Belchertown Police Department was not a hub of activity, and today was no different, with few people in earshot. But this was a personal telephone call and Detective Karen Ratcliffe had no intention of sharing its contents with the few colleagues that might overhear. She stepped outside. Snowflakes swirled around, sharp and icy where they touched her exposed skin. She ignored the discomfort. Somebody once had the great idea of constructing a skate park behind the police building; ordinarily the air would be filled with the high rattle of skateboard wheels, the clack of boards on concrete and the laughter of kids, but the cold spell had put paid to children having fun there for now. Ratcliffe took a walk across the expanse of buried asphalt that formed the station's parking lot, and stepped on the lawn at its edge. Yesterday's snow had frozen, the fresh layer on top made slipping and falling a firm probability. She trod down hard and her feet sank to the ankles through the icy crust into the snow. Her toes felt instantly frozen.

'It has been a while,' she said into her phone, while trying to stop her teeth from chattering, 'I wasn't sure you'd recall my name and where we'd met.'

'Under those circumstances, it should be no surprise that your name's indelibly written in my memory,' Tess Grey assured her.

'Yeah. I dined out for free on that story. At least I did until all the restaurants were ordered shut during the pandemic. You're probably wondering why I asked you to get in touch?'

'Well, I assumed that this is not an official call, otherwise you'd probably have contacted me via the office.'

Tess Grey subcontracted to a specialist inquiry firm attached to the Portland, Maine district attorney's office. 'I got your personal email address off the business card you gave me; it has been sitting in the back of my purse all this time. You were mainly doing genealogy work back then, but had recently crossed over into private investigations. I hoped it was a career move you'd followed, as it's something you seemed good at. Before contacting you I did some Googling; you've built an impressive resume in the last few years, Tess.'

'I've had help.'

'I remember. Are you and Nicolas Villere still partners?'

'In more ways than one.'

'Aah, so you're—'

'We're engaged to marry, if and when we get the opportunity. Now's not a good time to try planning *anything*.'

'Yeah, it's difficult.' Neither of them expounded on why organizing their respective lives was currently challenging. 'How's about Jerome Leclerc, your friend from down south, did he get over his injuries?'

'Pinky's hale and hearty and larger than life. Oh, and since last we spoke, he has moved here to Maine and taken over my apartment.'

'I'm happy to hear that. He was a good guy . . .'

'Despite what you might have learned about him afterwards, Pinky *is* a good guy. He's one of the best. And even better, he's given up his old ways, so you needn't concern yourself about having divided loyalties around him.'

Ratcliffe understood where it was best not to push a subject, and besides she was happy that Tess's assertion that Pinky had left behind his criminal lifestyle was the absolute truth. Had he not, would she still have asked for Tess and her friends to help? Yes, absolutely she would've.

'I'd like to hire you guys,' she said.

'Hire us?'

'Specifically you, but the way you just spoke about those guys I assume y'all come as a package deal.'

'I guess you could say that.' Tess chuckled at the idea, but her voice then lowered an octave, as she grew more serious. 'Karen, you're a police detective, why'd you need to hire me?'

'Not all problems can be solved by the police, Tess.'

'I guess not. So what is it that you want help with?'

Ratcliffe paused to check over her shoulder towards the police station. A uniformed patrolman called Henry Beets stood in the open door, flapping a hand to catch her attention. Ratcliffe gestured in reply, reassuring him she'd be back inside in one minute. She turned her back on him, but cupped the phone closer to her mouth, talking quieter. The snowfall deadened sound, but she didn't want to chance him overhearing. 'I've a sister . . . Joanne, and I need you to find her.'

'You've probably more resources than I have, why not—' Tess stopped mid flow. She was astute; she'd figured there was a reason why Ratcliffe couldn't conduct an official search for her missing sister. 'Conflict of interests?'

'Yes. Trying to help her might compromise my position within law enforcement.'

'She's done something illegal?'

'Allegedly. We're all innocent until proven guilty, right?'

'By your tone of voice it sounds as if she's already been convicted and the key thrown away.'

'It's worse than that, Tess, for what Jo has been accused she could face the death penalty.'

'They still have capital punishment over in Massachusetts?'

'Not since the early eighties,' Ratcliffe said, 'but for Jo they might make an exception.'

She caught her breath. She was exaggerating. Massachusetts had abolished the death penalty in 1984, and even after Dzhokhar Tsarnaev, the surviving Boston Marathon bomber, was sentenced to death the US Court of Appeals for the First Circuit later vacated his sentence. Her sister's alleged crime was heinous, but not on the scale of conducting a fatal bombing attack. 'Sometimes a death penalty can be carried out before there's a trial. I'd hate to see my sister gunned down before she's given an opportunity to prove her innocence.'

'What has she supposedly done?'

'You haven't been following the news?'

'I've been . . . distracted,' Tess said.

'Jo's the nanny alleged to have murdered those children. Death penalty or not, there are people all across the world would happily form a lynch mob and string her up from the nearest tree.'

Tess's silence could mean something else, but Ratcliffe feared the private investigator couldn't see beyond the alleged murders and was determining the best way in which to turn her down.

Tess surprised her. 'You weren't judgmental about Po's past or of our friend Pinky's, I'll return the favor and not prejudge your sister.'

'Tess, if I thought for one second that she was guilty of murdering those little ones I'd be at the head of the screaming mob demanding her death.'

Henry Beets was back outside again, this time tramping over the expanse of white enshrouding the parking lot. His big boot tracks seemed massive beside her daintier ones. Ratcliffe hunched over her phone. 'Tess, I must go for now, but can I have an answer one way or another.'

'I'll need some time.'

'I'd rather—'

'I mean to familiarize myself with the facts, it's like I said, I've been distracted lately. My answer's yes, I'll help, but it comes with a caveat; if I discover she is responsible for murdering those children I'll personally drag her to a gibbet.'

TWO

Tess ended the call and set her phone aside.

It was cold enough for a hat and gloves, but she'd momentarily forgone them while seated at a table overlooking Back Cove; it was difficult using a touch phone while wearing mittens. She sipped coffee, finding that it was still warm and very appreciated. It dispelled some of the chill but not the wedge of ice that'd inserted itself in her heart when hearing who Detective Ratcliffe wanted her to help find. Despite saying she wouldn't prejudge Joanne – or 'Jo' as Ratcliffe had repeatedly referred to her sister – it had been difficult, and a lie, because like most others who had seen the news reports, she'd already judged Joanne Mason a monster for what she did to those children.

'*Allegedly* did to those children,' Tess said aloud.

She checked around, ensuring she hadn't been overheard. She hadn't. For the moment she was the only one hardy, or foolish, enough to brave the cold while eating lunch. Sitting outside had not entirely been her decision. Her partner, Nicolas 'Po' Villere, stood about twenty yards distant, feeding his nicotine habit. The blue smoke from his cigarette formed horizontal striations in the crisp air. He'd wandered away to spare her from breathing his secondhand smoke. His food went untouched for now. If he didn't return soon she might liberate some of those sour pickle spears off his plate.

They'd both ordered Maine Italian sandwiches; sub rolls piled high with ham, peppers, American cheese, tomatoes, onion, green olives and said pickles. Ordinarily Tess wouldn't attempt eating a sandwich so large, but she was ravenous and if Po wasn't careful she might make a start on his sandwich too before he was finished smoking. She reached for her sandwich. She aimed it at her mouth, but didn't bite. She set it down again. Unconsciously she lowered her hand and caressed her belly, barely able to feel it through her insulated parka. It wasn't her that could gorge on two sandwiches; she'd a tiny passenger craving nourishment too. She'd entered the second trimester of her pregnancy, and although the fetus was now as big as an avocado, it wasn't showing much; not unless she counted the few extra pounds she'd added to her breasts lately. Maybe she should have mentioned her condition to Ratcliffe, because it could cause her to do more than prejudge somebody capable of murdering babies.

Po approached. He was a Southerner by birth, but had lived in Portland long enough that the Maine winters didn't trouble him much. But even Po blew into his cupped hands, then rubbed them furiously together. 'You want to go inside, Tess? I'll grab our lunch and—'

She batted aside his offer and aimed a nod at the empty seat opposite. 'Sit down, Po. There's a job I've agreed to and I'm unsure if it's something you want to get involved in.'

'Y'know I have your back, Tess. What's up?' He sat, and after a moment dragged his plate towards him. He didn't pick up the sandwich. 'This job got to do with . . . whaddaya call her, the cop?'

He knew about the request made by Ratcliffe for Tess to make contact, but was offering her an easy route into what was obviously going to be a troubling conversation. 'Detective Ratcliffe asked me to help her locate and bring in a fugitive, the twist being that the fugitive is her sister Joanne.'

Po shrugged and exhaled. He wore a black leather motorcycle jacket, the collarless type, with contrasting colored stripes down one sleeve. Ordinarily she enjoyed the aroma of warm leather and tobacco emanating from him, but today the leather was cold and stiff and the only scent she caught was from his caustic exhalation. She averted her face; she used to smoke, now she didn't, but it was her pregnancy that had given her a deeper aversion to the habit. After lunch Po would have to pop a breath mint before they returned to the confines of his car. 'Sorry, Tess, it smells that bad to you, huh?'

'I'm overreacting,' she admitted. 'Ignore me.'

'Kinda difficult to do that when you screw up your face and wretch.'

'Yeah, it's definitely an overreaction. Hopefully you don't react as dramatically after I tell you who Ratcliffe's sister is.'

Po eyed her steadily.

'All right, so you're not known for losing your sense of proportion,' she teased, 'but you might want to steel yourself.'

'Is she someone famous?'

'Infamous. You've seen the news lately, right?'

'Sure I have.'

'What do you make of the nanny who supposedly killed their mother and the children in her care?'

'You say supposedly, but the evidence is stacked against her. You tellin' me that Ratcliffe's sister is this Angel of Death character?'

'Yes.'

Po's right eyebrow rose and fell.

'I guess I kinda blew the surprise, huh?' said Tess.

'Nothin' people do to each other surprises me any more,' he said. 'But I must admit, those that hurt children are the worst of the worst in my estimation.'

'So you don't think you want to help her?'

'We're helpin' her? I thought Ratcliffe asked you to help bring in a fugitive.'

'Detective Ratcliffe isn't fully convinced of her sister's guilt. Can't say I am either, not after giving it some more thought. It's too convenient that the missing nanny was assumed guilty of the murders, right?'

'There was that case years ago where the British au pair was accused of shakin' a baby and killin' it. She was found guilty.'

'She was found guilty of involuntary manslaughter; Joanne Mason's been accused of multiple cold-blooded murders.'

'I can put aside my personal feelings till we find out if she's a monster or not' – Po nodded at where the table hid her marginally swollen belly – 'but are you sure you can . . . considering?'

'There were difficult cases where I had to remain neutral when I was a cop, I compartmentalized my feelings, and I'll do it again: being pregnant shouldn't affect my judgment. Besides, what if she is innocent?'

Po didn't answer.

Tess said, 'More importantly, are you going to eat those pickles?'

THREE

She forced the door closed and immediately snapped the security chain in its holder. Placing her back to the door she stood a moment, trying to regain her composure after dashing the final few yards in panic. She had heard voices, the scuff of shoes on asphalt and had feared that she was about to be pounced upon. She'd almost dropped the old-fashioned key on its oversized fob before she got the door unlocked and lurched inside her motel room. Outside, the footsteps continued, along with the low murmur of conversation. They dwindled. Apparently she was not the object of a trap, or if she were then she'd derailed it for a minute or two more. She listened a while longer, then crept to the single window and peeked between the vertical blinds. She could still hear distant voices, but there was nobody in sight.

Joanne Mason darted across her room to the bathroom: the only place where somebody could lurk out of sight. Nobody was there. She checked her room, trying to spot if anyone had snuck inside while she was out and if the place had been surreptitiously searched. She feared also that tiny cameras and listening devices could have been hidden inside sprinkler heads, smoke alarms or even the light switches on the walls. If a team had fitted any covert surveillance equipment in her room they were damn good at their craft, as they had managed to conceal the tech without disturbing the ratty, disheveled room. The light switch for the bathroom still hung partly off the wall, a screw missing, as it had when she first rented the hovel. Dust clung to the spiderwebs on the lampshade at the centre of the ceiling. The webs themselves, thickened and balled up in spots, caused shadows to be cast about, patterns missing from the uninspired cream paint on the walls. On second study, the walls weren't painted cream, maybe once they'd been nearer white, but the thousands of cigarettes smoked inside over the years had soured the paintwork. Joanne thought that the most recent tenant had probably smoked a thousand cigarettes judging by the smell that clung to everything. The dated wooden furniture felt tacky.

Next she opened the single closet and saw her meager belong-ings were untouched. She sorted through them nonetheless, ensuring no tracking devices had been slipped into her bag. She was being overly paranoid: anyone pursuing her wouldn't waste time with elaborate surveillance, they'd strike the instant they had eyes on her and she would be arrested or killed, depending on who found her first. She sat on the bed, the coverlet feeling as imbued with cigarette tar as everything else, and placed her face in her hands. It would have been easy to weep, to fall into despair, but she couldn't allow even a minute of weakness. Instead of crying, she cursed vehemently into her cupped hands. Her situation was crappy and it could only get worse.

She needed help, but it was a rare commodity.

Besides, whom could she turn to when even the person closest to her in the entire world couldn't help? Worse, her big sister might not want to help. Karen was in the untenable position of being a homicide detective and reaching out to her would engender a response that was impossible for Joanne to follow. Karen would do one of two things: she'd arrest her or she'd order her to give herself up and allow justice to follow its course. Whichever way she looked at her problem, Joanne couldn't see how the murderer of a young mother and her three babies would ever get a fair trial. Supposedly a jury was meant to be unbiased, but where would they find a dozen folk that wouldn't despise her the second they laid eyes on her? They would deem her no less guilty than if they'd witnessed her washing the victims' blood from her hands.

She flopped back on the bed. It creaked beneath her. Her heart beat a wild rhythm, felt within her throat and ears. The ceiling was no less tarnished than the walls. Joanne closed her eyes and allowed her anxiety to escape in a low wail that wouldn't travel beyond her room. To her, the moan sounded far too loud and might draw her hunters there. She sat up, clutching handfuls of the grimy bedding. She stared at the door, expecting somebody to burst inside. Even the footsteps and voices from before had diminished, but her pursuers might be approaching with stealth. She pushed up to her feet and returned to the window, again peeking out through chinks in the blinds. On edge, about to explode, anyone would think she deserved the turmoil and fear, because it would be slight compared to what her victims had endured as they were struck time and again with the claw end of a hammer.

Nobody was in sight. Voices were indistinct murmurs. Even the traffic noise sounded muted. And within her room, the walls closed in around her, squeezing the breath from her lungs. Joanne croaked in dismay. She couldn't stay in the room another minute. Thankfully she was disguised and her belongings were few. She grabbed her bag from the closet and returned to the door. She drew it open, took a brief check outside, then dashed for where she had parked her car, out of sight of the motel office and from traffic passing on the highway. The car had gotten her this far from Massachusetts. She had first planned on abandoning it in the motel lot and to use public transportation to move on somewhere far away, but paranoia had clutched her in its stranglehold, and her only hope of shaking it off was to put distance between her and the horrible motel room as quickly as possible.

The car wasn't hers. She'd found it unattended, with its keys in the ignition and had taken it. It was nothing special, not something she'd write home about. It was fourteen years old, an old gas-guzzler, but had proven to be a sturdy old workhorse and had never failed to start when turning the ignition key. Even as strung out as her nerves were, her fingers refused to shake as she turned the key and the engine sputtered to life. She had to manually turn on the lights and the old car came with a stick shift. She had her hands full as she maneuvered out of the motel lot and sat waiting at the side of the highway to find a gap in which to enter the fast-moving traffic.

Anxiously, she expected the manager to come running out of his office, to chase after her for failing to return the room key and its ridiculous fob, but how could he suspect she was fleeing when she'd paid for a week's accommodation up front? After winding down the window, she delved in her pockets, found the stupid key and dropped it on the road. If some homeless dude found it and gained access to the room and stayed there free of charge, so be it. If the key was quickly returned to the manager he could assume she'd dropped it accidentally; he wouldn't know she had fled until after she failed to return that evening, maybe not even before morning. She'd no fear of him growing suspicious about her sudden disappearance, not enough for him to put two and two together and realize she was a fugitive from justice; should he guess she'd ran away, he'd probably pocket the cash she'd paid for the worst room she'd ever rented and sell it again to another desperate resident.

She caught a break and pulled out, following in the slipstream of a truck headed for the turnpike that would take her across the state border from New Hampshire into Maine. It was several days since she had fled West Roxbury, an upmarket district of Boston, and made it almost to Portsmouth. Ordinarily a journey of that distance, even in her old car, should've taken no longer than an hour and a half. Sticking to the slow rate she'd set, it would take her another week to reach Portland, Maine, and a month beyond before reaching the Canadian border at Houlton. A treaty of extradition existed between Canada and the USA, but Joanne hoped that she could lose herself north of the border. The manhunt currently underway for her was hottest around Boston. She hoped that up in New Brunswick or Quebec territories, wherever her flight stalled, her assumed identity would hold for longer, at least until she could think and plan for a more permanent move.

She had waited, thinking that to dash for the border would be expected of her, but that was under the misapprehension that the manhunt would cool down as news of fresh atrocities overtook the murders of the young family. Now she realized that by stalling, all she had done was encourage her pursuers to sniff out her trail and to grab her before she'd completed even half of her journey. She put her foot down, urging the car to speed up. Not too fast, though. She stuck to just below the speed limit, tucked in behind the truck as it rolled northeast, in an attempt at attracting as little notice as possible. It was cold, the skies were clear, but further up in Maine the same cold front that had already dumped feet of snow on western Massachusetts and Vermont was moving in. Before reaching the border, she'd probably be driving through a blizzard. The thought pleased her, the blizzard would help hide her, and the Canadian Border Services agent would probably wave her through without leaving the warmth of their cubicle.

She by-passed Portland, and continued towards Bangor before the urge to visit a bathroom overtook her. She held on to the discomfort in her bladder. A good distance after Bangor she got off the highway on to a country road and pulled in at the next gas station. The air was frigid as she left the warm confines of her car, so she felt justified in pulling down her woolen hat and tightening a scarf around her features from the bridge of her nose down. She also turned up her collar. It would take the most sophisticated of facial recognition technology to identify her from what little of her face showed and she doubted the CCTV camera drooping off the wall of the gas station was up to scratch. Fooling an observant human being could prove more difficult. Fortunately, the country was coming out the back end of a pandemic, where it was still the norm for some fearful people to conceal their faces under surgical masks or knitted scarves like hers, so she wouldn't raise too much suspicion by keeping her face covered.

A polite notice instructed her to request the key to the washroom inside the adjoining convenience store. She'd been out shopping for provisions before paranoia had her fleeing her motel room. Thankfully she had not unloaded her foodstuff from the trunk of the car, so she was stocked up for a few days. However, she required more convenient snacks that she could eat whilst driving. It wouldn't be a bad idea to gas up either, as the gauge showed that the old car had drank half its fuel already, and she still had a-ways to go before reaching the border. She entered the shop, heard the electronic ding of a bell, and saw the clerk eye her from beyond Plexiglass. She nodded and raised a hand in greeting and immediately turned away to start rummaging at a counter stacked with candy bars and other treats. When she glanced back at him, the clerk showed her no more attention, more concerned as he was with fitting a fresh receipt roll in the cash register. Joanne chose several different sweet snacks and a cold bottle of spring water from a cooler and approached the counter.

'Do you need gasoline, ma'am?'

The gas station ran on a pay-first pump-second system. 'Forty dollars' worth,' Joanne replied and was surprised by the volume of her own voice: it was the first time she'd spoken directly with anyone since fleeing West Roxbury.

The clerk probably knew the makes and models of cars, so didn't ask the type of fuel she required. He dabbed at the buttons on the cash register and then craned to see what snacks she held. The Plexiglass screen was a holdover from when people stringently avoided breathing each other's germs. At its base was a narrow slot through which the clerk shoved a barcode reader, and complying with the unspoken instruction, Joanne held out each of her purchases until she heard corresponding beeps. She paid cash, to the clerk's slight perturbation, but there was nothing else for it. She had several items that identified her as Jo-Beth Sugden, but when stealing them she hadn't also taken Sugden's debit or credit cards. No way could she use her actual cards otherwise the police would be on to her trail within minutes.

'I also need to use your bathroom,' Joanne told the clerk.

He passed a key on a large fob through the slot. Immediately he squeezed sanitizer on his fingers and wrung his hands together. Joanne wondered what it was with keys and oversized fobs around these parts. 'Do you pump the gas or is it self-service?'

'I can do it for you, ma'am. Not as if I'm rushed off my feet, no how.'

'Thank you, I'm almost cross-legged. Keys are in the ignition.' She hurried out, carrying her purchases and the bathroom key, and dumped the former on the passenger seat of her car. As she headed for the bathroom, the clerk hobbled outside on what were obviously prosthetic legs. Joanne stared a second or two longer than was polite, causing him to stare back. While jostling with her purchases her scarf had slipped and he got a good look at her features, and she thought recognition exploded behind his eyes. She averted her face, rushed for the bathroom, terrified to look back at him in case he'd left the gas pump in its holder and gone inside to call the cops.

The bathroom was an addition added to the original convenience store, more or less a wooden box tacked on almost like an afterthought. She could probably throw her meager weight against a wall and the entire thing would collapse. She unlocked the door and pushed inside, immediately slipping the bolt in its retainer. Rather than go to the toilet, she rushed across the small room and laid her ear to the adjoining wall. There was no hint of a telephone conversation from beyond the wall. Then again, the clerk could have been whispering to avoid alerting her. There was a small window high up near the ceiling. Joanne clambered up on the toilet bowl, balancing awkwardly as she craned to peer outside. Her vantage offered little view of the clerk, but the angle of weak sunlight was enough to spot his wavering shadow. From what she could tell from the faint shadow, the clerk was busy filling up her tank. She exhaled and stepped down from the bowl, feeling jittery. Quickly she urinated and washed her hands; there was no automatic hand dryer, and under no circumstances would she ever use the grungy cotton towel hanging limp on a roller. She ran her palms over her thighs, slid open the bolt and stepped outside. She paused to pull up her scarf and settle the brim of her hat lower. Again the cold assailed her and she shivered. The quaking went right down to her bones and chattered her teeth; it had little to do with the temperature, more to do with adrenalin.

The clerk nodded to show he'd done as asked and the car was ready to go. If he'd been insulted by the way she'd stared at his false legs, then he didn't mention it. Instead, he thumbed at the kiosk, said, 'I could only fit thirty-five bucks' worth in your tank. If you'd paid by card I coulda—'

'Take the five dollars and my thanks for helping me out.'

'Was no problem,' he said. 'Say, d'you have a long journey ahead of you? Reason I ask is there's some bad weather forecast upstate.'

'So I heard,' she said. 'But I'm not going far.'

'Say, are you from Lincoln or from nearer abouts? It's just I thought I recognized you from someplace.'

An icy worm burrowed through her gut. 'I'm from Concord, over in Vermont. It's my first time here in Maine, so no, you must be mistaken.'

He nodded at her wisdom. 'You're right; I see so many faces passing through they all begin blending into one. If I stand around long enough I'll probably spot myself limping past.'

While he chattered his inanities, she ducked inside the car and got settled. She was relieved again when the engine turned first time. The clerk tapped on the roof of the car. 'Be seeing you, ma'am.'

Jo pulled away, and back on to the highway. 'Not if I see you first,' she said.

FOUR

Tess pushed away from her computer and stood. She wandered through the house from the converted bedroom office and into the open plan family room. Po had gone out on an errand without turning off the TV; it was tuned to one of the major syndicated news channels.

In the adjoining kitchen she poured coffee into a cup and turned towards the large screen TV. The latest piece on the 'Angel of Death' had ended, but the news was on a loop and would be repeated again within minutes. She had already caught an earlier bulletin but there'd been nothing new to report. Footage of police patrol cars and even of patrol officers with dogs on leashes was used to highlight how vigorously law enforcement were searching for the murder suspect. It was a total fantasy, as three days after fleeing the scene Joanne was probably many miles away and Boston's finest dog handlers wouldn't be chasing her down on foot. The footage aired was either seventy-two hours old or had been filmed at an entirely different crime scene.

A posse of officers like this rarely apprehended fugitives; usually their task was to find and secure evidence in order to prosecute said fugitive when they were later captured. Often an arrest followed when the fugitive made a mistake, got sloppy and lowered their vigilance. Mostly law enforcement were tipped off by a confidant the fugitive had made the mistake of trusting. From what she could gather from the brief discussion with Detective Ratcliffe earlier, Joanne was still to turn to her sister for help. That situation, Tess felt, would come to pass; it was just a question of when.

Ratcliffe was yet to get back in touch. Earlier the detective had been on duty with barely time to talk. Tess had given her space and very little intrusion, sending only a brief text message requesting Ratcliffe call her as soon as appropriate. In the meantime she hadn't sat on her thumbs. She'd checked the websites of various news outlets, getting a rounder, but incomplete, picture of what had occurred down in the affluent Boston neighborhood of West Roxbury. As was often the case, investigators were keeping much of the pertinent information to themselves, so the news articles tended towards supposition. What could be disputed was that they'd gotten it wrong when it came to the number of fatalities involved, the police having since confirmed that five victims were found at the scene: they hadn't released full details on the fifth victim yet, but some of the reporters had speculated on the manner of death, some said by knife, others a hammer, while one reported the cause of death as a broken neck. That was how rumors began, twisting the facts, and could sometimes taint even the minds of the investigators. Before she'd been given a chance to plead, Joanne had been named, and from there had quickly morphed into the prime suspect, a heinous murderer, and an angel of death: a devil. Cold-blooded infanticide was one of the worst crimes imaginable to most, and rightly so. Unconsciously Tess placed her free hand protectively over her belly. She sipped coffee again, but it suddenly tasted bitter and she set it down on the counter. She wandered into the family room, never taking her gaze off the TV.

The story had returned to West Roxbury where there was breaking news. A media helicopter hung in the air above a large house surrounded by snow-covered but normally lush gardens. The exclusive property boasted outbuildings, a swimming pool and a tennis court. It was the crime scene where the murdered family had been discovered, but instead of concentrating its cameras on the house, the chopper was now hovering at the boundary of the grounds and the camera zoomed in to try to gain a clearer picture of what was going on beneath the canopy of snow-laden branches. Several men and women huddled at one side, conversing, whereas another few stood nearer the base of a large tree. Something lay on the ground at the foot of the trunk, currently swathed in a blanket of snow, but the camera was sharp enough to pick out folds of clothing and a booted foot poking out. Apparently the murderer's tally had gone up by one more victim; Tess bit down on her bottom lip, wondering where it was going to end. If Joanne was responsible for six deaths, where three of the victims were adults, then she was more dangerous than the pathetic creature the media had initially painted her. Second and third thoughts assailed Tess about getting involved while in her current state.

'You're pregnant, Tess, you're not frickin' dying,' she said aloud.

Oddly enough, now into her second trimester, she felt more human than she had during the first. She supposed it was down to hormonal changes, but she didn't feel as tired or nauseated as before, the need to urinate wasn't continuous and even the tenderness in her breasts had abated, despite them growing larger and feeling heavier. Craving certain foods – she'd earlier snarfed down Po's pickle whether he'd wanted it or not – and being a tad unfocussed was a tiny price to pay by comparison. She felt slightly fatigued, but otherwise wasn't hindered by the few extra pounds she'd gained, and felt capable of handling the rigors of the case ahead. It was her moral compass that was having difficulty aligning with the job. She thought that when Ratcliffe got around to calling her back, she might politely decline any further involvement.

'Yeah, right! Who are you kidding, Tess?'

If ever she was going to turn down Ratcliffe's plea for help it would have been at the moment the detective revealed its nature.

Her cellphone rang in her office. She'd left it charging while she had recharged on caffeine. She went with no haste, carrying her almost empty mug with her. She knew without looking at the name displayed on the screen that it was not Detective Ratcliffe calling. The ringtone had been chosen to alert her to calls from Po.

'Hi, lover, what's up?' she asked and took a final slurp of coffee.

There was a pause, a gathering of breath before Po said, 'Do you have the news on?'

'Yeah, I just saw that another victim has been discovered at—'

'I'm not talking about *your* case, Tess; switch to a local channel.'

'What is it, Po, what's wrong?'

'Take a look and I'll tell you all I know after.'

A worm of unease squirmed through her gut. As she grabbed the TV remote and flipped channels, her discomfort grew from worm-sized to anaconda. She settled on a local news channel and felt as if that giant snake was squeezing the air out of her lungs. The main feature on screen showed a building spewing smoke, with fire crews battling to halt the blaze from spreading to adjoining properties.

'Is that Bar-Lesque?' she squeaked in dismay. Her question was rhetorical; she'd instantly recognized the building despite it being wreathed in smoke.

'That ain't all,' Po said. 'Charley's was also hit an' has gone up in flames.'

He meant Charley's Autoshop, where he worked occasionally

and where Tess had first met him. Head mechanic and manager
Charley had his name over the door, but Po was the owner of the
business, as he was with Bar-Lesque after turning it from a former
seedy strip joint into a bar/diner.

'What's this about, Po?'

'Couldn't say. But it doesn't take a detective to figure out that
I'm the target.'

'Yeah, fires at two of your businesses on the same day can't be
coincidental.'

'There's no official word yet on Bar-Lesque, but it seems that
the fire at Charley's was fueled by accelerants.'

'Yeah, but in a garage isn't that to be expected?'

'Fire chief said the way the fire spread, looks as if somebody
was inside and threw some gas around. He thought that some kids
out for their kicks maybe snuck in, got their hands on the jerry
cans we hold and decided to burn down the place. If this was an
isolated incident I might've agreed, but with Bar-Lesque goin' up
too . . .'

'Wasn't stupid kids,' she said.

'Nope. With the fire at the diner, the chief's opinion has also
swayed, and he's been givin' me the stink eye ever since. For all
intents and purposes, it looks like an inside job, right? As if maybe
I'm hopin' to cash in on the insurance.'

'Are you?'

'You know me better than that.'

'I believe you. So he knows you own both businesses?'

'I told him that I do.'

'How many other people know? It's not as if it's common
knowledge.'

'I've tried keepin' my involvement outta the public eye, but this
is Portland, Tess. It's a small town and people know each other
and often each other's secrets. Besides, since we partnered up,
I've ensured my business dealings are all aboveboard and legal.
Anyone with a mind to do it coulda gone into the town hall and
checked the records and gotten everythin' they needed on me.'

'That sounds like a stretch.'

'I know, I'm just sayin'. Point is, I'm not as invisible as I once
was, and it has left me open to repercussions. It's also put you in
the firin' line and that worries me most.'

'You know I can look after myself.'

'Ordinarily I wouldn't be as concerned, but we've got Junior to think about.'

She tapped her belly. 'Junior's safe and sound.'

'Yeah, and if anyone even thinks about harmin' either of you, they'll be sorry.'

'Po,' she said, 'promise me you won't go off on a rampage before we even know the truth. Accidents happen, and fires start all the time. It *could* be a coincidence.'

'Yeah, and I *could* be the next king of England.'

FIVE

The auto repair shop was toast. Literally. Although the equipment within was modern and mostly top of the range, the building that housed the workshop was old and the flames had fed hungrily on the walls and ceiling joists, bringing down the roof in an avalanche of flaming debris and smoke. Tess had often cautioned that the cavernous workspace was impregnated with oil and gasoline, a tinderbox ready to go up if Po was ever careless when discarding a cigarette butt or match; she'd been kidding, but now he had to concede the point. The repair shop, the equipment and tools and even the vehicles being worked on inside were replaceable. The loss would have been more painful if Charley or any of their crew had been working when the blaze took hold: thankfully the shop had been locked up for the weekend. The firefighters still had to check for any fatalities in the smoking debris, because, locked or not, the consensus was somebody had gotten inside to splash accelerant around, and it was not unknown for arsonists to be overwhelmed and consumed by the very fires they set. Firefighters poked through the collapsed building with axes and pry bars. For a second Po worried that the sudden cold snap had forced a desperate homeless person to seek shelter, and it was they that had inadvertently set the place alight. No, it had to be somebody that'd come prepared with the tools necessary to force an entry: nobody had gotten inside through a poorly secured door or window.

Po had answered the battalion chief's questions, been open and truthful in his replies, except for when the chief asked if he had any rivals that might be responsible for the fires. For starters, he would take up too much of the chief's precious time by listing his potential adversaries.

'Nobody I could point a finger at,' he lied, although his mind was already ticking through a bunch of people that might've chosen to make him an adversary.

Because of the deliberate nature of the fire, the police had already attended the scene. Po had given a brief statement to an officer who continuously shivered despite the warmth emanating from the smoldering ruin and it took a moment for it to strike Po that the cop was quaking in his presence. It was no secret that Po had served time in Louisiana State Penitentiary, but his reputation was not simply built on having killed his father's murderer, but on his involvement in several super violent incidents after pairing up with Tess Grey. He'd attained an almost fearsome reputation despite all his actions being directed at bad guys. There were some cops that feared him, some that despised him, but most secretly applauded him. Po couldn't say if this young officer's reaction was through fear, or through hero worship, but he suspected the latter.

Deciding that there was currently nothing more he could do there, Po rang Charley at home. Surprisingly, despite having an aversion to speaking on telephones, Charley answered. Po gave the mechanic the bad news; the old man was mortified. He was approaching seventy-eight years old and should've retired years ago, but he had refused to bow out. The autoshop had been his second home for decades, for many moons even before the business came into Po's ownership, and he couldn't foresee a future in which it didn't feature. Po suspected that Charley planned on simply keeling over one day at work, and dying happy with a smile on his face and a wrench clutched in his hand. The old man had already left instructions to roll his corpse into the inspection pit where it'd serve as his grave. Now – as whimsical as his funeral plan was – it was done with. He tried to control his emotions, but couldn't. Po had never heard the old mechanic as upset, certainly not openly weeping. If Po were pissed before about the attack on his business property, it angered him more the impact it would have on those that relied on the work, both for their wage and also the camaraderie. A childless widower, Charley had nobody waiting for him at home, his personal interactions all took place coming to, going from or while at the autoshop.

'We'll rebuild,' Po promised. 'We'll get set up again in no time.'

'It won't be the same. It *can't* be.'

Po knew he was right.

He told Charley about Bar-Lesque.

'Holy crap, Po, what's this about?'

'Wish I knew, Charley. I wish I knew.'

The old man's voice frosted over. 'You make it your mission

to find out who's responsible, and when you do, you make the sons a' bitches pay.'

'I don't need tellin' twice,' Po assured him.

He drove to Bar-Lesque in his vintage muscle car. Po had several cool vehicles at his disposal, but his 1968 Ford Mustang was his favorite. The make of car was not as rare as what the general public might think, because 1968 had been a good year for turning out more than 317,000 Mustangs. Many collectors of classic cars favor Mustangs, but it'd be fair to say that Po's was unique. If the mysterious arsonist attacked his car, it would be a more personal attack on him than on either of the bricks-and-mortar structures that had been burned to date. He considered putting the car into temporary secure lock-up until he got to the bottom of who had targeted him, and why.

'The hell I will,' he proclaimed aloud.

Collectible Ford Mustangs changed hands at around the $70,000 mark. Po's, with all of its modifications, couldn't be replaced for any less than twice that figure. It wasn't about the muscle car's monetary value to Po, it was a facet of his character, as much a part of him as any of his limbs. He wouldn't hide it out of sight, fearful of a coward that used flame to make war, he'd damn well cruise around town, with the windows rolled down and rock 'n' roll music blaring, and invite his enemy to try something.

The sight of Bar-Lesque took some of the wind out of his bravado. Unlike at Charley's Autoshop, the firefighters here had caught the blaze early enough to extinguish it without the entire structure being raised. Nevertheless, it was still a smoking shell with broken windows and a scorched sign over the front door. Inside, Po guessed, was a scene of destruction, the décor ruined, the furniture beyond salvaging, either burnt, smoke-damaged or both. Again, preliminary reports said that there were no victims, the firefighters having made a search of the premises already – their findings earlier relayed to him by the battalion chief overseeing the operation at the garage – and Po was thankful that his staff had not arrived for work before the arsonist struck. He looked around and saw several familiar faces in the crowds on the opposite sidewalk, no less those of Jasmine Reed and Chris Mitchell, his restaurant and bar managers. He couldn't choose which of them was most disconsolate.

Ordinarily he parked his Mustang around the back, but fire

trucks blocked access, and wherever there was a free space had momentarily been filled with several vans and cars from the local media outlets. He saw camera crews from both Channel 8 and Channel 13, and recognized several roving reporters creeping among the onlookers, seeking juicy quotes to headline the morning papers. Po had no intention of being cornered by any of them. He parked his Mustang a couple of blocks down and walked back, getting only close enough to beckon Jasmine and Chris to join him.

Chris approached with his hands raised in surrender. 'This isn't about me this time, Po.'

On previous occasions, Po had to deal with a bunch of homophobic thugs who'd targeted Chris, and also with a violent moneylender and his henchmen to whom Chris owed cash. He doubted that, this time, the attack on Bar-Lesque had anything to do with Chris and was firmly on his own head.

Po thumbed over his shoulder. 'Let's haul ass outta here before somebody sticks a damn microphone in my face.'

They found space on a bench situated at the next intersection, where Portland's older residents could rest. Chris and Jazz both sunk down on to the bench, but Po paced to and fro, deciding he needed a cigarette. Smoke from the fire fouled the air; to Chris and Jazz his tobacco smoke might smell equally bad so he was considerate and stayed downwind. His employees waited. Jazz's eyes were brimming with unshed tears. She dabbed at them with the back of her wrist, avoiding smearing her make-up; as was her usual case, she'd dressed like a 1950's starlet but with modern attitude. Usually Chris also looked as if he could front an old-time Rockabilly band, but today the image was slightly tarnished; his normally coifed hair hung in bangs and his eyelids were puffy and reddened. He wore a thick winter coat over his work clothes. As an afterthought, Jazz had to be freezing.

'I won't keep you guys too long,' Po promised. 'Until the fire crews get done, we won't know what we're workin' with. It's my intention to bring the place back to life, though. I don't know how long a rebuild or renovation might take, but I don't want to lose either of you in the meantime. Whatever happens, you guys and your employees will be paid fully. Say, Jazz, d'you want my jacket?'

She was too shocked by what had become of Bar-Lesque to

notice her extremities were pimpled with goose flesh. She either shook her head in the negative or she shivered.

True to his word, Po didn't make them sit around in the cold for long. He emphasized his promise that nobody would go short of cash, but in the meantime they should stay clear of Bar-Lesque, until things had been brought to a satisfactory conclusion with whoever the hell was attacking him, then he wouldn't risk putting any of them in the crossfire.

After that, he sped home, worried that his house would be next on the arsonist's list and Tess could get trapped in the flames.

SIX

'You stink like a dumpster fire, you.'

'Talk about stating the obvious,' Po grunted at his friend Jerome 'Pinky' Leclerc as he pulled his Mustang away from the curb. 'I've stood in the cinders of two fires already today. How'd you expect me to smell, Pinky?'

'Like pulled pork?'

Po shook his head in mock disbelief.

Cumberland Avenue was devoid of moving traffic, but then it was Sunday afternoon; churchgoers had returned home, while those that put their faith in partying rather than religion were yet to surface. Po aimed his car for home again and within minutes they crossed Tukey's Bridge, with the calm waters of Back Cove on one side and the more turbulent open sea on the other. Clouds had enclosed Portland and they had a strange ochre cast to them.

'There's a blizzard coming,' said Pinky.

'F'sure,' said Po.

There had been only light flurries of snow in Portland, but there were parts of New Hampshire, Massachusetts and further north in Maine, that were already blanketed under drifting snow. Forecasters warned that a winter bomb cyclone could conceivably dump several feet of snow on them within the next twenty-four hours.

'I've seen snow before, me,' said Pinky, 'but nothing like they're warning about.'

'Yep, it's time to put on your sturdy boots, podnuh,' said Po. Pinky, although he'd donned a quilted parka on his way out of his apartment, wore a tracksuit and sneakers. He had been on a fitness trip for several months and chose to dress accordingly. Po wouldn't knock him for working to regain some fitness he'd been lacking for the past decade or more. Pinky was a big man, strong and deceptively agile, but he'd be the first to admit that his aerobic fitness was diabolically bad. Po smoked like a chimney, and was as fit as a coonhound; Pinky on the other hand was overweight and often troubled by swollen legs. Correction: he used to be. These days Pinky's silhouette was no longer as bottom heavy, and it seemed that his new exercise regime had helped relieve his chronic lymphatic condition. Pinky had reformed from being a downbeaten convict, to head a criminal network in Baton Rouge, but since relocating to join his friends in Maine, had reformed again in order to put his criminality firmly in the rearview mirror. Part of this reformation was his drive to get fit and healthy; how could he ever be criticized for taking care of himself?

A gentle flurry of snowflakes dotted the windshield. They were mere minutes from Po's place and he wondered if they'd make it indoors before the winter storm broke over them.

No sooner had he given it thought than hail slanted sideways, driven by gusts of wind off Casco Bay. Po crept the Mustang the final fifty yards and parked on the hard-pack outside his ranch-style house. His home was at the dead end of a road nestled in woodland adjacent to the Presumpscot River. When the spring melt came, he was close enough to hear the rushing of water over the Presumpscot Falls, but for now the river ran low and was almost frozen over in places. Last time he checked, the waterfall comprised a jumble of ice-encrusted rocks through which the river barely trickled. Usually a favorite spot for anglers, they'd hung up their rods and tackle until the return of the warmer months. It suited Po. Especially with the oncoming blizzard there would be few valid reasons for anybody to be out in the woods, so – blizzard conditions aside – spotting a suspicious interloper should be easier.

The reason for bringing Pinky to the ranch was two-fold. Simply and plainly, Pinky was undeniably the best friend Po had ever known so was always a welcome visitor; he was also the person he trusted most to protect Tess if he was unavailable. His fiancée had proven tough and resilient, and she didn't shirk from a fight, but presently she was not in a fit condition for brawling. If Po's fears proved true, the arsonist's next target could be closer to home. Before bringing Pinky to the ranch he'd explained he needed him to house sit, because he anticipated there'd be plenty of times when Tess accompanied him, making the ranch vulnerable to attack. Pinky hadn't exactly packed for the weather, but he had for a fight. In the footwell between his splayed sneakers there was a gym bag containing a couple of pistols. Before leaving Louisiana Pinky had quit dealing in illegal weapons, but was still all for expressing his constitutional right to bear arms.

Tess was through in her office when they went inside, but hearing their arrival she dropped whatever she was working on and came out to greet them. She looked crestfallen – only broken for a second when she smiled at the sight of Pinky – and moved to meet Po. They embraced briefly, before she stood back and peered up at him.

'I've been watching the TV,' she said, 'and have seen footage from both fires, but it's from a few hours ago now. What shape are the buildings in by now?'

'The damage to the diner's mostly cosmetic, but as far as Charley's Autoshop goes, it has literally been raised to the ground.'

Nothing he said was news to Tess, but their previous conversations had been over their cell phones, this was the first time they could emote openly. Tess had no shame about weeping in front of Pinky, but she was made of sterner stuff. Her eyes shone with unshed tears, and she controlled a tremble that threatened her bottom lip.

'This is absolutely the worst time for this to happen,' she said.

'No time's a good time, but you're right. With our babe on the way—'

She cut him off. 'I confirmed with Detective Ratcliffe that I was going to help find her sister. But now, with an arsonist on the loose, how do I concentrate my efforts on Joanne when my priority should be helping you?'

'You leave the arsonist to me,' he said. Then with a nod at Pinky, he continued, 'Rather, with us. Most of your search will be data lead, I'm assuming, but I'll be yours as and when you need me.'

'Ditto,' said Pinky. He aimed an exaggerated thumbs-up at her, his other hand encumbered with the bag containing his pistols.

'I guess that bag doesn't contain your packed lunch?' Tess said, inspecting the way it hung heavy in Pinky's grasp.

'Why'd I need to bring lunch when I fully intend raiding Nicolas's refrigerator, me?'

'*Mi casa es su casa*,' said Po, 'but that doesn't extend to the leftover meatloaf in the fridge. If you're hungry, you can call for take-out.'

'Sure, because Taco Bell is gonna deliver in a blizzard.'

Po grunted. 'That's a fair point. *Mi meatloaf es su meatloaf*, podnuh.'

Pinky grimaced. 'I hate meatloaf as much as I do collard greens.'

'Sacrilege!' Po croaked. 'How'd you call yourself a Southerner and not love collard greens?'

'You forget, you, my folks were so dirt poor, the greens we ate were fit only for compost.'

Po's upbringing had been a tough one. His mother had left them and his father had raised him before he was murdered by one of his mother's stepsons. Before his pa's death, they'd lived off low income and hard work, and there was little by way of home comforts or special foods to be enjoyed. But compared to Pinky's early life, Po accepted that by comparison his was blissful. Pinky once told him that the best thing about being incarcerated in the Louisiana State Penitentiary was that he enjoyed three square meals a day, the beatings and rapes not so much.

Seemingly their joking about food had already lost interest for Tess. She turned to the TV and stood before it. The sound had been muted and the stories had moved on from the suspicious fires that had struck Portland in the early hours of Sunday morning; nothing on screen seemed pertinent to either the arsonist or Angel of Death cases. Tess used the clicker to turn off the TV.

'Have you upset anyone lately?' she wondered aloud.

'Not especially,' Po said.

'Arson's a strange weapon to choose,' she said, voicing her thoughts.

'Cowardly,' Po stressed.

Pinky added his wisdom. 'Any punk-ass can drop a match and walk away, hey, there's no need to face you head-on when they can watch from a distance.'

'Maybe they're afraid of a direct confrontation,' Tess cautioned, 'but the threat they represent shouldn't be underestimated. We must also consider that the fires were lit, not as attacks against you, but as diversions. To get you looking one way when the real attack is going to come from another direction.'

'So I'm not the priority target?' Po hadn't considered that anyone but him had gotten somebody's back up enough to illicit having his businesses burned down. He squinted at Pinky.

'Don't look at me, Nicolas, I've been a good boy, me.'

'If anyone could attract a revenge attack, I suppose it'd be me,' said Tess. 'If that's the case then maybe you should return home, Pinky, cause that's where the arson might strike next.' Pinky was currently residing in Tess's vacant apartment above an antiques and curios shop.

'Can't see him going anywhere near Cumberland Avenue,' Pinky said, 'not during daylight hours. He's already proven to be a cowardly punk, him, so probably won't risk showing his face where there are witnesses.'

'Right now it's all speculation,' Po said. 'We shouldn't assume anythin' until we know for sure who the target is and who the hell's targetin' them. Way I see it, we're all here right now, and remote enough for the scumbag to maybe try burning the ranch down with us in it.'

Pinky was yet to set down his holdall bag. He held it up for emphasis. 'Let him try, hey!'

SEVEN

Joanne Mason, no, *Jo Sugden* as she must continually think of herself, had formed a misassumption. She'd believed it would be a simple enough task to slip through the border patrol checks under cover of the blizzard. Not so. It appeared that the agents were taking more notice of those determined to cross the border in this hellish weather. There were few road users as it were, but luckily she'd noted that those before her were being waved into the customs loop for pointed questioning. Panic struck her afresh and she began shivering as she gripped the steering wheel, but it didn't hamper her enough from completing a turn in the road and heading away from the controlled area. Hopefully nobody had noted her hasty retreat and decided to follow up on her suspicious maneuver. The snow was not yet a blizzard, but it was falling heavily enough that it should have obscured any view of her registration plate by the CCTV cameras, not so the make and model of her car. She simply must get rid of the car she'd used since fleeing Boston; she'd taken too much of a risk holding on to it this long. If her speedy change of direction had caught the wrong attention and was reported to local law enforcement, a roadblock ahead could cut her off. She began seeking an alternative route, one that would take her off the main highway and – hopefully – to a crossing into Canada that was not assiduously guarded.

She'd gone against her original idea of attempting the crossing at Houlton and had elected for the quieter route into Canada over the Vanceboro–St Croix River Bridge, so was immediately funneled back through the small town of Vanceboro. Residents had battened down the hatches, in anticipation of the winter cyclone bomb about to explode over them, so she didn't see another living soul, which suited her. She avoided taking Route 6, by chance getting on to a narrower road that largely paralleled the St Croix river; she wondered if she might come across a boat she could use to cross, and then source a replacement vehicle once she was in Canada. A couple of miles beyond the town limits she realized the folly of taking the route. It wasn't paved nor plowed, and there was no way it'd take her to a secret crossing place as she'd hoped. Rather she found the tires on her car had no traction and steering became almost impossible. She tried turning and the back wheels fell into a ditch and that was as far as her car would ever take her. As if in punishment that some vengeful god had decided to throw at her, the blizzard arrived.

Since escaping Boston, Joanne had grown light-fingered, despite never stealing beforehand. Her thievery was necessary in assisting her flight because she only had a few hundred bucks cash and no way to safely access her bank account. She had not found her inner kleptomaniac, rather she stole what she needed where it wouldn't do harm to the owner of the goods. Case in point was the car she'd fled in. Along her route she'd collected clothing she might require and had amassed a pile of various different garments she could use to rapidly change her appearance. She had stolen a coat off the back of a door at a gas station washroom, and initially found it was far too large for her. However, now it was a godsend, but probably not from the same deity that sent the storm to bury her car under a snowdrift. She couldn't stay with the car as she'd probably freeze to death before her supplies ran out, but without the voluminous coat she couldn't brave the elements. Already she had accumulated several different hats and scarves, and she made use of them, pulling on several of each, and then she got out of the car to pop the trunk and retrieve the coat. The temperature had fallen to sub zero. She hurried into the coat. It smelled faintly of a stranger's body odor and stale cologne, but worn over the top of her own coat it didn't feel as ill-fitting. With the addition of three woollen caps, the scarves and extra layers of clothing, she no longer resembled her athletic self, rather she shambled away from the abandoned car, squat and bulky, unrecognizable.

Within twenty yards she wished that one of her thefts had been of a sturdy set of boots. Her shoes had been fit for completing childcare tasks in a West Roxbury mansion, not for trekking through snow. Slushy ice compacted the inner sides of the shoes. The cuffs of her jeans and her socks were soaked and painfully cold. She seriously considered returning to the car and hoping to sit out the storm, but what then? She must still make off on foot and the snow would only be deeper and make walking the road much more difficult. She clenched her teeth, squinted against the icy flakes batting her eyelashes and forged on. Within another hundred yards she caught herself making strange whimpering noises with every other step. In fact, she was ready for screaming in discomfort, but in this storm nobody would hear. She shrieked and then shouted a string of curse words that would ordinarily make her red-faced. The layered scarves muffled her frustration. The dampening effect of the falling snow muffled what the scarves couldn't contain. Jo shuffled on, realizing that screaming didn't help.

It was still day, but you wouldn't know it. She was under the boughs of trees that had lost their foliage but not their dense networks of branches. On the branches snow already piled up. She trod through a twilit tunnel. To her right the St Croix River was quite a formidable barrier, and it kept her from escaping into the neighbouring country. Ice had formed on the river during the cold spell preceding the blizzard, but it was not yet fully frozen over; she daren't make the fatal mistake of trying to cross from one ice flow to another. Right then her only hope of survival was reaching shelter and warmth, not dumped in water so cold the shock might feasibly stop her heart, and most definitely would make her hypothermic.

The blizzard was of epic proportions, falling harder than she'd ever personally seen before, but in the next instant she realized that there was worse to come. The wind grew exponentially, whipping the snow around so that keeping track of direction, including up and down, was difficult. She threw an elbow across her face to avoid being blinded. Twice she stumbled off the road into the same ditch that had already claimed her borrowed car. The second time she fell on her hands and thorns buried beneath the snow pierced her palms. She had wished for sturdier boots, now she wished she'd appropriated some protective gloves. After scrambling out of the ditch and finding firmer ground underfoot, she stuck her hands under her armpits and continued, eyes slitted almost shut.

It seemed like forever, but was probably no more than ten minutes, before she was hemmed in on one side by the river and on the other by a cemetery. The wind battered her, plucked at her oversized coat and invaded even the bottom-most layer of her clothing. She shivered so hard that her teeth grew painful. How far had she driven from Vanceboro? She couldn't fully recall, so couldn't begin to approximate how far she'd shuffled back towards town. It didn't take much figuring that she was not going to make it there without first succumbing to the icy cold. She veered towards the cemetery; if she were about to perish she may as well save the undertaker the job of carrying her there. A metal gate blocked access, but was more symbolic than anything else. The wall to either side had fallen down and even with snow piled on top was no barrier. She scrambled over the lowest part, kicking through a drift to gain the ground on the far side. The wind grew stronger, pushing her before it. She staggered but welcomed the assistance as it ushered her towards what was probably a family mausoleum.

The memorial was the first stone-built structure she'd come across since abandoning her car, the only shelter to offer protection from the storm. A worm of unease crawled through her bowel at the thought of taking shelter alongside the moldering corpses of the dead, but it was still more appealing than sitting down with her back to a headstone and freezing solid. She searched for the way inside. Thankfully the mausoleum was built to accommodate several generations, so the building was equipped with a door for easy access. It wasn't locked, but the doors, wooden, braced with bands of iron, were heavy. She barely had the strength to push inside, astounded by how rapidly the storm had sapped her vitality. Whoever it was that designed the mausoleum had given thought to both its recipients and the living left behind. Small windows had been installed either side of the door and also a third window sat high up towards the ceiling on the back wall. There was enough daylight filtering inside so that she wasn't walking into the pitch darkness of a subterranean tomb. Before shoving the door closed behind her, Joanne took in her surroundings in one long sweep of her gaze. She shivered, chilled to the bone, but also from an uncanny fear of the dead interred in individual crypts arranged around the room. It wasn't the dead she should be fearful of, it was the living.

Wrapped in several layers of clothing, sheltered inside a stone-built building out of the wind's reach she shouldn't have to worry about hypothermia, and yet it was an absolute threat. Her shoes and trousers were soaked, her feet so cold they were painful, and she had carried in an accumulation of snow on her coat and hats. She shook off the coating of snow and stamped her feet. In the mausoleum the sounds were unnatural and a shiver of dread rode through her again. She looked for somewhere best to rest. She wouldn't avail herself of any of the raised crypts, so she went instead to the back of the room and found a plinth: once it might have been used to display wreaths and other floral tributes but was now bare. It was raised up enough to make sitting more comfortable than directly on the floor. She pushed her back to the wall and allowed it to assist her as she sank down on to her backside. A fire would have been very welcome, but she had no way of building one. One way she could warm up was by consuming food and, hopefully, the coffee she'd left in a thermos was still warm enough to reach her core.

'Shit!'

Rather than lug them to town with her she'd left her provisions in the car.

Thankfully she'd had the presence of mind – even in her haste to dress against the weather – to fetch her purse, which she'd shoved deep into a pocket of the outer coat. Inside the purse were what little cash she had and also a cell phone she'd lifted off the table in a café when its owner was distracted. How had she ever believed she had a hope of escaping her dogged hunters when she made such reckless mistakes and become stranded in a blizzard? She had yet to use the cell phone and was concerned that by now it might have been reported stolen and the service canceled. She must reach out for help.

Without a plug-in cable to keep the cellphone charged, she'd turned it off to conserve what power was in the battery. It was a relief when the screen lit up and cast cold blue light around her. Its owner hadn't protected its contents with a security pin number. The screen saver was of a trio of laughing children, and though they looked unlike her previous charges, it was still enough to send a spear of guilt through her.

She had to dig through her memory for a number; as was the case with most people, her personal cell had been filled with dozens of contacts whose numbers she didn't need to memorize when she could call them at the press of a single button. The same could be said for even those closest to her. She had no hope of dredging up a number she'd once input into her phone, so instead she decided to go old school and phoned a landline instead: this number had been instilled in her memory since childhood.

EIGHT

'Unexpectedly she rang our parents' telephone number,' Detective Ratcliffe relayed to Tess, 'so I was able to speak with her for a few seconds before warning her to hang up.'

'You're afraid that your parents' phone has been bugged? I can't imagine it—'

'I should explain. Our mom and dad don't live here anymore, they moved to Florida for the better weather. I kind of took over the family home at their bequest, so in effect, I also inherited their old landline. These days I rarely get anything other than marketing and scam calls on it, but have kept it in operation for if my parents ring home.'

'I see, and there's a possibility that your calls are being monitored?'

Po and Pinky were inside, attempting to figure out who their enemy could be, so Tess had taken her cell phone outside to hear better. She sat on the swinging seat Po had installed on the front porch, a place she could often be found when mulling over problems. The snow sifted beyond the overhanging porch roof, settling on the crushed shells on the drive. Po's Mustang already wore white caps on its hood, roof and trunk. Tess pulled a knitted shawl over her thighs.

'It sounds paranoid, but I'd say it's a probability rather than a possibility.'

'Is bugging a person's phone something you've ever done as a detective?'

'No, but that isn't to say it has never happened. You used to be a cop, Tess, you know what law enforcement is capable of.'

'Bugging phones and hacking computers and such is for Hollywood and the FBI, not for a county sheriff's department in sleepy old Maine.'

'I'd guess that Boston PD has more resources than your sheriff's office and my police department ten times over. I might have been overly cautious, but it wasn't a chance I was willing to take, for

Jo's sake. I noted the number she was ringing from, told her I'd call back from a secure line, but unfortunately when I found a working payphone I was unable to contact her again. A recorded message announced she couldn't take my call; I assume her cell's battery probably died. I'll have to wait until she charges it again, or makes contact by other means.'

'By your actions I've the feeling that you're less and less convinced of her guilt and more inclined to help her evade capture,' Tess probed.

'Before she hung up she asked me to help her. It doesn't matter what lies are being spread about her, she's my kid sister and it's my job to protect her. Besides, you've seen the latest developments over in West Roxbury, right? The more I've heard what Jo's supposed to have done, the less plausible it sounds. Two more unidentified male corpses . . . for Christ's sake, does killing them sound like the actions of a kiddies' nanny?'

'It doesn't take a trained assassin to pick up a rock and smack somebody over the head,' Tess said. 'But, no, I'm in agreement with you; this does not sound like the actions of a nanny. At first when the story involved the murder of the children, then, yeah, maybe, but then the mother was added to the equation, and now two more grown men? To begin with, Jo has been a handy scape-goat for the real killer, but surely the charade can't be kept up now.'

'I don't know about that, even some of my colleagues still think her capable.' Ratcliffe snorted in self-deprecation. 'They say if she's half as tough as I am, and desperate to escape, then she can probably kick the ass of anyone that gets in her way. I don't consider myself tough, it's the fact I carry a badge and a gun that I've managed to get by; Jo doesn't have the benefit of either.'

'Sometimes the most unassuming can be the most surprising.'

'Yeah, especially if we are talking about Tess Grey. You've proven you're a bad ass, Tess, but beyond some scratching and hair pulling, I don't think Jo's ever been in a real fight. You on the other hand . . .'

'I've usually had help from Po,' Tess insisted. 'One of the few times I didn't I almost had my hand chopped off by a drugged-up guy who would probably blow away on a stiff breeze. Please understand, I'm not trying to make a case that your sister's a murderer, but we can't fully discount it either. What if she had an accomplice?'

'No, I don't buy it. She's no angel, but that doesn't make her a devil. Jo's incapable of the crimes she's been accused of, and I'm more certain of that every passing second.'

'Good. It will make helping her less difficult if we're convinced of her innocence.'

'I'm convinced, what about you, Tess?'

'I'm getting there. As long as Joanne gives me no reason to change my mind, then all's well.'

'I'm happy to hear it.' Again Ratcliffe snorted, but this time it was at her reticence to fully trust Tess before. 'We actually shared more than I admitted to earlier before we ended our call. Are you confident that your cell is secure, Tess?'

'I'm as confident as I can be.'

'Jo's in an even worse predicament than before. Has the blizzard hit you yet? It has where she is and she's gotten herself stranded. If I could, I'd fetch her myself, but you're much nearer to her, Tess. Is it safe for you to go and collect her?'

'Safe traveling in this whiteout? I'd say no, but Po might be of a different opinion. He mostly does our driving these days, and even the harshest weather doesn't seem to faze him.' As if to prove that it was the dominant force, not Po, the storm grew wilder, with hearty gusts of wind bending the creaking treetops, and the snow falling in flakes as large as silver dollars. 'However, I can't promise to go without first speaking with him. He has problems of his own to contend with right now.'

'He has? In relation to . . .?'

'We're unsure. But before you ask, it can't be connected to Joanne's case, because this stuff Po's dealing with started before you contacted me.'

'Right,' said Ratcliffe. It sounded as if she hadn't space in her head to waste on thoughts of anything else but getting her sister back safely. Tess understood. There was nothing more important to the detective than Joanne's safety.

'Are you going to tell me where she is?' Tess prompted.

NINE

'Another dead end,' said Bruce Harper as he slipped into the passenger seat. The car sank a few inches on its suspension. He was a huge man, thicker about the waist than his barrel chest, and sporting the scarred eyebrows and malformed nose of an unsuccessful boxer. His eyes were the color of glacial melt over slate, just a touch darker hued than his thin hair.

The driver of the car, a freckled woman who insisted her name was pronounced Sh'von and not See-oh-barn, pinched her mouth at the news. She'd heard similar from him at the dozen or so other gas stations and diners they'd checked already. Harper knocked snow off his hair with leather-gloved fingers, allowing it to fall in the footwell of the car as he squinted across at her.

'You think we're wasting time, Siobhan?'

'Like I said already, Harper, I trust your instinct. You'll get a hit, just you wait and see.'

'Told you, this ain't about instinct, and no sixth sense either, just plain ol' logic and detective work.'

'I hear you.'

'You should. I've proven my method works on past hunts.'

'That you have, Harper, that you have.'

He brought up a map on his smart phone.

The police in New Hampshire were following up on a possible sighting of Joanne Mason at a crummy roadside motel a few miles shy of Portsmouth and the state border. Supposedly she'd fled the scene in such haste that she literally dumped her room key on the road outside; had she returned it to the site manager she wouldn't have raised any suspicion, but once her rashness had been highlighted, the manager – a would-be armchair sleuth – had gotten to wonder and had pulled up CCTV footage of her on first arrival. Comparing the images on his computer to those depicting the wanted Angel of Death, he'd jumped at getting his hands on the reward that'd been offered for information leading to her arrest. He guessed that Portsmouth PD was currently sharing images with the local FBI office, determining through the feds' facial recognition software if the disguised woman was Joanne Mason or not. They were welcome wasting their time, Bruce Harper decided, because if she hadn't fled the motel only to hole up again nearby she'd have probably kept on driving. From what he'd learned about those on the run, those panicking tried putting distance and often a barrier between them and their pursuers. Once across the Piscataqua River Joanne would've been in Maine, but still within spitting distance of Portsmouth – too close – so had probably kept on fleeing, watching New Hampshire diminish in her rearview mirror. In her shoes, he thought he wouldn't stop before reaching Canada, and perhaps not even then.

While the cops in Boston, and now in Portsmouth, pecked after old crumbs, Harper decided that he'd catch her only if he was hot on the trail. He'd crossed into Maine and foregone any of the major towns and cities she could have gone to, instead plotting several routes she could've taken north. Again, figuratively squeezing his size twelve's into the fugitive's shoes, he had determined how she'd plotted on crossing the border unchallenged. Somebody more resourceful than a glorified babysitter might find any dozens of passages into Canada, but he'd bet she would stick to the roads and hope that whatever bogus identity she'd assumed held up. There were five or six official ports of entry into the country on the north and eastern borders of Maine, with others to the west if Joanne took a hard left and headed for Quebec province. On her current trajectory, though, it was more plausible that she'd strike out for New Brunswick, using roads other than interstate highways where there was more possibility of being pulled over by the state police. After checking on a map, he thought she would choose between three crossings: those at Houlton, Vanceboro and Calais/St Stephen – he discounted the crossing at Lubec as it would take her on to Campobello Island and no further, unless she decided to row a boat up the Bay of Fundy.

'Let's try that way,' he announced after studying the map. He aimed a finger at the map and Siobhan had to lean across to see his instruction.

'You want me to take Route Two?' she checked.

He grunted affirmative.

Already they'd progressed beyond Portland, Augusta and Bangor. By now, most hunters would've given up and turned back, but that wasn't in Harper's playbook. He often sneered at Siobhan's assertion that he was 'a goddamn human bloodhound', and wouldn't admit aloud to her that often he was simply very lucky. If a hunch struck him, he wasn't the type to ignore it: maybe he was being guided by some divine power from above, his very own eye in the sky. Yeah, right! He followed logic and clues, not only gut feeling, and found that as a trinity they served him well.

'Can't see her trying for the Calais to St Stephen crossing . . . towns are too built up,' he said. 'I think she'll try somewhere with less traffic.'

'Surely it'd be easier trying to blend in with a crowd than at a quieter crossing?'

'Ordinarily that might be the case, but from the way she's acted till now, she has avoided other people. She's changed her appearance twice now that we know of, and has probably done so again: she's afraid, paranoid about being recognized. In her mind, she probably thinks the fewer people see her the safer she is. You and I know that is not always the case, Siobhan.'

Sometimes, bored guards tended to be more particular once given something to do. Rather than a passing glance at her, Joanne would probably be questioned and studied at length, to determine why she'd chance traveling in this hellish weather.

Siobhan tugged Harper's wrist, angling his phone towards her, studying the immediate route on the screen. 'D'you have a sense of where it is she's likely to go?'

'If it was me, I'd try for the Orient crossing –' he dabbed a finger at a spot at the very top of the map, before moving to the extreme right – 'or right here at Vanceboro.'

Siobhan studied the map, tracing the road from the border back across country. If she got off the highway at Lincoln, then it was a fair assumption that Joanne had made for the crossing over the St Croix River at Vanceboro. 'So if we stay on this road to Lincoln, then . . . that must be at least fifty miles, Harper.'

'I'd say so. But there won't be fifty gas stations on route. We can check them all in maybe an hour or two and then if we've learned nothing . . .' Harper paused, considering his next move. 'Nah, let's not be negative. Something's going to come up. I can feel it in my water.'

'I thought you didn't put any stock in that mumbo jumbo,' Siobhan teased. 'Men of your age just tend to pee more often in cold weather, that's all.'

He scowled, but then his face lost its deepest ridges. He smiled. With his lopsided nose and thick lips, he was reminiscent of a big friendly ogre. Those that knew him for real wouldn't be fooled: there wasn't a friendly cell in his body. 'Hit the road,' he growled.

She drove, undaunted by the heavy snowfall.

There was good reason that Harper had paired with Siobhan Doyle for the hunt; it was for her driving abilities. Whether he found redheaded, green-eyed women attractive was neither here nor there.

None of the stops bore fruit, until they were beyond Lincoln, for which Harper found he was thankful. Now they were on a country road, rather than a highway or Interstate, it narrowed the choices of which crossing the fugitive was heading for to one: Vanceboro. Harper enjoyed it when his method was vindicated.

Siobhan had barely arrived at the gas pump before a middle-aged clerk hobbled out of the convenience store. First the man eyed the lowering sky, and then he eyed Siobhan a little time longer. He was unaware of Harper seated within her large SUV because of the tint on the windows and the amount of snowflakes swirling under the canopy over the pumps. Colored light from the store and roadside signage gave the snow a kaleidoscopic unreality.

'It's cash up-front, ma'am,' he called. 'You going far?'

'Far enough for a refill of the tank,' she replied.

'This ain't the weather for traveling,' he told her.

'I've got my snow tires on and the heater blows hot air, so I think I'll be good. How much do you need?' She took out her hip wallet and opened it to display several credit cards.

'Like I said, it's cash up-front.'

'Don't you charge?'

'Normally I do, yeah, but not in this blizzard. Phone lines are down, so's the Internet. If you want gas we're gonna have to do it the old, reliable way.'

Siobhan shivered. Inside the SUV she had been immune to the storm. The wind cut sideways under the canopy, dotting her with huge flakes. She checked her wallet for bills. She could barely scare up twenty-three bucks and that little gas wouldn't take them far enough. 'Gimme a second, will ya.'

She returned to the SUV and appraised her passenger. 'Do you have any cash with you, Harper?'

'How much do you need?'

'How much is a tank of gas these days?'

When you charged everything to your employer's account you rarely took notice of the small things like the price per gallon of diesel. He dug a wad of bank bills out of his trouser pocket and peeled off a hundred bucks in twenties. 'I want that back.'

'Add it to your expenses, Harp, it isn't my goddamn debt.'

She returned to where the clerk waited on unsteady legs. Handed him the wad. 'Keep pumping till that runs out,' she instructed him.

'You've got a traveling companion with you, huh?' he asked.

'Why? Would you try abducting and raping me if I didn't?'

The clerk staggered at the weight of her question.

'Chill out, for feck's sake, I'm only kidding,' she said.

'It's just you're not the first young woman today who looks like they're driving into trouble.'

'Trouble, huh? What kind of trouble?'

The clerk nodded at the snow and refused to expound.

'Why was she heading for trouble, she wasn't equipped for the weather?'

'She wasn't equipped for anything except a hard fall. I warned her about driving in this storm.'

Siobhan thumbed at the SUV. 'That big ol' thing won't be stopped.'

'Hundred bucks, you said.'

'Keep pumping till the tank's full. You got a bathroom?'

'I'll have to fetch the key.'

'That's fine. It's not for me. It's my buddy, by now his bladder's the size of a cantaloupe and fit for bursting.'

Taking his cue, Harper pushed open the passenger door and stepped out. His body unfolded out of the confines of the SUV, exaggerating his size. He caught the fractional widening of the clerk's eyes and smirked. He evoked fear in some people, but he could tell the clerk wasn't intimidated, only surprised by his size.

'Where's the key?' he asked. 'I'll get it while you pump the gas.'

His offer wasn't up for debate. He continued past Siobhan and the clerk towards the convenience store. The clerk watched him, suspicious for about three long seconds that Harper might try stealing the cash from the register while he was kept busy outside. By the cut of the duo's clothing, and their truly expensive ride, he doubted either required the few hundred bucks he'd taken that day. 'It's hanging on a hook on the counter,' he called after Harper.

Harper showed no sign of hearing. Instead he cast his gaze around, spotted the old-fashioned CCTV camera where it drooped off slack fixtures at the corner of the building. Often the systems installed in some places were outmoded and there was little chance of recognizing his mother if she waltzed across the screen the picture was so grainy, but, being targets of robberies, gas stations tended to keep better systems than this one. Out of the way, in the ass-end of Maine he doubted there was much need for security measures. The clerk probably kept a baseball bat under his counter for when some asshole got lippy with him.

The chime of a bell announced his presence to a store otherwise empty of people. The place smelled like damp cardboard. He ignored the candy and chocolate bars on the nearest rack and went without invitation behind the service counter. A single sheet of Plexiglass was all that served to protect the clerk from a stranger's expelled spittle, and nothing to do with halting a robber. Distractedly Harper knew it was a shield erected during the pandemic and the clerk hadn't gotten round to doing away with it since. He plucked the washroom key and its huge fob off its hook and shoved it in his coat pocket. He'd no interest in relieving himself yet. He looked at the small CCTV monitor and control box perched under the counter. The camera had been positioned more to alert the clerk to anyone out by the pumps than in the store. Harper grunted. Thankfully it was live and recording. To conserve run time, he saw that the system had been switched to a motion detection mode and was right then filming the clerk and Siobhan outside. Harper saw that the clerk had his back to the store. Good enough. He hit the stop button and relayed the film back through other snippets of footage filmed earlier. The gas station had seen very few customers, so it was less than thirty seconds of spooling before Harper allowed the footage to play out. He smiled as he watched Joanne Mason alight a car and make the amateur's mistake of immediately checking out the camera; he got a full frontal shot of her worried face. She'd taken pains to cover up, to disguise herself under layers, but Harper was intimate with her features and immediately recognized his quarry.

'You shouldn't be behind there, buddy.'

Harper glanced across at another man that'd exited a back room:

perhaps a dry storeroom or walk-in chiller, making no odds to Harper. He was younger than the first clerk, taller, built.

Harper was unmoved. 'Just fetching the washroom key, pal.'

'Doesn't take all that time to find the key, not with that big ol' rubber brick hanging off of it.' The young man set down a crate of plastic-wrapped cola bottles. He dusted off his hands as he moved toward the counter. As Harper stepped out to meet him, the guy visibly faltered in his step. He was a big, muscled guy, athletic, but Harper defined raw power, and his face hinted at the thousand fights he'd had.

Harper dug in his pocket and slipped out the key. The fob was indeed styled to look like a red brick, though it was only an inch thick and four inches long. 'Found it,' he announced.

The clerk gave him a quick once over, perhaps checking for stray dollar bills poking out of hastily stuffed pockets.

'I didn't touch anything but this,' said Harper, wagging the key.

He would've probably gotten away with his snooping, except he hadn't had time to return the CCTV footage to the present, or hit record. As he moved aside the clerk swerved past him and in behind the counter. He first checked the cash register, and was visibly relieved to see that it was untouched. He wasn't yet convinced of Harper's innocence, though.

'If it's a problem, I'll give you back your damn key and go take a leak at the side of the road.' Harper moved around the counter, holding out the key, and by reaction, the clerk turned to accept it.

Harper dropped the key and clutched the man's outstretched hand too fast for the move to register. Before he could attempt to flinch back, Harper snapped his own elbow back, drawing the young man off balance on to his toes and directly into the headbutt aimed at the bridge of his nose. Harper's lumpy forehead smashed the cartilage flat and blood droplets sprayed as the man exhaled in agony. The strength went out the clerk's knees and he was fit for folding, but Harper shouldered him aside, throwing the man's bleeding face against the Plexiglass. At the same time, he stamped down on the back of the guy's bent leg, driving the knee all the way to the floor. The clerk collapsed on the ground, with Harper standing over him. He was verging on unconscious, which was not satisfactory to Harper. He stamped the man's head, twice for good measure, and decided he was no longer a threat.

The short, sharp, violent incident hadn't escaped notice.

However, prepared for such eventuality as Harper silencing potential witnesses, Siobhan had taken charge of the old gimpy clerk. She forced him inside the convenience store with the barrel of a gun jammed against the nape of his skull.

The clerk knew the depth of trouble he was in, but it was also apparent to Harper that his immediate concern wasn't for his welfare.

'Where's Tyler, what have you done with my boy?' he demanded.

'Quiet!' Siobhan hit the older man between the shoulder blades with the butt of her gun. He was propelled forwards on his prosthetic legs. Harper left Tyler lying where he was, instead coming back out around the counter to lend a hand to the father. He grabbed the old clerk by his jacket and dragged him, throwing him down alongside his son.

'Tyler! Ty?' he cried out and shook his unresponsive son.

'If *Ty* hadn't gone and stuck his nose in my business, all would be fine. We'd have left and you'd be a hundred bucks better off than before. Thing is, Ty here brought a different fate avalanching down on you both.'

'Don't dare hurt my boy again.'

Harper peered down. 'By the looks of him he's beyond pain. Fact is, he looks beyond *anything* except maybe a pine box.'

Siobhan chuckled at Harper then stopped.

He wasn't joking.

The clerk struggled to rise, but his position in the cramped space made getting up almost impossible.

'What you going to do?' Harper asked. 'You think you can fight me.'

'I'm not afraid of a bullying son of a bitch like you. I've been to war with real enemies.'

'You're a veteran, eh? That how you lost your legs?'

'Two tours in Iraq,' the clerk said, with a thump of his chest. 'Fucking IED sent me home, after Saddam's men tried and failed to kill me. Do you think I'm afraid of a piece of crap like you?'

'Fear is a useful emotion,' Harper told him, 'kind of reminds you when to keep your mouth shut and not insult the man holding your life in his hands.'

'Let me up, even with these metal legs I'll kick your ass.'

'Thanks for the head's up. I don't think I'll be letting you up any time soon.'

Harper stamped on the clerk's stomach. It almost forced out his innards. The clerk tried to grapple his leg in vain, but Harper was a powerhouse by comparison and simply walked over him to stamp again, this time on the man's throat. Behind him, even Siobhan – who could be a bloodthirsty bitch in her own right – winced and exclaimed at Harper's savagery.

Harper bent down and rifled the man's pockets. He plucked out the hundred dollars given to the clerk for fuel, and then turned his attention to the cash register. He hit buttons until the drawer popped open, and then he grabbed the notes and some of the coins out of the drawer. He allowed some to fall and scatter around the two clerks, both of whom he was certain were dead.

To Siobhan he said, 'Throw over some of those racks and scatter stuff off the shelves. I'll grab some of the smokes and booze.'

His instructions were to make it look as if the clerks had died during a robbery gone wrong. Before grabbing the cigarettes and booze a desperate robber might snatch, he yanked out the CCTV system's control box and jammed it under his armpit. He didn't need it to study the hours-old footage of Joanne Mason again, he'd gotten what he needed from what he'd already viewed; taking it was about destroying the footage showing his and Siobhan's arrival at the pumps.

'Want me to drop a match or two?' Siobhan offered. 'Burn this place to the foundations?'

Harper shook his head. Luck had favored him – discounting the fact he'd had to murder two men to cover their tracks – he didn't want to test it now by trying to outrun a flame to the gas reserves, and the petrol station turning into an inferno before they were clear of it.

'Robbers that had just stomped two guys to death wouldn't hang around to watch the place burn, best we don't either.'

Back in the SUV he pointed down the road they'd initially followed. 'Before I was disturbed back there, I watched video of Mason drive off. I was right to aim for Vanceboro.'

'You sure you aren't part bloodhound, Harp?' Siobhan asked.

Straight-faced he replied, 'Are you suggesting my momma made out with a mutt?'

'It's either that or she got jiggy with a freakin' psychic space alien.'

TEN

P o had swapped out his Mustang for a vehicle more capable of contending with the deepening snow. Some of his small fleet of cars had burned down to their wheel hubs along with the autoshop, but he had still accessed a Kia Telluride SUV and already it had taken them beyond Yarmouth over the Royal River. The snowfall in Portland had been heavy enough; further up the coast it was worse.

Tess had dressed for the blizzard, pulling on extra layers and a beanie hat and fur-lined boots. Po was in his usual attire of high-topped boots, jeans, T-shirt and leather jacket, with the addition of an un-tucked blue plaid shirt. The SUV came with heated seats. His intention, he'd made clear, was to spend as little time outside the car as possible.

Tess checked the time on her cell phone. She guessed that they had less than an hour's daylight before nightfall. Actually, *daylight* was a bit of a misnomer, considering the storm had already blanketed them in a weird twilight. 'How long do you think it will take us to get there?'

'Ordinarily,' Po estimated, 'it'd be about a four-hour drive; stickin' to posted speed limits, an' all. It will be longer because of the storm. I'm not so sure the roads will even be passable the further we go.'

Tess nodded at his ETA: Portland to Vanceboro was around two hundred and forty miles. Much of the journey could be made on the Interstate and freeways, but there was no avoiding having to get off at some point on to routes less traveled. Pains would be taken to keep the major highways open, but the same couldn't be expected of some of the backcountry roads.

'We'll make it,' she asserted, more to bolster her confidence than his.

'Your best move is to tip off the cops in Vanceboro and let them fetch Joanne in.'

'Under any other circumstances you'd be right, but not now. I swore to Detective Ratcliffe that I wouldn't involve the cops, not until after we can prove that Jo's a patsy for somebody else's crime.'

'So you don't doubt her innocence now?'

'Not after what has come to light since, y'know, about the other murders?'

Po shrugged. He knew that some women were equal to or more capable than many men in a fight; he was looking at one of them. 'Joanne could be frozen to death by the time we reach her. What's worse, that you break your word to Ratcliffe or her sister perishes because you didn't?'

'I can't believe you've even asked,' she said. He was an ex convict by virtue of avenging his murdered father, not because he lacked morals: Po laid a lot of stock in loyalty, his word being his seal. 'Neither scenario is palatable, and it's unfair of you to make me choose.'

'Hey, chill out, Tess, I'm *making* you do nothing. I'm only suggestin' other ideas seeing as I think it's goin' to be a bitch reachin' her.'

'We must try.'

'F'sure. I'm up for tryin',' Po assured her, 'I'm just not too confident we'll make it there.'

'I've faith in your abilities.'

'If I was driving a snowplow, yeah,' he agreed, 'but even this car has its limitations.'

'You're worried that we might get stuck overnight and another attack will happen back there in Portland and you won't be able to stop it.'

'I'm not gonna lie,' he said. 'I'm conflicted.'

'A young woman's life takes priority over—'

'You don't have to point out the obvious, Tess. I'm gonna try my hardest to get us to Joanne in time, I just don't want to make a promise that's impossible to keep.'

'I understand. Let's not concern ourselves with what ifs, they don't help.'

'You're right.'

The blizzard waned as they by-passed Augusta and they made decent time towards Bangor. Afterwards they followed the Telluride's built-in GPS navigation. It diverted them off the Interstate on to US Route 2. Through Orono, Old Town and Milford the going was slow, despite the roads being plowed, and it grew slower again as the highway followed the course of the Penobscot River upstream towards Lincoln. Only one lane was clear for traffic moving in both directions, and they were fortunate not to meet a truck coming south. To either side the snow was banked high, and fresh snow had fallen since the last time the snowplow had been through. The Kia Telluride equipped with its winter tires held the road surprisingly well.

Going by Po's earlier estimate, they should've reached Lincoln within three hours, and it was gratifying to find that the blizzard had only added about half an hour to their expected journey time. Alas, once beyond Lincoln they would be driving through hill country, and the rise in elevation would favour the storm. All told, Joanne had taken shelter about six hours ago; hopefully they'd be with her before the clock struck eight hours.

Po pushed on through Lincoln and took the road towards the border crossing. It had not been plowed: several vehicles had cut their own routes through the snow, and Po followed their wheel ruts. Under their tires the sound of crunching and squeaking became an annoying accompaniment, but there was nothing to do about it.

'D'you need to take a break?' Po asked.

They hadn't used a toilet since leaving home, and Tess had to admit that the urgency of emptying her bladder now outdid that of reaching Jo. Chewing down on her bottom lip, she nodded and Po began looking for a stopping place.

'I wonder what happened here?' he said shortly.

Tess spotted the unexpected activity ahead. There were several cop and sheriff's cruisers at the roadside. It had grown dark hours ago, so their lights flickered and strobed, turning the falling snow to coloured confetti. Initially she believed they'd come across a road traffic collision, but as Po slowed the Telluride to creep past, it was apparent that the police activity was concentrated on a gas station adjacent to the road.

Other than emergency vehicles, there were no cars at the pumps or parked on the snow-blanketed hardpack that would normally serve as a stopping point. She caught movement behind the windows and doors, but it appeared to be cops investigating something inside the small convenience store.

Burglary? Robbery? Whatever had gone on inside, Tess decided, it wasn't their business, and could have no bearing on them

collecting and bringing in Joanne. She was dying to know what
had befallen those inside, but satisfying her curiosity would delay
them too much. She squeezed Po a grimace. 'You'd best keep on
going; I'm just going to have to hunker down behind a bush.'

'You'd best make it quick,' he said with a smile, 'otherwise I
might have to dig you out.'

They made a quick stop a mile out of town. Tess ducked down
alongside the car while Po stood guard. He needn't have, because
now there wasn't a single impression in the most recent snowfall
to mark a vehicle's passage, so she was unlikely to be seen. He'd
foregone the warmth of the heated seats to have a quick cigarette.
Back inside once more, he turned down the collar of his plaid
shirt, the only concession he'd made to fight the chill. His hair
was dotted with melting snowflakes, as must her beanie cap. Tess
rubbed her hands, watching the ruddiness grow mottled with
patches of paler skin. It was verging on sub-zero temperatures
outside, so Joanne simply had to be suffering by now.

'We've gotten this far,' she announced, 'are you more confident
of making it to Vanceboro now?'

The snowfall grew heavier. Sound was muted and visibility was
close to a few yards at best. The glow from the SUV's headlights
seemed to be absorbed by the conditions. Po hit the windshield
wipers, to bat away the accumulation that had gathered in the past
few seconds. Instantly the snow piled up again.

'What was that you were askin'?' Po asked, deadpan.

ELEVEN

B ruce Harper stood alongside Siobhan Doyle's SUV, peering through the tattered net curtain of falling snow at the approach to the border. In the minutes he'd observed, nobody had crossed, but he'd spotted staff; shoveling snow off the sidewalks, but they were still active. He questioned if Joanne Mason had made an attempt at slipping past, but didn't think it was likely. Being suspected of several murders, her face would be plastered all over law enforcement and federal government alerts. She might have disguised her looks, but he'd bet that single women were coming under extra scrutiny, and an overdone disguise would be an immediate giveaway to agents trained to single out the unusual. He wondered if she had stood nearby, as he did now, assessing her chances of crossing unchallenged into the neighbouring country, and realizing how hopeless her chances were. He turned to study Siobhan. This time she'd alighted the car to stand alongside him. She shivered all the way down to her boots, hands tucked under her armpits against the painful chill.

'What's your built-in radar saying, Harp?' she asked, teeth chattering.

'Couldn't rightly say. If she got past then she's in the wind by now,' he said. 'But I don't think she crossed. From what we've learned about Joanne, she's prone to panic, and when it hits, her only recourse is to run.' He nodded at the small cluster of buildings housing the US Customs and Border Protection Agency, almost mirrored across the bridge by the Canadians', and said, 'I'd bet she didn't run in that direction.'

Harper thought that even during clement weather the traffic load on this border crossing would be negligible, mostly local residents and vacationers. He'd bet good money that the guards knew those crossing during the winter months on first-name terms. Trying to bluff her way past would be a big fail for Joanne. She neither held citizenship nor Native American status, so to enter Canada she'd be required to produce an Enhanced Driver's License or Enhanced Identification Card, failing those a birth certificate in combination with a government-issued photo identification. He very much doubted she'd been able to source any fake documents during the few days she'd been on the run.

He turned and perused the road on which they'd approached the crossing. He was confident that after leaving the gas station outside Lincoln that Joanne had plowed on through the storm to reach Vanceboro, therefore he was equally certain that she had been within grabbing distance of where he stood within the past few hours. If he were she and had suffered a collapse of confidence, where next would he have turned? Would he try to retreat the way he'd come or attempt to find another route? Would he seek someplace close by to hide and gather his wits after abandoning his original plan? Would he simply flee blindly, allowing paranoia and fear to guide him?

'We should check all hotels and guesthouses on this side of the river,' he stated. Without waiting for any counter suggestions from Siobhan, he returned to the car, sitting in the passenger side as before. He ignored her as she climbed back into the driver's seat, bitching noisily about the cold, and instead concentrated on his cell phone screen.

He had brought up a map, on which colored pins indicated various different services. He searched for anywhere that Joanne might have holed up to escape the storm. To his surprise there were very few hostelries in the vicinity, although a few locals offered Airbnb accommodation.

'Well, checking these shouldn't take us much time,' he said.

Siobhan said, 'We should think about booking lodgings, because whatever happens next, I don't see us traveling much further tonight.'

She started the SUV's engine and the automatic wipers kicked on. Harper looked out the windshield. The heaters were working overtime to keep it clear of condensation, but did little to melt the snow missed by the wipers; it had built up a good deal, standing a few inches deep now.

Harper didn't agree. 'I checked the forecast earlier. It promised heavier snowfall than before. Could block the roads. D'you want to get us stuck here in the ass-end of nowhere? I won't be happy.'

'How's getting caught in a goddamn winter cyclone suddenly my fault?'

'It's nobody's fault, not yours or mine, because it hasn't

happened yet. I intend locating Joanne Mason and putting her in the ground. If she isn't here and has moved on, we need to stick hard on her trail. I'm only giving you fair warning that I won't be pleased if your need for a comfortable bed allows me to lose her.'

'So forget I mentioned it, for fuck's sake. If the worst comes to worst, and we get stuck in a drift, I can always drag that blanket outta the trunk, and at least we've got each other to share body heat, right?'

Harper snapped a glare on her that made her instantly regret her sarcasm. Harper abstained many worldly desires, especially those of the flesh: never in adulthood had he engaged in sexual activity, or even bared his flesh to the caress of another person. He could appreciate Siobhan's beauty, and did – she was a fiery Celtic goddess in his eyes – without ever wishing to partake of her womanly pleasures; the very thought of snuggling naked under a blanket with her made his gorge rise and his skin crawl.

'OK, so book rooms,' he grunted. 'Separate rooms.'

'On whose tab?'

'What, you think the host will demand cash too?'

'I meant, are you paying for your own room or—'

'Do you think somebody paying us to find and eliminate the threat to them is going to quibble over the cost of a couple of flea-infested rooms in a goddamn rat's nest?'

'Was hoping for something two star or above at least,' Siobhan quipped, attempting to lighten his mood, but he was done with her prattling for now.

'Siobhan. Rent rooms, don't rent rooms; I seriously don't give a crap. I am, however, intent on bagging the reward on Joanne Mason's head before any of the others do. Don't let anything you do distract you – or distract *me* especially – from the hunt.'

'We can use enquiring about renting rooms as an excuse for asking about Joanne Mason,' Siobhan suggested. 'We can pretend she's a friend we are supposed to meet here before crossing into Canada, and inquire if she has booked in yet?'

'Suit yourself,' Harper grunted, 'but whose name d'you suppose she's using? Hmm, it's just as I thought. You didn't really think that through, did you, Siobhan.'

'So how are you going to get answers,' she sneered. 'Stomp them outta every hotelier you come across?'

'The situation back at the gas station called for that level of violence, Siobhan. I had to make things look like a robbery gone wrong, once that younger guy spotted me eyeballing the CCTV . . .'

'You don't need to remind me, Harp. All I was suggesting was approaching things subtler this time.'

'Maybe I should leave things to you, huh?'

'No, I only—'

'That's right, Siobhan. You *only*. You are *only* a fuckin' driver, being paid to drive. So do what you're here for; drive *here*.' Harper stabbed a thick fingertip on the nearest pin on the map.

He didn't give further instruction. He was over her and her smart mouth. Siobhan also stayed silent while she turned the SUV and followed the road back into Vanceboro. The road hadn't been plowed in a while. The snow squeaked under the weight of the SUV's thick tires and with each high-pitched noise a tic jumped in Siobhan's cheek, drawing up the corner of her mouth. In profile, her mouth dragged up into the leer of a demented clown. Siobhan seemed to have lost the attractive qualities he normally found in her features. He turned his head so she was merely a blur in his periphery. He forced down the urge to reach across, enfold her slim neck in his paw-like hands and throttle the life out of her.

TWELVE

If she didn't get warm soon Joanne was going to die. She was already mildly hypothermic, despite being indoors and beyond the freezing fingers of the wind. Before it had been cold, with nightfall the temperatures had dropped another twenty degrees. Her breath not only misted before her, it also crystalized on the scarves around her face and on the brims of her hats. Inside her oversized coat, and the several layers of clothing, she should have been warm, but she'd fallen into torpor allowing the cold to permeate through. She shivered violently, a small blessing: she had heard that in cases of hypothermia once the shivering stopped death quickly followed. She'd heard also that some hypothermic people often felt too hot and ripped off their clothing, making themselves more vulnerable again to the cold. For now she huddled as tightly as possible in her clothes, shivering, wincing at the pains darting through her extremities.

People talked about the cold of the grave; well, Joanne had experienced it for sure, and it was truly awful, something she hoped to avoid for a very long time. She must get her blood pumping, force some warmth into her limbs or they were going to fall off! Her feet felt worst, due to the snowmelt soaking them earlier. She told herself to get up. She didn't move, beyond squirming in pain again.

It had gone dark beyond the tiny window high up in the mausoleum wall. But as was often the way during heavy snowfalls, there was an unusual glow that lit the terrain. The weak light streaming in the windows was enough to pick out shapes and forms by. Joanne finally pushed on to her hands and knees, waited a few seconds for her sluggish blood to fuel her muscles, and then she pushed up to stand swaying and groaning in her oversized clothing. She rammed her hands under her armpits, took them out and blew on her palms, rubbed them furiously, then jammed them under her armpits again. At once she began stamping. Her knees creaked and the pain was almost unbearable in her feet, but she kept marching on the spot. She was still desperately cold, but even to be moving was a small victory and she emitted a sharp yelp and kept marching. Soon she was shaking her hands out and flapping her arms. She began cheering and goading herself on. Around her, the other residents of the mausoleum stayed silent, cold in their graves.

The thought gave her pause.

Was she somehow disrespecting the dead? Was her noisy exuberance for life somehow a desecration of their final resting place? Instantly that sense of dread she'd experienced for days returned, tenfold. Before she had thought she was the subject of unseen eyes, of being watched, now the sensation felt uncanny. Immediately she fell silent, halted her stomping and arm-flapping. She told herself it was because she had grown a little warmer, not because she could be the subject of disapproving ghosts.

She hurried to the door.

Earlier she'd tried pushing it all the way shut again, but it had stuck open a few inches on a warped flagstone. The windows flanking the door were opaque, so Joanne peered out of the crack against the jamb, unsure what she hoped to see. Desperate, with nowhere else to run, and nobody else to turn to, she had given in and called for help. Karen had not been a police detective in that moment, she'd been a loving sister, and she'd promised to help her through this, whatever people were accusing Joanne of doing. There hadn't been time to plead her innocence, nor much else. The battery was dying on her cell, so Joanne had told Karen where she was. Karen said she'd send help, but Joanne had no idea in what form the help would be. For some time she'd thought Karen would have no other recourse than send law enforcement out for her, but apparently that wasn't the case: even in the blizzard, cops would've been dispatched if they knew a wanted child murderer was on their patch. The place would have come alive with lights and sirens and Joanne marched out at gunpoint. She was reasonably certain that Karen hadn't called the cops. Outside the snow hadn't abated, it had grown stronger. A virgin expanse stretched back towards the narrow road alongside the river, even her footprints from before had been concealed under several inches of fresh snow.

To conserve her battery, Joanne had switched off her cell.

She was sorely tempted to switch it on, to check if Karen had tried calling her with an update on the rescue mission, but she got only as far as holding her trembling thumb next to the power switch. She put away the phone into her pocket.

She was layered in scarves, but she still felt the prickling of skin on the back of her neck.

She spun around, hands at her mouth now, expecting some loping presence to appear from the dimness, a denizen crawled up from the crypt, to grab her and haul her to hell where all child murderers belonged.

There was nothing there.

Of course there was nothing.

It was simply her heightened senses spinning on overdrive now that she had gotten her blood flowing again.

It made no difference. She cried into the dimness of the mausoleum, as though her accusers would hear. 'I didn't do it. I didn't harm those babies. I swear it wasn't me!'

Those were words she had barely been able to express before. Not because they were untrue, but because she didn't have a sympathetic ear to cry to. Her brief entreaty for help from Karen hadn't included an innocent plea; her sister assured her it wasn't necessary for her to help save her life. Karen hadn't promised not to hand her over to the police, but hopefully Joanne could convince her of her innocence before she was duly led away in handcuffs.

Joanne stared into the dimness. The weak light from the back window was faintly golden. It cut through the room in a bar. Rather than motes of dust, tiny crystals of ice danced on the breeze making its way through the partially open door. She should shove the door fully shut with her back and legs doing all the work, but instead she faced the door and her gaze again swept the virgin snow outside. A cry caught in her throat: the expanse was no longer pristine, deep footprints spoiled it.

Her first instinct was to flee to the darkest corner of the mausoleum, but she denied the impulse to hide. What if those were the footprints of the savior sent by Karen, not one of the hunters who'd dogged her tracks since West Roxbury? She approached the door tentatively, then placed her head close to the gap. Craning from one side to the other she had a wider view of the cemetery. Beyond falling snow there was no hint of movement. The track cut past the mausoleum as though their destination was much deeper within the burial ground.

Joanne was undecided.

Her rescuer might well have missed her hiding place, and carried on further into the grounds. Should she save them both a wait and go outside and track him down? His tracks through the snow should assist her to reach him quickly. Should she simply go outside and holler into the darkness, hoping he'd hear her over the blizzard? No. She must follow neither idea, because she'd no idea whose tracks those were. It was difficult to think why anyone else was out in this storm unless hunting for her. But what if this hunter's intentions weren't in line with Karen's? What if this person chose to grab her and hand her over at the Washington County Sheriff's Department in exchange for a reward? Worse, what if the one hunting her was the same monster that'd slaughtered the young family and other staff in the house, and had chased her through the gardens with a bloody hammer in his huge hand. She'd narrowly escaped when another member of staff had darted from concealment, and he'd gone after the man instead of her. What if he had resumed the chase, and was as relentless and dogged as she feared? Was it him that now prowled through the graveyard with a hammer poised to crack open her skull?

'For frick's sake, Jo,' she moaned. 'That's just insane, and impossible. How could he possibly be here? How would he be able to track you hundreds of miles across three states and find you here, in a blizzard in the middle of nowhere? He's a monster, but he's a human one, he doesn't have fricking supernatural powers!'

Then why not go outside and shout, bring her rescuer back in her direction?

She wavered a few seconds longer, but her need to get warm trumped her fear of the unknown.

She tugged the door open by increments. Snow had built up at its foot, and some had blown in under the corners and at the open crack. It wasn't as easy opening as she'd first thought. She of course had left her supplies in the abandoned car, and had not as much as taken a sip of water in . . . how many hours? She was weakened, frozen almost to the core, so even the simplest tasks would prove more wearing on her. The flagstone she'd earlier strained to close the door against now held on to the door and she wondered if it was simply being obstinate for the sake of pissing her off. She cursed and tugged and almost fell on her backside when the door suddenly jumped open. She scrambled to regain balance, grabbing this time at the door for support. She wondered how much racket she'd made and if it would be enough to draw her rescuer back to her.

Stepping outside, the full blast of the storm hit. Her oversized coat snapped tightly about her like a shroud. Her hats and scarves threatened to fly away in the wind. Her cheeks felt blazing hot, but the sensation would last only seconds before the wind dug in its icy fingers and froze her exposed flesh. She bent at the waist, throwing one shoulder into the wind and pressed through a drift of snow towards the corner of the mausoleum where the footprints angled past. The snow was fully in her face for several seconds, and it both confused and disconcerted her equally. She bleated in discomfort, and pushed harder and then was around the corner. The building did little to break the storm, as she was still in the reach of the wind and snow, but moving horizontally to its force wasn't as difficult as it was head on.

Her wholly unsuitable footwear was immediately chocked with icy slush. Her trousers had not fully dried out from earlier and grew wetter than ever, the seeping cold was painful. But Joanne forced her mind to shut out all the bad stuff and concentrate on locating a possible savior. She high-stepped through snow now knee-deep, making for where the single line of footprints cut through the grounds. She checked back from where the prints originated. If she could spot the person's vehicle she'd head directly to it, wait for him there. The blizzard thwarted any attempt at spotting anything beyond a hundred feet. There were trees and sculptured topiary out there, but could she see any of them? No. She made out humps in the snow that could have been buried markers on graves, and to her right there was a large memorial depicting a winged angel. As the heavy snow sifted down it gave the statue a semblance of subtle movement. Despite the subject matter, it was still a discomforting image.

She shuddered and checked in the other direction. She spotted a darker shade flit beyond the falling snow. She moved to follow, but came to a halt. Wandering out into that snowfield was not a wise move. Instead she called out. 'Hey! Hey, you out there. Can you hear me?'

She could barely hear the words leaving her throat; she couldn't expect anyone else to hear. Her shouts would be muffled by the snowfall to anyone more than an arm's length distant. She must make a sharper noise, something more likely to carry. If she picked up a rock and struck it against the mausoleum wall, she could perhaps make an alarm distinct enough to draw in her rescuer. It was a good plan, but for two reasons. First, where would she find a rock under feet of snow, and second, where the hell was the mausoleum? She couldn't see it for the volume of falling snow. Panic crawled from her chest up into her throat.

She wasn't lost. All she needed to do was reverse her direction and follow her own trail back through the snow. She'd be back within relative safety in less than thirty seconds. But that was too logical a strategy for a panicked mind to concoct. She floundered through the snow, gasping and falling to her knees before scrambling up once more. She croaked in alarm, barely able to breathe, and realized that she had lost direction with her own tracks and had come across those of the original person to cross the graveyard. She hoped that their direction would indicate the way back to her shelter. She looked for boot prints; the heels should aim back the way in which she should go. But there were no heels. The tracks showed the hint of two sharp points, cloven hooves. She had misread the tracks as those of a human rescuer when they belonged to a damn moose or other ungulate.

'Damnit!' she cried.

Some panic subsided, as she could still follow the tracks in reverse through the blizzard and relocate the mausoleum. However, she'd made a stupid assumption and it had almost proven her downfall. Her rescuer hadn't arrived yet, and she'd no real sense of when, or even if, they'd make it here through the blizzard. She'd swear that she had seen a human figure flitting beyond the nearest gravestones, but it couldn't have been. Other symptoms of hypothermia could be delirium and hallucinations; maybe she was suffering worse than she first thought, and she had followed her own wishful thinking out there into the storm.

Stumbling into the moose prints, she followed the furrow it had cut through the snowfield, and soon enough was back adjacent to the mausoleum. It was an icebox, but it would support life longer than if she stayed outside. The door was still open as she'd left it, and her first instinct was to check for fresh wet prints leading inside. There were none. The only indications of passage were the tracks she had made. Before entering fully, she turned and peered hopefully over her shoulder towards the road, wishing to see a car's lights heralding rescuers, but the weight of snow thwarted her.

She set her back to the door to help push it closed, but again the buckled flooring caught and held the door ajar. Earlier she could see enough with the golden light filtering in through the small windows, but having been outside her eyes must adjust again: it was inky dark inside. And the stone was frigid. As soon as she sat, huddled with her arms around her knees and chin buried under her scarves, she could feel the cold seeping through to her bones. Her little outdoors adventure – and leaving the door open – had possibly cost her severely.

THIRTEEN

Pinky Leclerc muted the volume on the TV.

He'd assumed a position on Po's reclining chair, feet up on a small stool, his ankles crossed. He had ransacked Po's fridge, seeking something to eat that'd be satisfying without threatening his weight-loss diet. He'd body-swerved the leftover meatloaf Po – or perhaps it had been Tess – had plated up and wrapped in tinfoil, and chose instead to chow down on some sliced breaded ham and pickles. If only he had known that Tess was so protective of the pickle jar she'd fight to the death for it, he'd have chosen more wisely. Tiny crumbs flew off his chest as he jerked upright and turned to face the front door. He set aside his food. He tiptoed towards the door, a fully loaded pistol in each hand.

There had been a clunk from outside. It was not so much the sound that had alerted him, more a sense of impending doom. He was no psychic, or prophet, but he trusted his gut when it warned of unseen danger: it was an ancient instinct bred out of many modern humans, but after being the target of dangerous enemies most of his life, his instincts had been fine-tuned. He crept to the door and set his body to one side. In the door Po had installed a fisheye lens, through which there was a panoramic view of the front yard. It was OK for checking if a pizza delivery had arrived, but Pinky wasn't keen on using it when there could be somebody with a gun pressed to it on the other side. He'd seen too many movies where assassins slayed their targets through such ploys, to know it was rather implausible, but to hell if he was the dope going to get caught out. He remained to the left of the door: if anyone was to burst inside, then the door would swing towards him, concealing him long enough to launch a counterattack.

He was tall enough to crane and get a peek outside via the small arch of toughened glass at the top of the door. The glass was semi-opaque, but through it he hoped to spot movement. There was nothing obvious, not when the dancing snow obscured everything else. Pinky remained there a moment longer, then sidestepped away, moving from the open-plan living area towards the rooms at that side of the house. There was a guest bedroom with en-suite bathroom, a utility room and also a small vestibule that led to storage closets. He checked them all without turning on any lights, making only cursory investigation to ensure no windows had been pried open. Once his search was completed, he cut back across to the large island that marked the transition from living room to kitchen. His position allowed a view of the back door and also out of the kitchen window. On this side of the house were Tess and Po's bedroom, plus a spare room she used as an office, and also a larger bathroom. Pinky usually avoided their private rooms, but this time was different. He was charged with keeping the ranch safe from harm, and it was a task he wouldn't shirk from. He moved down the short access corridor and came first to Tess's office. The light was doused but she'd left on a couple of computers: colorful screen savers danced and whirled in kaleidoscopic patterns in the darkness. He ensured he didn't dwell on the writhing patterns, not when they could leave afterimages burned into his vision. He checked that the window hadn't been forced, then immediately moved on to check the master bedroom and bathroom. In the latter a window was left cracked open to allow fresh air inside, but it was latched on a security feature so that it barely opened an inch. An inch, as the saying went, was as good as a mile, when it only took an arsonist to push a tube through the gap and feed accelerant inside the house. Pinky swiftly jammed one gun in his waistband at the back, freeing a hand to secure the window.

A crash resounded from the front of the house.

Pinky loped through into the kitchen, from where he could see the entirety of the open-plan area. For a second he expected to find the blazing contents of a Molotov cocktail thrown through a window. The room was untouched, and there was no sign of what had caused the crashing sound. He swiftly returned to his position beside the door and again craned for a look outside. A raised porch ran the length of the house. To Pinky's right Po had erected a swing seat, on which he had spent many hours enjoying the company of his friends. The swing was moving, but Pinky thought that the wind was to blame. It hadn't been the seat bashing against the house, as there was plenty of clearance on the deck to swing unhindered. Nothing else caught his eye.

He unlatched the door and pulled it open a fraction, still concealed by its inward arch. When nobody lunged to force a path inside, he stepped back and allowed the door to swing open. A few errant snowflakes swirled in on the draught, but nothing else. Pinky moved through the doorway toward the seat; that way he didn't highlight his silhouette in light for longer than a second. He checked the rocking of the swing by pressing a thigh against it. All the while he listened and peered towards where Po's Mustang sat under a thick blanket of snow. He could barely make out its shape beyond the heavy snowfall, but spotted a hunched figure darting for cover behind it.

'Whoever you are, you'd best show your hands, you.' Pinky aimed the single pistol he held, sighting down the barrel to where his shout had caused the figure to jerk down.

There was no response.

Pinky's gaze darted, seeking others. He spotted a set of footprints cutting in a zigzag pattern across the yard. It appeared that the one who had made the tracks had completed a circuit of the house – probably while Pinky had been conducting his own search inside – before returning to the yard and moving around the parked muscle car.

Pinky strode to the edge of the deck, the pistol never wavering. 'I don't give second warnings, me. There's no good reason for anyone to be out in this weather, so I have to conclude you've snuck here for malicious reasons, you. Kinda gives me the right to put a bullet in your gut and watch you bleed out, eh?'

Whoever had ducked behind the car, they didn't reply.

Pinky glanced at the snow. His sneakers weren't fit for the conditions, but he didn't have time to go and find suitable footwear. He went down the steps gingerly, ensuring he didn't slip on his ass, and never lost sight of his intended target. Snowflakes batted his eyelids and melted on his lips. He snorted to clear his nostrils. He didn't allow the blizzard to deter him. Rather than head directly for the car, he took an oblique angle across the yard, which would put anyone crouching behind it in his sights, without him getting too close. Who knew, perhaps he was not the only one armed and prepared to shoot.

He crouched slightly as he aimed directly at the spot where the stalker must be hiding. There was nobody there. Yet the churned up snow confirmed that his eyes hadn't deceived him. While he'd been throwing out warnings and making his cautious way across the yard, his quarry must've squirmed away on their belly through the snow. He saw that a messy furrow led to the edge of the property and under the boundary fence that separated Po's land from the woods at the riverside.

Concerned the disappearing act could be a ploy to draw him away from the house, he paused a moment, took a quick look back at the rectangle of light – all he could distinguish of the house now – and thought he should've shut the door behind him. Anyone could sneak inside while he was out in the storm, seeking whoever had crawled away on their belly like a slug. He almost backtracked to the house.

Something crackled nearby and he swung forty-five degrees to peer into the woods. The skulker had apparently entered the trees, then sought cover from where they could spy on him. Pinky's grip on his gun was solid; his index finger lay alongside the trigger guard. It would take only the fraction of a second to adjust his finger and shoot. He moved towards the source of the crackling: low hanging branches were being broken and were shedding their burdens of snow. By comparison, Pinky's scalp, his shoulders, and even the barrel of his pistol all carried thin layers of snowflakes.

'Going to give you to the count of three, and if you don't come out, I'm coming in shooting, me.'

More crackling of branches indicated a swift retreat.

Pinky lunged after his prey and within seconds was entangled in the same type of branches that encumbered the other's escape. He checked for signs of movement, could hear nothing now except the wind in the treetops, but spotted another trench dug into the snow. It led deeper into the woods, towards the frozen river. Was his prey desperate enough to try escaping across the ice? Here, Po had told him, the Presumpscot River was tidal. Heavier salt water lay on the bottom, with fresh water on top. The fresh water was prone to freezing over during the coldest winters, but not the saline beneath: in the past several people had fallen through the thin ice and perished. Pinky thought that drowning could prove the perfect antidote to a goddamn arsonist.

He checked behind once more, but now couldn't even tell where the woods ended and where Po's yard began. He felt certain he'd neither get lost nor freeze to death in the next few minutes, so went on, intending on pushing the stalker to the steep, slick rocks at the riverside. His feet sank to the ankles in the ground layer, his sneakers offering little protection from the seeping cold.

Nothing about the circumstances spoke of innocent behaviour: whoever was out there it was for the wrong reason and he felt no qualms about pushing them into the freezing river, or in fact putting a bullet in them if need be.

The kicked-up snow made following simple enough; even as heavy as the blizzard was it wasn't fast enough to obliterate the trail. Pinky pushed harder, intent on catching up and forcing answers from whoever it was out there. He spotted movement, a blur of motion and color against the white.

'Hey, you! Stop right there!'

The figure didn't halt, it kept going. Where it disappeared, Pinky guessed the bank began its steep slope to the river. He almost expected to hear a croak of alarm, followed almost instantly by a splash. Neither sound rewarded him. He pushed forward, up to his shins in snow. His trousers were soaked through and his sweatshirt failed to keep out the chill; his vitality was being leached with each step.

Coming to the edge of the river, Pinky found his footing precarious. Shelves of rock were laid one atop the other, each slick with ice and tapering icicles thick and long enough to easily pierce a human torso. The trail he'd followed disappeared at the riverside, several feet below him, and it was obvious that his quarry had used rocks exposed by the low water level, and thicker ice patches, as stepping stones to cross the Presumpscot. On the other side of the river there was a public park. There was no way on earth he'd trust the ice to support his bulk. The lurker most likely was out of Pinky's reach. He stood a moment longer peering across the river, trying to determine movement among the trees on the opposite bank, but saw nothing.

'Yeah, you goddamn bitch, you'd better keep running, you,' he called and wagged his pistol, barely confident his words would carry through the dampening effects of the blizzard.

Nobody replied, but he didn't expect one.

He stood a moment longer, trying to look menacing, but all he achieved was another gathering of snow. He turned and headed back, following his own trail through the woods. On the way out he'd been full of expectation, keen on catching up with the lurker and teaching them a lesson. On his return to the ranch it was chewing on disappointment. He felt the cold twice as much, walking as he was into the wind. Acrid smoke billowed around him before he saw the flames.

'No, no, don't you dare, you,' he croaked, and he charged through the trees and spilled out into Po's yard.

Thankfully the house was still intact, but Po's pride and joy, his vintage muscle car, blazed ferociously.

FOURTEEN

Compressed ice squeaked under the Telluride's tires as Po brought the vehicle to a cautious halt. There, in Vanceboro, the streets had been plowed, but since then more snow had fallen and local traffic had dug ruts in it that had since frozen, forming traps for the unwary that could catch a tire and resist steering. Po had found the last ten miles difficult going, even for a man that prided himself on superlative driving skills. He got out of the car to smoke a cigarette and to calm the jitter in his chest.

Inside the SUV, Tess remained snuggled in her winter coat and beanie hat. The heater was on full, but she still experienced the external chill after Po's rapid opening and closing of the driver's door. She could see him through the accumulated snowflakes on her window, shivering and kicking at the white mound at curbside while sucking down on his well-earned cigarette. She looked away, concentrating again on her cell phone. Detective Ratcliffe had given Joanne's location as a cemetery outside Vanceboro, but couldn't be more specific than that. Tess searched the Internet and brought up a map. The only cemetery indicated on it stood adjacent to the St Croix River, maybe two miles outside of town. She tried orienting the map to her current position, but couldn't make out a street sign from where Po had parked. Ahead and to the right there appeared to be a gas station, currently closed judging by the lack of lights. Tess made a quick adjustment to the search criteria and brought up the gas station. They'd stopped on Water Street, a continuation of Route 6, on the approach to the border crossing. The cemetery was behind her, more or less due south.

The screen display changed and the ringtone she'd specifically assigned to him tinkled, announcing Pinky was calling.

She answered. 'Hey, Pinky.'

'Oh, Tess, I'm glad I got you. I wasn't sure if Nicolas was driving so I rang your number instead.'

Pinky had dropped his quirky manner of speech, an immediate indicator that something was very wrong.

'What's wrong? What . . . has something happened, Pinky?'

'Is Nicolas there with you? I swear to Jesus, when he hears what they did to—'

'Are you hurt, Pinky?'

'No. But if Nicolas chooses to punch me in the nards, I'll deserve it.'

'That doesn't sound good.'

'I messed up, Tess. Big time.'

'Is it the arsonist again?'

'Yeah,' he wheezed, 'but that should be arsonists. Plural. I stopped them from burning down your house, but they double-teamed me and, well, damn it, you'd better get Nicolas.'

Tess rapped her knuckles on the windshield. Po squinted back at her, saw her urgent gestures and got the message. He flicked aside his cigarette and lunged to get back inside.

'Whassup?'

'It's Pinky,' Tess warned him, as she held out the phone for them both to hear, 'and something bad has happened.'

'I'm sorry, man, I tried, me, but—'

Po cut him off. 'Let's establish something important first, Pinky. Are *you* OK?'

'No, I'm smarting with shame, but I'm physically unhurt if that's what you're concerned about.'

'OK. That's good. Nothin' else is more important than you're OK, podnuh.'

'You might not think that once I tell you what's happened.'

Pinky delivered the news that Po's precious car was now a smoldering hunk of scorched metal, burned wires and melted plastic and rubber. 'I swear I tried putting out the fire but it was hopeless. It was already burning furiously by the time I got back. I was a fool, Nicolas; I was tricked, me, so's the firebug could attack your car while I was off chasing shadows.'

The awful news was greeted by silence. Tess had a tough time absorbing the magnitude of what had occurred, let alone how Po must feel. He loved that car. It was as much a part of his persona as his laconic voice and the motor oil ingrained in his knuckles. She reached to touch him, the only offer of support she could make just then. Po's reaction surprised her, and most definitely Pinky. 'This kinda forces my hand,' he said, calmer than anyone in their right mind would be expected to react. 'I was thinking of trading my Mustang against a car more suited to fatherhood. A muscle car with a baby seat in back ain't the ideal vehicle for doing the school run in.'

Tess gawped, but only for the split-second it took to understand he was trying to lessen Pinky's pain. His normally turquoise eyes seemed so dark they were bottomless. She squeezed his forearm in consolation and could feel how tense he was.

'Nicolas,' Pinky went on, 'I don't know what to say to make things better, me. I promised I'd protect your home while you were away, and my pledge included protecting your car. I know how much she meant to you and I feel almost as bad as if I'd failed to save Tess's life.'

'It's an inanimate piece of machinery,' said Po, 'and doesn't compare to how I feel about Tess, so don't fret, podnuh.'

'Yeah, maybe it was a poor comparison, but still—'

'Did you see who was responsible?'

'Sorry, not once, me. While I chased one of them towards the river, his buddy must've snuck in behind me and set fire to your car.'

'You didn't get eyes on any of them?'

'No, bruh, I didn't. It's blizzarding back here. Well, one of them ducked down behind the car and I took off after him, but I never once got a look at his face.'

'Man or woman?'

'Couldn't say for certain, me. But in my mind it was a guy, and nothing he did gave me reason to think otherwise.'

'He ducked behind the car, then you chased him. How'd he escape?'

'He belly-crawled away, then once in the woods he must've stood up and run like a jackrabbit, him. I heard movement and followed his tracks down to the river. It had frozen over in places and there were enough stepping stones for him to have gotten over to the park.'

'Sounds as if they intended luring you away, meaning they expected to find you at home and planned accordingly.'

'How'd they know to expect me, eh? Maybe when they lured me out they were expecting you to be the one runnin' around in the woods?'

Tess interjected, as everything concerning the latest arson attack was pure speculation and couldn't be verified. 'Don't you think we should call the cops?'

'Not my usual style,' said Po, 'but under the circumstances, and the previous attacks, I must involve them.'

She noted how haunted his features had grown. The loss of his car was bad, but sat much lower in his priorities than the safety of her and their unborn child did. He was worried that his enemies had struck as close to home as this, and by what target they might choose next in order to hurt him. 'Pinky,' he said, 'I'm gonna get in touch with Alex, and have him send over a squad car. If you can make the preliminary report to the cops I'd appreciate it. You OK doing that?'

'Yeah, man, sure. The cops around here treat me with more respect than they did back home in Louisiana, but that ain't saying much.'

'I'll ensure Alex knows it's you at the house so there's no misunderstanding.'

Alex Grey was one of Tess's elder brothers, currently a patrol sergeant with Portland PD. He knew Jerome 'Pinky' Leclerc beyond his rap sheet, but the same couldn't be said for some of his colleagues. Sadly, Pinky still lived in a world where a black man with a criminal record discovered in a white man's home could be treated with instant suspicion and perhaps an over-zealous response.

'Chances are,' Tess said, 'that they won't risk coming back again tonight, but maybe you should go home to your own apartment. I'd hate for you to maybe fall asleep and be burned to death if those idiots do make another try at the house.'

'I hear what you're saying, pretty Tess, but no. I'm not running from them, and I swear I won't shut my eyes, not even to blink, till you guys get back.'

'We're in Vanceboro now,' Po informed him, 'and will hopefully have the girl in the next half hour. Drivin' conditions are real bad, but I think we'll make it back to Portland again. Can't swear how soon, but I wouldn't bet on seein' us till morning light.'

'I've got my guns, and I'm spiked on adrenalin, me. No way I'm sleeping tonight.'

'Don't go waving round those pistols until after the cops have left,' Po cautioned.

'I don't have no death wish, me,' Pinky reassured him.

As the men finished up their conversation, Tess remained silent, allowing Po to guide Pinky through, among other things, the process of filing a police report that would satisfy his motor insurance provider. Po had fetched some of the cold inside with him, but the heater had soon dispelled it. She was beginning to feel hot inside her coat and beanie hat. She shifted, allowing some of her body heat to escape her coat's confines and considered cracking open the window to let in some fresh air. She didn't, because the blizzard kicked up again, the wind squalling around the nearest rooftops, so all their warmth must be conserved. She noted headlights glittering through the falling snow, and saw a large SUV prowling along Water Street towards the Telluride. Nothing in the car's approach should have raised her hackles, and yet she felt itchy, as if her body reacted subconsciously to impending danger. A sharp exhalation escaped her. The SUV hove alongside, and for several seconds she met the scrutiny of the driver. It was a woman, perhaps aged in her late thirties. She was undeniably attractive, a natural redhead with green eyes, and a spray of freckles across her nose. However, there was something sour about the woman's squint and dismissive twist of her mouth as she gave the SUV more gas and plowed on past. Beyond the woman, Tess caught a hint of her passenger, but only as an amorphous hulk that almost filled the far side of the car, topped by a huge square head Frankenstein's monster would be proud of. She gained the impression that he – she assumed it was a male by his brutish build – had also studied Tess with as much interest as the woman had. Studied and then dismissed her as inconsequential. Tess twisted in her seat, trying to spot the SUV again, but beyond a few glimmers of light was thwarted by the blizzard.

Po had ended his call with Pinky.

'Did you see that?' she asked.

'The Chevy Tahoe that went past? Sure did.'

'What did you make of it?'

He shrugged. 'Do I even get a clue?'

'There was something about the occupants that got my hackles up. The driver looked at me as if I was a piece of dog crap.'

Po checked for any sign of the SUV. 'They've gone. Probably just locals with no truck for strangers crazy enough to drive here in this darn storm.'

'Yeah, maybe that's all it was,' she said without conviction.

FIFTEEN

Taking off her shoes was the latest of the stupid mistakes she'd made since fleeing the murder scene. Joanne had resisted the urge and the bone-deep chill, but in the end the pain in her toes had grown excruciating and she had struggled out of her shoes to try rubbing some warmth into them. Her socks were sodden and had taken some effort to pull off with fingers equally as pained as her toes. Her skin was pale blue below her ankles and worryingly there were strange grey-white blotches on several of her digits. Fear struck her so suddenly that her stomach somersaulted and acid spouted up her throat. The blotches were precursors to the flesh turning necrotic through frostbite. Most often the cure for frostbite was amputation, and how would she escape her pursuers when missing several toes on each foot? She rubbed and massaged and then rubbed some more, hoping the friction was enough to invigorate the tissue and stave off greater problems. The warmth she built was fleeting, and probably a totally pointless exercise when she wrestled back into her socks, the damp wool instantly sapping the warmth from her flesh. Her shoes wouldn't easily go back on. She didn't believe her feet had swollen, or that her shoes had shrunk, but it became a challenge fitting one into the other. Finally she had to stand and employ gravity to help settle her feet in her shoes again and the pain caused her to cry in despair. She forced her legs to move and she shuffled stiff-kneed across the icy paving, encouraging sluggish blood to circulate.

After completing several revolutions of the cramped space, she stood next to where she'd originally sat and shambled on the spot.

'Where are you, Karen?' she cried, as if her sister might appear at the door with a warm blanket and cup of steaming cocoa.

There was of course no answer.

She shambled a minute more, feeling as if an eternity had passed, and cried out again in wordless frustration. She staggered towards the door and pulled it open a few inches. Often snow flurries in Maine fell as tiny, sharp fragments of ice, blown side-ways out of the north-west to bite and sting exposed flesh; the snow that fell now was the big fluffy type beloved of Christmas movies. There was nothing festive about the killer storm. Nevertheless she would rather fight it than give in to the hopelessness of being rescued from that icy tomb. She hadn't driven too far, maybe two miles at most, from town, but had no delusion of making it back to town before succumbing. But during the drive, while contemplating passage across the river into Canada, she'd been vaguely aware of passing several homesteads built on the slopes above the road. If there were a house within a few hundred yards, she would throw herself on the mercy of the occupants. Some houses and businesses in Vanceboro had appeared decrepit, abandoned, and the same might be said of some of the homes out here in the wilderness, but it didn't matter. Finding shelter in one of those collapsing structures, where she could at least get a fire going, was preferable to freezing in this crypt of icy stone.

She pulled her several layers of clothing around her frame again, hugging them to her stomach. Bent at the waist she again challenged the storm, but this time headed directly downhill, away from the tomb and the footprints in the snow towards the road. It was so cold it hurt to breathe. Did she have the fortitude to travel a few hundred yards through the hellish storm? The wind chittered among the denuded treetops down alongside the river, and she could swear that it was the elements laughing at her stupidity. She literally swore vehemently at those unseen spirits, and pushed on, turning towards the distant border town but hoping to come across shelter much nearer.

Previously the wind had been at her back. Now she fought against it, and each step was an effort. The snowflakes that got under her hats plastered her face and made seeing difficult. She blinked frozen eyelashes, cursing again, swearing so harshly was not in her usual vocabulary, but spitting out the coarse words helped flush her cheeks and add some steel to her spine. Angry, she battled on, conjuring words to make a sailor blush.

Her curses became whimpers in short order.

She staggered on, moaning, setting one foot in front of the other in the tire tracks she'd made coming this way. Already they'd been buried under a layer of snow, but were still definable in the weird gloom. By following her tire tracks she hoped not to blunder off route and lose the road. The cemetery was lost to the swirling void behind her, ahead was as featureless. It was only after trekking for what felt like another eternity that she grew aware of the change in direction of the wind. Before it had been at her back, but without warning it pummeled her from her left side. Rather than turn from it, she hunched into the wind and tried to make sense of her surroundings. The ghosts of giant trees loomed to each side, but there was an expanse of barely broken white sweeping up to meet the clouds. At the center of the open ground she could make out the faint delineation of a wire fence and assumed that the trough alongside it signaled an unplowed road. She couldn't recall exactly where she'd spotted homesteads on the drive in, but this was reminiscent of the entrances to many of the housing plots. She took a final lingering look in the direction of Vanceboro and knew it was out of reach: she turned and trod through shin-deep snow, using the low fence as a marker to keep her on the track. The wind battered her, slapping and pummeling, but she set her jaw and bent into it and continued uphill.

She went down on all fours.

What? Why was she crawling?

She tried to push to her feet, again setting her chin and peering into the blustering wind. Flakes invaded her eyelids and she crunched her lashes shut. It was much easier to stay down on all fours, that way her balance wasn't as compromised. She crawled on, then tried rising but fell again. Stay down, stay down, don't go hurting yourself, she counseled. She crawled on but the exertion was too much. It was all those damn clothes she'd layered on top of each other, too constrictive. She dragged off the hats and cast them aside. Tried worming out of her over-large coat, but the effort wasn't worth it. She needed to rest. She rolled on her back, comfortable on a cloud of snowflakes and laughed at the tickle of the storm's touch across her features, and how its fingers tousled her hair. She tugged at her coat, feeling warmer now and happy; happier than she'd ever felt before; happier than she'd any right to be. She wept and her tears turned to ice on her cheeks.

The snow continued falling, and Joanne didn't rise. Soon, she thought, all her troubles would pass.

SIXTEEN

'They could be cops,' Siobhan Doyle suggested to her taciturn passenger.

Bruce Harper grunted, gave a scornful shake of his head.

'How can you be certain?'

'I didn't get a cop vibe off them.'

'You put too much trust in your gut, Harp. One of these days it might be your undoing.'

'Gut instinct and the application of logic has gotten us this far. My hunches haven't failed me yet, have they?'

'Who's to say? I mean, we haven't found Joanne Mason yet, and there's nothing to say that she's even within a hundred miles of here.'

Harper thumbed back the way they'd come from. 'You're dismissing those two too quickly.'

'They looked out of place,' she admitted, 'but if they aren't cops, who else could they be?'

'I thought that some of the others had beaten us here, chasing the same reward that I am, but no, I don't think that's the case now. How could any of them beat us here to Vanceboro without access to the same clues we had.'

'We had clues?'

'We gained information.'

'Yeah,' she said. 'That reminds me, let's find someplace to get rid of that hard drive from the gas station before what's recorded on it comes back to bite us.'

'There isn't time for that now. I need you to take us back, I want to check out that couple in the Telluride again.'

'The woman had a good look at me,' Siobhan said. 'We might make 'em suspicious if we pass them going in the other direction.'

'So take us someplace where we can see them but they can't see us.'

'This is a ghost town, not many places I can hide the car or blend in.'

'Siobhan, take a look outta the goddamn window: there's enough cover from this storm to hide a parade of pink Cadillacs.'

'I guess,' she muttered, although the blizzard wasn't all it had been before, and they'd be spotted if she got too close.

She retraced their route back through town. Houses were set back on private lots, some high up on the slope above the road. It appeared that the recent lockdown hadn't been kind on the livelihoods of some of the locals; most of the business premises they passed were either closed or simply falling into ruin. A short distance from where they'd passed the Telluride earlier, the road doglegged through some tight ninety-degree bends; Siobhan considered stopping at the last corner from where they should have a view of the target vehicle.

Snow danced on the air, but the fury had momentarily left the storm, so they could see a fair distance along Water Street. The gas station on the right indicated the vicinity in which the Telluride had previously been parked; it had been tucked against the curb facing the gas station and the approach to the border beyond, as Siobhan recalled.

'Well, problem solved,' she muttered. 'They've bugged out, Harp. Could be miles into Canada by now.'

'Drive to where they were parked.'

'Why?'

Harper curled his lip and growled like a mean old junkyard dog.

Siobhan threw up her hands. 'I'm your driver. You want me to drive, I'll drive.'

She returned to Water Street and crawled the SUV along, coming to within ten feet of where the Telluride had previously been parked.

'Stop,' Harper instructed. 'Look.'

Siobhan could see what he was interested in. It was apparent from the fresh tire tracks in the snow that the driver had broken free of the icy ruts and performed a three-point turn in the road. Fresh tracks led past them, but didn't follow the bend in Route 6, they continued directly ahead. Siobhan thought the narrow track was some kind of service trail.

'Follow them,' said Harper.

'They could be locals who—'

Harper slammed a palm on the dashboard. 'Do not second-guess me.'

'Fair enough. I won't. I'll do *exactly* what you say, Harp.'

Fuming, Siobhan stared forward as she followed the tire tracks on to the minor road. It left the outskirts of Vanceboro in no time and then followed the contours of the St Croix River, before angling slightly further inland. Hill country, crowned by snow-laden trees dominated the scene. The momentary lull in the storm ended and it was as if the blizzard was more determined than ever to bury everything. Finally, Siobhan darted a glance across at Harper. His huge face in profile reminded her of a gnarly tree stump, more correctly a scarred chopping block. He either refused to return her glance or her feelings really were as insignificant to him as she believed. She concentrated on the road, ensuring a moment of distraction didn't ram them into a drift.

The Telluride's fresh tracks were being obliterated with every passing minute, but it didn't matter. There were few turn-offs and no suggestion it had followed any of them. They drove past several homesteads perched on the hillside to their right but again there was no indication the couple in the Telluride had returned home to any of them. Siobhan kept the SUV moving, the windshield wipers battling furiously to keep her view clear. Ahead in the dimness she spotted lights, lost to her a second later. The blizzard helped obscure their prey, but also the fact that she and Harper were following. The Telluride must only be fifty or less yards ahead. She cleared her throat, catching Harper's attention. When he scowled across at her, she nodded ahead.

'Yeah,' he said, 'I saw them. You'd best drop back, but not far enough to lose them.'

'I'd have to try hard to lose them,' she grumbled under her breath.

Harper must have heard. He said, 'Don't tempt fate, Siobhan.'

She slowed but without losing any traction. The SUV pushed on, its tires in the Telluride's tracks. They passed a broad expanse of hillside from where the forest had been cleared. Wind buffeted them, rocking the SUV on its chassis. Siobhan gripped the steering wheel tighter. There were faint tracks on a road leading uphill, but a vehicle hadn't formed them: probably an animal had made them. The tire tracks they'd followed kept on going.

'Cemetery ahead,' Siobhan announced.

Harper acknowledged the same road sign she'd read with a jerk of his chin. Snow clung to it, but most of the sign was discernible in their headlights.

'Check it out,' Siobhan said.

'I see them.'

Not far ahead the Telluride had stopped and its lights had been doused. Two figures stood shin deep in snow near the cemetery's low boundary wall. They turned to face the SUV and were painted in the glow of its headlights. Siobhan checked out the same woman as before, noting that she was shorter and stockier than the first impression she'd formed. However, that could have been down to the fact her male colleague towered over her. He was tall and slim, but there was nothing frail-looking about him. His shoulders were broad and his arms thick and long; she surmised he might swing a hammer or axe for a living. Both eyed the SUV suspiciously.

'Should I stop?' asked Siobhan.

'And give the game away that we're following them? No, carry on, nice and easy and go past.'

'If we play dumb, they'll for sure know we're following them.'

'You're right. You got your gun handy?'

'Seriously?'

'Maybe we won't need it. Stop adjacent to them, but let me do the talking. You keep your pistol ready but out of sight. If there's any shooting to be done, you can pass the gun to me.'

Siobhan drove and pulled up so their hood was close to that of the Telluride. The couple had observed their approach, but without moving to meet them. It was notable that the tall guy stood slightly forward from the woman, so he was between her and potential danger. Siobhan was on the left of the car, so it was Harper's big, florid face that greeted them when he powered down the window. From her angle she saw a deep pit form in his cheek when he graced the couple with a broad, friendly grin; Siobhan was familiar with his faux joviality, he reminded her of a leering hyena about to bite clean through flesh and bone.

'Having a bit of car trouble, fella?' Harper asked the tall man.

'We're good,' the man drawled.

'Thought you might need a little help. Weather's atrocious, isn't it? Couldn't just drive on past and leave you stranded out here.'

'I appreciate your concern, bruh, but no, we're good.'

'You visiting the cemetery at night in the middle of a storm?' Harper grinned again. 'You on a ghost hunt or something?'

'I can see how it might appear weird to some,' the tall man replied. 'But no, we just stopped so's my girl can relieve herself. Wasn't expectin' anyone to come along here, see? Not at night in the middle of a storm.'

Touché, thought Siobhan.

'Saw you guys back in town,' said Harper.

The guy read his meaning without him having to spell it out.

'Couldn't find anywhere open. We drove down this trail looking for somewhere private.'

'You've come aways outta town,' Harper pointed out.

'Yeah, noticed your lights behind us and hoped you would pull into one of those homes back there. Things got a bit desperate, so we stopped here and hoped you'd get on past.'

Siobhan noted that the woman was unfazed by her partner's blunt honesty about seeking somewhere to take a leak. She stood with one hand cupping the slight swell of her belly, the other dug deep into her coat pocket. She shivered in the cold, feet straddling wider than her shoulders. She wasn't as stocky as Siobhan had first thought; her bulkiness was due to her clothing and the way she stood. Pregnant, Siobhan deduced, so the story about her needing urgently to pee rang true. She set down the pistol she'd taken out when instructed to by Harper, ensuring it was not within his immediate range. She wouldn't put it past the psycho to shoot the couple simply for the hell of it.

'We'd best be on our way then,' Harper announced to Siobhan's surprise, 'and let your girl do what she desperately needs to do. There's no need to go clambering out of sight over that wall once we're gone. We live down the road apiece so you've no fear of an audience.'

Harper hung an arm out of the open window. He clapped the side of the car, an indication for Siobhan to drive. He flicked the couple a brief wave. 'Be seeing y'all,' he said. 'Stay safe. Stay warm.' He caught a nod from the tall guy in response.

Siobhan steered the SUV away, unsure what their next move might be. Of course, it would be whatever Harper decided it would be. He muttered under his breath, now out of earshot of the couple. 'What a pair of lying bastards they were. Siobhan, take us far enough away that they can't see or hear us, then turn around.'

SEVENTEEN

There was little possibility of hearing the Chevy Tahoe over the keening wind, but Tess cocked an ear after it all the same. 'What did you make of that BS?'

'If that wasn't suspicious I dunno what to call it,' Po said. He too stared after the SUV, but it had disappeared beyond the whirling curtain of snow.

'I'm trying to hear if they've kept going or not,' Tess said by way of agreement. 'That guy's story about living further down this track was as lame as ours was for stopping here.'

'You should pee.'

'Eh? To add validity to our story?'

'No, it's because you probably really are fit to burst. Besides, both of us don't have to go into the cemetery. I can go fetch Jo without you havin' to scramble through two feet of snow as well.'

His suggestions made sense, but Tess thought that Joanne would be more responsive to her than if Po arrived alone. Most women could be wary of trusting a stranger, more so when of the opposite sex, more so again when – according to Ratcliffe – Joanne was so paranoid she believed everyone wished to skin her alive. 'Just give me a minute and I'll come with you.'

'You sure you're up to the walk?'

'Po, I'm pregnant, I haven't had my legs broken.'

He shrugged and allowed the subject to drop. Nowadays there was a fine line between chivalry and male chauvinism and he didn't intend crossing it.

She made fast work of relieving herself, then kicked fresh snow over the evidence. All the while she'd fretted that the SUV would suddenly loom into view and she'd be caught in all her glory in its headlamps. Po stood guard, having scratched out a cigarette from a crushed packet in his jacket pocket and lit up. His attention had fully been on where he'd last watched the SUV disappear. There was little to nil chance that anyone else was traveling this remote track in the awful weather, right? She couldn't fully discount it, because those living thereabouts were probably used to inclement

winters, prepared for the hardest snowfall, and still had to go about
their business.

'Ratcliffe said that Joanne's gotten herself holed up inside an
old family mausoleum,' she recalled as Po steadied her so
she could clamber over the low snow-capped wall. He flicked
away his cigarette and then stepped over after her into shin-deep
snow.

'Can make out some tombstones. Can't see anythin' resembling
a mausoleum,' he said.

'What's that?'

'Topiary or shrub,' Po said, discounting a nearby mound. 'Up
there looks more promising.' He indicated a route from the locked
gate, assuming that the road was a central artery that served the
rest of the cemetery.

Tess also traced the route of the road; low embankments of
snow marked its verges. Many headstones were clustered nearer
to it than towards the hinterlands of the burial ground. Centuries'
old trees dotted the area, also more tombstones. Many of the
markers were probably toppled, or small enough that the snow
had already piled over them. Gusting wind caused a change in the
direction of snowfall and Tess spotted what could possibly be
Joanne's sanctuary. It was a low, squat building, incongruous
among the modest memorials surrounding it.

Po had spotted the mausoleum and without comment started
towards it. Tess high-stepped through the drifts to follow.

Before reaching the mausoleum, they both spotted the tracks.
There was evidence that Joanne had come and gone from the
building on a couple of occasions, but a final, fresher trail went
downhill towards the road again. She had left the sanctuary
of the tomb and gotten who knew where? Po wasn't satisfied
with the evidence of her flight: he shoved the door inward and
entered the echoing space of icy stone. His breath billowed,
visible against the darkness within.

'She's gone,' he stated the obvious.

There was no need for discussion. They followed her trail back
towards the low boundary wall. She'd left the grounds little more
than twenty feet beyond where they'd parked their car. Joanne's
footprints were distinct enough in the snow on the road. They
went under the Telluride and continued towards Vanceboro.

'How'd we miss her tracks during the drive here?' Tess asked.

'We were following directions, not lookin' for the prints of some fool girl wanderin' about in a blizzard.'

'We didn't see her on the way here. Do you think she might have' – Tess didn't want to say *died* – 'succumbed?'

'We'd have come across her corpse on the road. We didn't. That isn't to say she hasn't wandered off into the wilderness and perished out there, 'cause it'd be darned easy to get turned around in this weather.'

'I won't accept she's dead unless we find her body,' said Tess.

'So let's look. Jump back in the car, we may as well warm up while we can.'

He turned the Telluride and picked up the faint trail of footprints. By now they'd mostly been obliterated by a combination of gusting wind and falling snow. The car's headlamps were of little use against the swirling snow, but their angled light caused shadows in the scuffs dug into the snow by Joanne's trudging progress. She'd made it a couple hundred yards before slipping and crawling through the snow. She'd made it back to her feet. Her tracks led off the road and on to the verge. Some distance on, she'd fallen a second time, and within ten yards had fallen again. Po crawled the Telluride along as they again watched her tracks zigzag off the road and on to a hillside cleared of forest.

Here there were fresh tracks, but neither of footprints or tire. They looked like skids on a sled, placed either side of a caterpillar track. 'Snowmobile,' Tess said unnecessarily.

Po pulled the Telluride on to the track that Joanne and the snowmobile driver had followed uphill, but immediately its tires began to lose traction. 'Best not get us stuck,' he muttered and allowed the big SUV to roll back. He used the momentum to help turn it back on to the road. 'You want to wait here and I'll go scout things out?'

Tess peered up the slope. The blizzard was cutting through it, throwing snow downhill towards them. Climbing into the face of the storm would be a bitch. 'I should come with you.'

'Better if you try contactin' Detective Ratcliffe and seein' if Jo's been in touch.'

Tess made a perfunctory check of her cellphone. No missed calls. 'She'd have called if she'd heard from Joanne. I'm coming with you, Po.'

He didn't argue this time, for which she was grateful. His depth of care for her and their unborn child was unquestionable and she didn't require constant reassurance. Following the first time they'd worked together as a team, and despite his chivalrous sensibilities, Po had never treated her other than as an equal and she didn't want him to start mollycoddling her now.

The hike uphill was tough. Each step was paid for with effort and her face felt as if knotted threads were flailing it. She dug her chin deeper into her scarf and ensured her beanie hat covered as much of her ears as possible. Po went ahead, blazing a trail and she tried stepping into his prints to alleviate the exertion. Midway up the rise he halted and peered back at her. 'You should see this.'

Tess moved to stand alongside him. It was apparent that Jo had fallen again, and gone to her hands and knees for a short time before finally succumbing to the cold. Whoever had come along afterwards on the snowmobile had carried her off on the machine because there was no hint of her tracks beyond that churned-up spot. Thankfully, the snowmobile rider's destination wasn't miles off. From their new vantage on the hillside, the roofs of a house and outbuildings were visible between the snow-laden gusts. 'Hopefully she was found in time,' Po said. 'You know how weird this is gonna look, us turning up like this in the middle of the freakin' storm of the decade?'

'Whoever found Joanne, they've taken her in, I don't think they'll turn us away either.'

'Who can say unless we go and knock?'

'Lead the way,' she said.

He nodded, but didn't move. He peered downhill, but the road and their car was obscured to them.

'Those two in the Chevy still troubling you?' she asked.

'Yep.'

'Me too,' she admitted, though she couldn't fully explain why. Their appearance and subsequent manner of approach could be explained by neighborly behaviour, but she didn't buy it. The man acted friendly enough, smiled broadly, but with all the sincerity of a cat playing with its prey. The woman had first checked Tess out the way a bitchy love rival might, but next time had appeared marginally concerned for her. They'd continued driving, but it felt wrong to Tess, as if it was a sham to cover up deliberately following them out of Vanceboro.

EIGHTEEN

The car stuck in the drift at roadside had caused Siobhan to halt sooner than even Harper planned. While she sat with the engine idling, he got out and made an inspection of the car. From the slight tension in his shoulders, he perhaps expected to find Joanne Mason curled up asleep inside. Siobhan didn't entertain such fantasy: if she was inside, then she was a frozen corpse.

Harper moved around the abandoned vehicle. By now its tire tracks were buried under a foot of fresh snow, so there was no hint at how it had gone off the road, but the reason was immaterial. He moved around checking doors and finding them locked. He scraped accumulated snow off the windows and leaned close to peer inside. Frost on the inside thwarted a clear view but from his slow reaction there obviously wasn't a corpse, let alone a living person, inside. He moved to the back of the car and scraped a handful of snow off the trunk. Next, he crouched and scratched at the licence plate, disclosing it. Siobhan watched his ugly visage crinkle in thought. He stood, walked around the side and picked up a foot. He heel stomped the side passenger window and it imploded. He leaned inside the car, hitting the lock and then he wrestled open the door against the accumulated snow. He dug around for a while, reaching across to the driver's side on one occasion and also delving about in the back. He must have hit a lever, because Siobhan saw the trunk pop open. Harper checked its contents.

He returned and slid in alongside her. Siobhan felt the cold radiating off his clothing. His hair and shoulders again held a layer of white. He scraped it off into the footwell and then rubbed together his hands; she doubted it was to warm up, but to simply dry them. If he was as cold as he was callous-hearted then he was a block of ice.

'It was hers,' he announced.

'You're certain?'

He turned and appraised her with steel in his jaw.

'I'm not second-guessing you, Harp, just wondered what you'd found.'

He grunted. Lifted his hands and checked off on his fingers. 'One: car has Massachusetts's plates. Two: papers in the glove compartment showed Boston addresses too. Three: I found a crumpled receipt from a cash register where she bought supplies, and it corresponds to the neighborhood of the motel she fled south of Portsmouth in New Hampshire. Four: on the passenger seat there was a paper sack containing a half empty bottle of spring water and the wrappers of some candy bars and shit. The bag, and you probably know what's coming, was printed with the name of that gas station where I'd had to silence that gimp and his son.' He touched his thumb. 'Five: I checked the trunk. Inside it there was more provisions and they were likely what she purchased down in Portsmouth, but then neglected to take with her when she stumbled away from the wreck. I'd say the car was abandoned hours ago, but it also tells me that we're hot on her heels and Joanne still remains within grabbing distance. She's close by, Siobhan, and logic tells me she's around here, sitting tight until somebody can pick her up.'

'Those two strangers being at the cemetery makes sense now,' Siobhan admitted.

His thick lips turned down at the corners, conversely a show of happiness that she'd gotten his point. 'Better get us back there quick then, huh?'

She took care turning around. Joanne's car had reversed off the narrow track into a drift; from the way its trunk nosed down the snow covered a drainage channel or other form of ditch. Back on the straight again, she picked up speed.

'Take it easy, we don't want to take a spill,' Harper cautioned.

'I've got this,' she said.

Within a minute they approached the cemetery. Snow billowed and danced on the wind, but it wasn't falling as thick as before. 'They've left already.' Siobhan stated the obvious.

'Yeah. Keep going, they can't be too far ahead.'

Harper smacked his lips and then smiled, almost as if the taste of victory was already in his mouth. Siobhan on the other hand couldn't help thinking that his pleasure was premature. If the strangers had picked up Joanne, then where might they have gone? Possibly their sole purpose was to help smuggle her across the border into Canada. If that were the case, then the hunt would continue, but for how long? Sooner rather than later she hoped to return home; damn it if she didn't have a potted plant that required watering!

Her concern about a prolonged search withered and disappeared as a car loomed out of the blizzard. The closer she got, the more details she could make out. It was the Kia Telluride belonging to the strangers. It was parked at roadside, at the foot of a deforested hillside. There was snow on the roof and hood, but that gave no indication of how long the car had been there; however, fresh snow adhering to the windshield and side windows showed an accumulation of inches in places. It was likely that they were only minutes behind their prey.

She stopped behind the Telluride and Harper again reached out. She passed him her pistol.

'Wait here,' he instructed.

'They aren't in the car,' she said.

'You're probably right, but I'll check anyhow.'

'Suit yourself,' she said, then before he could respond to her sarcasm, she added, 'you're the boss, Harp.'

She could tell from the footprints in the snow that the couple had gotten out and not yet returned. It was dark, but the snow added a weird nimbus to everything, making the scenery glow. Their tracks went uphill to where they joined another trail. From her position, she thought it could be a snowmobile track.

Harper walked around the Telluride, poised to shoot. Siobhan was confident she was correct, that the car was empty, but had to admit that Harper had learned a lot from his cursory check of Joanne's car. He might learn something important about their prey by a similar investigation of theirs.

He shook his huge head, dislodging snowflakes that had piled up on his hair. The move had nothing to do with shedding the load, but at having found nobody in the car. He checked the doors, but they were locked. He spied uphill; Siobhan wondered if he was contemplating smashing inside, but it could set off an alarm and alert the couple. With no idea where they were it was probably best not to alert them to their presence. Harper made a second pass of the vehicle, this time gently touching the back hatch door, but it was locked too. He scowled at her through the windshield as if he'd just twigged on to her sarcastic comment of a minute ago. He pointed at the couple's tracks and how they led up the slope, meeting and then blending with the skids and caterpillar track of the snowmobile. There was one logical reason why they might have followed the snowmobile upwards, to reach shelter over the crest of the slope.

Harper returned to the SUV. He stood by her driver's window until she powered it down. They were in the full blast of the storm, Siobhan's hair whipping around her ears. He by comparison was unmoved by its force.

'Their car has all-wheel drive, and a three-point five-liter V6 engine. It could have easily managed that slope, even in this much snow. They chose to climb the hill on foot. Tells me they spotted something worth closer investigation.'

'I doubt it was Joanne on that Ski-Doo,' Siobhan said.

'It wasn't, but maybe somebody gave her a ride. We have to check it out, Siobhan, see where those tracks lead.'

'You're going to make me climb up there in this storm?'

'Can't take the Chevy and alert them we're coming,' he said. 'If you brought extra clothing now's the time to put it on.'

Siobhan had a coat and hat and, thankfully, gloves. Harper took his own advice and pulled into his gloves again. He turned up his jacket collar: he had no hat, but already his bristly grey hair was dotted with flakes and he seemed untroubled by the idea of gathering more.

He passed her the pistol. 'I don't need that,' he said, more as a personal reminder than for her.

Siobhan buried the gun in her pocket and kept her hand on its butt. She almost crabbed uphill, with her left shoulder braced into the wind, her face averted. Harper went ahead, shambling upward like some big old grizzly bear, his shoulders swaying from one side to the other with each step. Siobhan tried getting directly behind him, so that his larger form might block the worst of the blizzard, but he snapped instructions to fan out and make a second approach to the crest of the hill. Admittedly, he made sense. Without discussing a plan, it had been assumed by her that their only reason for scaling the hill was to ambush the couple and to take away Joanne if she was in their presence. Harper, again without having said so, wouldn't wish to leave behind any live witnesses. She was expected to flank and then shoot them given the order.

Earlier Siobhan had moved the pistol out of Harper's reach

when realizing that the woman was pregnant; knowing his disregard for life, she didn't put it past him to shoot her in the belly because of, rather than despite, the baby she carried. Siobhan had killed before and was not in a business where apathy could exist, but in her opinion murdering an unborn child overstepped a mark she'd prefer not to cross. That was not to say she wouldn't kill the pregnant woman, just that she wouldn't take any satisfaction from it the way Harper would. She'd do things clean, though, and spare her from Harper doing a dance number on her like he did to that cripple at the gas station.

NINETEEN

Joanne Mason woke up clutching a bloody claw hammer. She had no idea it was in her hand until she attempted to stand and found she only had the use of a single hand. She dropped the hammer, pushed up to her knees and peered down at it, as if the tool was an ancient relic left over from time immemorial; although if that were the case it would not be tacky with fresh, vibrant, red blood. A swollen lump behind her left ear indicated how close her skull had come to being shattered, but not, with the offending weapon before her, how she'd been spared.

She looked around, her throat constricting as memories flooded in. The sharp recollections were a kaleidoscopic assault on her senses and she cried out as if witnessing each again in real time. Without conscious thought, she lurched up and stumbled away from the murder weapon, reaching for and smearing a door handle with her bloody fingerprints. She staggered out into the second-floor hallway. Her skull was ringing from the blow she'd taken and pain shot daggers to the backs of her eyes and down her neck. Her right hand, the same one that had been clutching the hammer, felt numb, while her arm stung as if with nettle rash. Her discomfort was nothing compared to the dread clutching her heart.

Behind her were the open doors to Lacey Blackhorse's bedroom and those of her children. Joanne didn't look back: there was nothing she could do for any of them now and nothing she wanted to see a second time. It was bad enough finding her employer with her head beaten to mush, but incomparable to the horror of seeing those smaller blond heads broken like egg shells on their pillows. She thought whenever she closed her eyes in the future, nightmarish images would assail her. She was supposed to care for those children, to nurture and protect them, and yet she had failed. What future could she expect? A future for her wouldn't exist unless she got the hell away as quickly as possible. She could still hear the murderer inside the house and once he learned that the blow he'd struck her had failed to kill her, he'd surely return to finish the job.

Below her a door slammed as loud as a gunshot, and voices babbled, one of them high-pitched with fright, the other guttural. A scuffle and a door slammed again, was yanked open, and the voices diminished as the killer pursued his next victim. Her first thought was that while he was chasing another then the murderer couldn't trouble her. She must find a phone and call the police.

Her cell phone was in her purse in her bedroom, on the next floor up. She mustn't climb the stairs and trap herself up there. Lacey Blackhorse owned a cell phone, but where it was, Joanne had no idea. It could have been on her person, or deposited anywhere in the large house. Lacey was hair-brained forgetful and regularly lost things. When she wasn't caring for the children, Joanne's tasks included searching for Lacey's misplaced belongings. There was a landline in the kitchen, but that was too near to where the murderer had chased his latest intended victim. Carl Blackhorse, Lacey's husband and stepfather to the children, had an office in an annex to the main house, and she was pretty certain he'd had a landline installed to necessitate his work. He'd made his first millions through asset management via pooled investment funds, but he'd added to them through less conventional practices – criminal practices, she'd concluded – so required privacy from possible eavesdroppers. One time she'd been chased away by an angry Carl Blackhorse when she'd mistakenly pursued one of the kids into his office; afterwards she received no apology, only a warning from Lacey that he wasn't the type of man to say sorry. Ordinarily she'd avoid his office as instructed, but not under these circumstances – and besides, Carl wasn't home, he was on a business trip to Atlantic City, or more likely with an escort on his arm in one of the casinos.

She went along the hall on shaky legs, holding her breath. Her head felt twice its normal size. Her arm still stung like crazy. A sharp memory of taking a horrendous slap from an unseen assailant came back, explaining the numbness and tingling of returning circulation. She wondered now if the murderer should be thought of in the plural because that slap had come from someone other than who'd struck her with the hammer. If that were the case then the second attacker could be anywhere. She came to a halt, emptying her lungs in a protracted cry. She could be heading directly into the path of the second killer. She must forget trying to reach Carl's office, escape the house instead and run to a neighboring property, seek help there.

It was odd. She'd lived and worked at the Blackhorse house for months, and knew it intimately. Fleeing under duress, the house was an unfamiliar maze. She got turned around more times than there were directions to go, and she finally ended up catching her breath while leaning against a wall on the ground floor. A view through an open door and large window showed gently falling snow shrouding the garden. The snow was virginal, white and pure. It didn't last. A figure hurtled past, arms windmilling as it tried to ward off another figure following in determined pursuit. Joanne only saw them for a second or two, but her confused mind couldn't define sharp enough detail to tell who was chasing whom. Kicked-up tracks now destroyed the pristine snowfall.

Joanne pushed off the wall and staggered the length of the front vestibule. In her role of nanny to the Blackhorse children she was still nevertheless an employee, so didn't use the front door during her usual comings and goings. Even then, as she sought safety it felt alien and not a little forbidden to leave the house via the front door and she stuttered to a halt. At least now she had gotten back her bearings and knew it was a simple matter of cutting across the large kitchen and into the adjoining utility room to reach a second exit door. It allowed direct access to an adjoining parking garage where the Blackhorses stabled their mechanical steeds.

There was no possible way that she could use one of the Blackhorse cars to escape in. Their luxury vehicles weren't the type to be left with the ignition keys behind their sun visors. Besides, she didn't trust herself to safely drive just then, not with her brain in turmoil; she'd probably crash within seconds of setting off. Her idea was to gain the access door on the far side of the garage and flee across the grounds in the opposite direction from where she'd just watched the murderer chase his latest victim.

A figure blocked her escape. She cried out into the palm of her hand and backpedaled away. It was seconds before she understood the hands grasping for her were not to snare her. The owner of the hands was in equal need of support as she. She recognized Toby Hillman. He was little more than a youth, but was a talented cook and was employed by Carl Blackhorse to serve up more appetizing dinners than Lacey could dream of making. Toby was stricken with terror, eyes wide and mouth drooping as he reached *for her. She understood his mind was in as much turmoil as hers and he grasped at her for direction. She shooed him back the way he'd come, gesturing at him to stay silent. From somewhere behind them came the crash of breaking glass.*

She squeezed past Toby, urging him to follow and they sprinted through the garage, dismissing Lacey's Lexus as a getaway car, and she lunged for the exit door. Unlike from outside, it had no need of a key, and it opened to her by the briefest twist of the handle. The air was frigid, but Joanne was overheated by then and was unaware of the chill. She ducked out briefly, checking both ways, then turned to Toby. He was directly behind her, almost looming over her shoulder. His hot exhalations buffeted her hair. Each rasp of breath was enough to lead the killers to them.

'You must be quiet,' she whispered urgently.

'Wh-what are we going to do? Who are those people? Why—'

'Shush, Toby, be quiet or they're going to hear you.'

Tears rolled down his acne-dotted cheeks. He squirmed, ready to bolt away screaming.

'This way,' she instructed and grabbed his elbow. She tugged him outside and with a shove propelled him into the garden. There was enough snow on the lawn that the killers would spot where they'd ran, but if they could keep ahead of them, make it to the perimeter wall and escape into the neighboring property . . .

Joanne was running. She was unaware that somebody pursued, until she was barged aside and a burly form grabbed Toby and lifted him bodily in some kind of bear hug. Toby was swung around and then in the air, his legs forming a pendulum, and then he was savagely tossed to the ground. Joanne found herself on the ground too. Rolling, then scrambling for her life on her hands and knees. She made it partly to her feet as the killer stomped Toby's head into the earth; the soft cushion of snow wouldn't save him. Then Joanne was up and she lurched to get past, still intent on making it to the joining property. The killer swung for her and his huge hand grazed her shoulder. The force was enough to knock her off her stride and she staggered a few steps before catching her balance. She hurdled the wall into a graceless dive. Her fall ended in a spongy pile of fallen leaves and a thin crust of rime. For a second she lay there, gasping, and her gaze was drawn to the top of the wall. A huge head, as big as a propane gas bottle, leaned towards her. Huge, blunt fingers gripped the top of the wall.

Joanne croaked and rolled away. She bounded up, watching, fearful that the giant would step over the wall and pursue. He did not, only his mocking words chased her.

'That's right, Joanne, you can keep on running, girl, but you'd better believe I'll find you and when I do . . .'

He has found me!

He had his horrible hands on her, shaking her. He shook her firmly; perhaps intent on fooling her a moment before grinning his weird fixed grin, as she came to understand that her promised doom could not be avoided. She should open her eyes and face her death with courage. She kept them squeezed tight.

'Can you hear me?' asked a voice.

Joanne turned her head aside, mewling in anticipation of a crushing stomp to her head, the way in which she'd watched the killer murder Toby.

Craning away from him, her face should have pressed into the icy snow she'd collapsed into. Her cheek pressed something soft, but it was warm. The voice was exhorting her to wake, and she thought it odd that the killer's gruff tones were now more melodic, belonging to a girl and not a brutish Neanderthal. She cried out softly again, knowing deep down that there was no hope of mercy, but reaching out to this more gentle side of his psyche.

'Can you hear me? Are you awake?'

Joanne's gummy eyelids unzipped open. A figure loomed in her peripheral vision, amorphous and shadowy, backlit by a dim yellowish glow. It had several heads and more than the expected pair of arms. She cried out, horrified that her notion that a giant had chased her was only a partial truth of his horrifying monstrous form. She tried squirming away, but there'd be no escaping his multi-limbed reach. He'd warned her, said he would find her, and she'd believed that his words were prophetic . . .

She sat up abruptly and stared aghast at the figure crowding her . . . correction, at the figures. It was not some kind of nightmare creature looming over her, but a pair of women. They stood so close together they appeared almost intertwined, but it was only because both wished to help wake her.

Joanne knew them.

She didn't know them by name, but partial memories of them finding and then dragging her here on a sled towed behind a snowmobile flickered back. The women had manhandled her to get her inside and out of her half-frozen clothes. They had stripped her almost naked, leaving her only her underwear for modesty's sake, then set her in front of a stove to warm up. However, Joanne mustn't have had the energy to remain seated upright on the stool they'd furnished her with, because next she recalled being carried, arm-and-a-leg style, into this bedroom and subsequently buried under blankets. At some point, she must have kicked off some of the bedding because they were now balled up beside her. The heating must've been cranked up to roasting, because it had grown so hot in the room that it was stifling. Now, instead of freezing to death she was in danger of spontaneous combustion. Sweat poured from practically every pore, but failed to cool her.

'You were dreaming,' one of the women said, 'crying in fear.'

'It was as if you were having a *terrible nightmare.*' The other added potency to why they'd wakened her.

'Who are you?' Joanne croaked, and she pulled at the blankets, trying to cover her nakedness. 'Where am I?'

'We found you outside, you'd collapsed in the blizzard,' said one of the women.

They parted, one each approaching her on either side of the bed. Joanne switched focus, one from the other, then back again, and found it disconcerting. They looked so much alike they could be the same person: twins, she understood.

'You're in our house,' the one on her right explained. 'It's just outside of Vanceboro in Washington County, Maine.'

Despite her confusion Joanne blinked at the specific nature of the woman's words. 'I'm where?'

'You're in our home and are welcome,' said the woman on her left. She patted Joanne's knee through the blankets.

'No, I meant . . . I remember being near a cemetery.'

'Yes, that's nearby,' she was reassured by the same woman. 'You appear to have tried walking here and fallen on the way up the hillside.'

Joanne touched her hands to her face. Her previously blue fingers were now pink and healthy. She feared to check her toes. She yawned, a release of pent-up anxiety.

'We'd have let you sleep, but . . . well . . .' said the first woman.

'You said I was suffering a nightmare,' Joanne croaked, 'and you were right. I was, and it was horrible.'

'Oh, dear,' said the woman on her left.

'Oh, dearie dear,' said the one to her right. She also rested a hand on Joanne's leg through the blankets, squeezing gently to comfort her. 'You needn't give it any more thought. It was a horrible dream and that is all. Nothing to bother about now.'

'You were lucky we found you when we did,' said the other.

'Yes, you were. Lucky indeed. Who knows if you'd have survived before your friends found you.'

Terror clutched Joanne. She scrambled up in the bed to set her back against the headboard. She grasped the covers to her chest. 'My friends? Who . . . what are you—'

'There's no need to be afraid, young miss,' said the one to her right. The woman had moved in closer and for an illogical second or two Joanne fully expected the woman to throw her weight across her to halt her escape. The other woman peered back towards the open door that let from the gloomy bedroom into what must have been a vestibule or hallway. Joanne anticipated more figures to crowd the doorway.

They didn't.

'Hush now, you needn't be frightened,' said the woman nearest her. The old woman's features crinkled in a mix of concern and genuine kindness. 'They claim to have been asked to collect you because your car had broken down.'

'Who . . . who are they? Do they look . . .?' She didn't know what to say. How did those seeking her look? She was certain that the monstrous guy she'd barely escaped at the Blackhorse home, and again very recently in her nightmare recollection of the event, hadn't arrived to carry out Karen's bidding.

'Here,' the woman nearest said, and took from her shirt pocket a business card. 'Your friend said to show you this.'

She held it before Joanne, who finally reached for it with trembling fingers and drew it closer to her eyes. She read the name on it: Teresa Grey. It claimed she was a private investigator from Portland, Maine. For all Joanne knew, this private eye could very well be chasing a bounty on her head, or maybe simply to win kudos for turning her in to the real cops. No, that was her paranoia talking: she believed that Teresa was the same 'Tess from Portland' that her sister had mentioned on several occasions in the past. A few years ago, Tess, and a couple of her associates, had helped Karen to close a case involving serial rape and murder, and to date was one of Karen's most successful high-profile career wins. Karen had admitted to Joanne that if not for Tess, then she doubted that she'd have solved the case on her own merits; she was beholden to the Portland private eye.

Joanne pushed aside the blankets and leaned forward, as if moving a foot or so would allow her to see where Tess was.

'We left her and her gentleman friend warming themselves in our kitchen,' the first old woman explained.

'There's a man with her?'

'Yes. Is that a problem?'

At first her paranoia warned that it was the giant and he'd coerced Tess Grey to play along and hand her over to him. She shook off the illogical thought and instead indicated her state of undress.

'Oh, dear,' said the first woman.

'Oh dearie dear,' said the second. 'Let us go and check if your clothes have dried yet.'

TWENTY

They were an odd pair, Tess thought as Joanne's saviors bustled into the kitchen. They darted about, fetching different items of clothing from where they had been drying. One of them went as far as touching Joanne's trousers to her cheek, in an effort at determining how damp they were; she clucked her tongue and began wafting them as she checked on the progress of the other woman. The second one had folded a T-shirt, sweater and socks into a neat bundle she'd then tucked under her arm. Spotting Tess watching them, both of the women's faces crinkled into smiles.

'Shouldn't be too long now, dearie,' said the one holding Joanne's trousers.

The other finished her proclamation for her: 'And we'll have your friend dressed and ready to go.'

Tess smiled in acknowledgement. She found them odd, yes, but in a disarming manner. The women stood together, touching shoulders and hips. There was an intimacy in their closeness, but not sexual, more as if the women were a couple of mutually, unmarried sisters perhaps who had never sought the company of husbands. They could be twins, or just sisters aged similarly with few years between them. They both had the leathery skin and sinewy build of people used to a life spent outdoors, with plenty of toil. She found their way of ending each other's sentences cute, realizing it was because they were so close that they were finely tuned and worked mostly as one unit. She'd caught a bemused grin from Po after the women had eagerly invited them indoors out of the storm, and guided them to warm themselves in front of their stove. Now she saw that her partner wasn't as interested in the odd couple as before; he'd moved to a position where he could see outside.

The old women darted away.

Po glanced after them but immediately returned his attention outside.

'What's troubling you?' she asked.

'You know what . . . or rather *who*.'

'Any sign of them?'

'Nope. Doesn't mean that they aren't out there, waitin' to make a move.'

'We should be out of here and on the way back to Portland in no time.'

'I should git on down the hill and bring up the car. Even with the snow I think it'll manage that incline.'

'Going downhill should be easier than it was on the way up. We should walk, and not chance getting the car stuck.'

'You checked the blizzard lately?'

She moved to see past him. Beyond the kitchen window flakes the size of quarters fell. Already a fresh layer of pristine white had obliterated the tracks they'd made approaching the house. 'Too heavy to walk through, but it's OK to drive in? How does that work?'

'According to those old gals, Joanne had collapsed and was nigh on frozen to death when they found her, walkin' her downhill in this storm could finish her off. And then there's your state to be mindful of.'

'I'm OK.' She rubbed her abdomen through her coat. 'Junior's snug as a bug, too.'

Po refused to argue further. He adjusted his damp collar; finger-combed his damp hair off his brow. His preparation for another trek through a blizzard was simple.

'If you think it's safer for—'

He shook his head. 'There's no need for compromise, Tess. You're right. We'd best not gamble on makin' it up here without gettin' the car stuck. If we work together and move as one, we can make it safely down to the car and get outta here.'

One of the women appeared in the kitchen doorway.

'You don't mind me asking?' she said.

'Asking what?' Tess prompted.

'Is she in some kind of trouble . . . your friend, Joanne, I mean?'

Tess had already noted the absence of a TV or computer, and the only concession to modern communication devices appeared to be an old-style landline and – she assumed – the old women would have access to a two-way radio to hail assistance for when the telephone lines inevitably went down. If they'd heard about the 'Angel of Death' killings it might be through a transistor radio or gossip alone, so they'd have no way of matching Joanne Mason's face with the girl currently recovering in their bedroom.

'Not now, she isn't,' said Tess, without expounding. It must be apparent to all now that the initial suspect in the murders of Lacey Blackhorse and her children was actually a victim who had fled in terror. There was the matter of Joanne's fingerprints being found on the murder weapon and her bloody footprints leading from the crime scene, but Tess bet those could be easily explained. She allowed the old woman to believe she was referring to the fact they'd come to collect her after her car had gotten stuck.

The woman wasn't convinced though. 'I couldn't help noticing that you're a private detective and, well, uh . . .'

'I can see how you might think Joanne's involved in a case I'm investigating, but no, truly we're here only to collect her as a favor for her sister.'

'It's a hell of a favor, if you don't mind me saying. Driving all the way here from Portland and back in this awful weather.'

Tess thumbed at Po and gave the woman a conspiratorial wink. 'All I have to do is sit back and enjoy the ride, my partner's the one who might think the drive's a hellish one.'

Po acknowledged his part with a nonchalant shrug. But his attention barely shifted from the view outside the window. To the woman, it must appear he was judging the severity of the blizzard before starting their return trip.

'My sister Ellie was making soup, to help warm Joanne through. There's plenty in the pot for all of us if . . .'

'That's very kind of y'all,' Po piped up, 'but we should be getting' back on the road as soon as possible.'

'It would be no bother to put up a flask of something, dearie, while Joanne's getting dressed.'

'Don't want to inconvenience you more than you've already been put,' said Tess.

'Isn't any inconvenience, I assure you,' said the woman. 'What kind of Christian would I be to turn my back on anyone in need of help?'

The other woman appeared in the doorway. She'd been the one to test the dryness of Joanne's trousers by touching it to her cheek. She was called Ellie. Ellie offered up the other woman's name. 'Felicity's right, y'know. It's absolutely no inconvenience to us to fill you a flask or two of soup for your journey back. I'd bet that Joanne will welcome something warm in her belly.'

'Sure, if it's ready then why not?' said Tess.

Po gave an almost imperceptible shrug.

'I'll get it.'

Rather than Ellie, it was Felicity who darted towards the cooking range and began moving around pots and pans. The other sister returned to the bedroom to help speed up Joanne. Tess checked with her partner and saw that his forehead was creased with concern. How much of it was to do with the suspicious couple they'd met and with what was going on back in Portland she could only guess. It was bad enough that arsonists had targeted his garage and his diner. She thought he'd take those attacks on the chin, but she didn't buy for one second that the destruction of his Mustang wasn't eating him up inside. She approached and put her arms around him.

'You OK, hon?'

He dipped a swift kiss to her forehead, but immediately returned his attention to the view outside. 'Sooner we get back the happier I'll be,' he admitted.

'You're worried those idiots might try again?' She stepped back, and allowed her gaze to also switch to the window. 'Other than the house, what else is there they can burn?'

He had his fingers in several business pies, but the arsonists would have to be determined – or connected – to find out about them. Po's involvement in Charley's and Bar-Lesque had become common knowledge but he'd taken care to keep his other dealings under wraps. Once his business dealings might have erred on the shady side, but not since committing to his relationship with her: he had promised to stay above reproach and his word was solid.

'I'm worried that Pinky's back there alone and we're at the ass-end of Maine and in no position to help him.'

'What are the odds those bastards will try again?'

'What were the odds they'd be brazen enough to set fire to my ride?'

'Pinky's on high alert and the cops must've been there by now. I'll ask Alex if he can't have a patrol car stick around.'

'Pinky won't welcome a babysitter, 'specially when it's a cop.'

'What he doesn't know won't harm him.'

'I'm surprised, Tess. Y'know if Pinky has another run-in with our enemies he won't strictly abide by the law; he didn't fetch those pistols for show. If there are cops around he *needs* to know.'

'Yeah, of course, you're right.' She held up her cellphone and checked the screen. 'Besides, I think it's moot any way. I don't have any coverage and I'd bet you don't have any either. Joanne was lucky to have gotten off that call to Karen when she did because there'd be no hope of doing it now.'

'It's the hills at the back of us,' Felicity injected from across the room. 'It blocks the signal from the towers over in town. Once you get back into Vanceboro you'll find your cells will work just fine.'

The woman carried over two silver thermos flasks. She set them down on the counter next to Po. 'That flask's soup, the other's coffee.' She informed Po. Then she looked directly at Tess. 'If you need to urgently call somebody I can drive you down to the valley on our snowmobile. The signal's hit and miss down there but not wholly blocked by the hills.'

Po elected to answer for them. 'Once Joanne's ready we'll all be leavin', any calls needin' made can wait.'

He sounded abrupt even to Tess, but Felicity was astute enough to know his shortness of temper wasn't due to her offer. Tess and the older woman exchanged smiles. Felicity, it appeared, had figured out that Tess's ruddy complexion wasn't solely down to coming in from the cold. She said, 'How long until your babe's due, honey?'

'Oh, we're aways off yet,' said Tess noncommittally.

'You need to keep that little one nourished.' Felicity nodded at the flasks, still untouched by Po, and Tess took the hint.

Tess picked up the steel flasks and dropped one each into her coat pockets, keeping them safe for the trek downhill. She forgot instantly about the drinks, her attention drawn to the door from the bedroom. Felicity's sister Ellie led the way, encouraging Joanne to follow. Understandably there was some trepidation in the younger woman: she didn't know Tess and Po or how they would judge her considering the awful nature of the accusations levied upon her. To Tess the woman looked unlike her photos splashed over the media and web. Instead of the pretty, rosy-cheeked girl Tess had come to expect, Joanne Mason had become a twitchy, hollowed-out shell. Dressed in what appeared to be thrift-store seconds that were far too large for her frame, she appeared diminished: apparently the days she'd spent on the run had been taxing on both her physical and mental well-being.

Joanne went to speak and Tess preempted what was sure to be

denial of the murders. The sisters seemed oblivious to their guest's identity and Tess preferred it to stay that way. She flashed the young woman a cautionary look and spoke before her.

'Joanne, hi, I'm Tess. This is my partner, Nicolas. We came because Karen wanted to ensure you're safe.'

Joanne appraised Po with what amounted to growing terror. Her gaze rose from his boots to his face and remained locked on his turquoise eyes. He smiled and those eyes lit up. A breath rattled from her chest and she visibly wilted when she saw there was nothing to fear from him. Tess deduced it was something about his height that had first perturbed the girl, but other than that, there was nothing about him that had rang her internal alarms.

'I . . . I've been such an inconvenience,' she said. 'To all of you.'

'You were no trouble, dear,' said Felicity, waving aside her concern.

'No trouble whatsoever,' added Ellie. 'In fact if anything you've been a pleasurable distraction from the boredom. We don't get much company out here, so when we do, we try to make the most of it.'

'You can say that again,' said Felicity. 'You've told all your jokes a million times and they were lame the first time I heard them.'

'Ditto,' said Ellie.

Po said, 'We've a car waiting down the hill. If we leave now we can be back in Portland before daylight.'

Tess suspected that his announcement was as much for her ears as for Joanne's. He would never turn his back on helping her, but then again reciprocation should be mutual. 'I'm ready to go. Joanne, are you ready to leave?'

'I . . .' She looked at each of the old women in turn. 'I don't know how to thank you enough.'

'We don't need or expect thanks,' said Felicity.

'But if you hadn't found me I would have frozen to death. You saved my life. I should—'

'If you need thank anyone then just thank the Lord, honey. He sent you to us and helping you was our Christian duty,' said Ellie.

'Snowfall's weakened,' Po said. 'Now would be a good time to go.'

Even to Tess, Po's announcement sounded impatient. Joanne

hadn't had time to come to terms with being rescued by the sisters, let alone absorb that she was now about to be whisked to Portland to a rendezvous with her own sister. Tess understood his urgency, but giving Joanne a minute shouldn't make a difference to their return trip. Before she could say so, Po turned back to the window. She watched a frown flicker across his brow and his stance sank a few inches as he bent for a clearer view through the steamed-up window. A sour taste flooded Tess's mouth, even as he turned to her and flashed her a warning look. He walked his fingers in the air, miming somebody leaving their tracks in the snow. Picturing who had made the tracks was easy for Tess.

They'd been distracted for a minute at most. It emphasized how as little as sixty seconds could make a massive difference, especially in the cut and thrust flow of battle. Battle sounded too forceful a word to describe what had gone before, but their meeting and subsequent maneuvers around the suspicious couple in the SUV had always felt like the preliminary jostling before conflict ensues.

'Joanne,' said Tess, holding out a hand to the young woman. As soon as Joanne accepted her help, Tess guided her around so that she was between her and Po. She tried keeping things subtle, but there was nobody in the room fooled by her nonchalance.

'What's wrong?' Joanne asked.

Ellie moved quickly to stand near Po's shoulder. She spotted the fresh footprints. 'We have more visitors?'

'What's the big concern?' Felicity asked, but she knew; the atmosphere had grown almost palpable.

A trinity of knocks resounded through the house.

'Don't answer the door,' Tess warned.

'Why ever not?' Ellie asked, but she didn't move.

The power went out.

TWENTY-ONE

N ot long before Tess and Po were plunged into darkness Pinky had sat in darkness too.

Actually, it was only partly true. He sat outside, surrounded by the night, but it wasn't completely dark. The snow glowed as if from its own internal energy. Across the yard from him, the snow had been turned to dirty mush by the police cruisers and fire truck that had recently left the scene. Po's pride and joy was now a smoldering hunk of discolored metal and melted rubber. The tires had exploded and the wreck had sunk to its belly in the hardstand of crushed seashells. Pinky imagined that when he squinted at the muscle car it still radiated heat, but the fire crew hadn't left until they were confident they'd completely extinguished the blaze. The lingering smell was enough to remind him that the fire had been intense and fed by accelerant; at once it was a sharp stench that pricked the nostrils, in the next moment a heady cloud of toxic fumes. A pulse throbbed behind his ears.

Pinky closed his eyes.

He fancied he could see afterimages of the fire on the internal screens of his eyelids, but the glow it had initially burned into his retina must surely have faded by now. He didn't feel vulnerable with his eyes closed. If anything his other senses were heightened and he doubted he'd be caught wrong-footed a second time that night. Earlier he'd carried two pistols in pursuit of the arsonist that'd fled across the frozen river. One of them had been tucked in his pants, the other in hand. Now he gripped a pistol in each hand, ready for the more than one arsonist out there. Initially he'd thought there was a single enemy to contend with, but had quickly reassessed and decided on two because he'd been drawn away by a second skulker when he'd gotten too close to the first. He'd had to perform a recount: both those sons of bitches had led him a merry dance down to the riverside, so it was unlikely either had been responsible for smashing a window on Nicolas's Mustang and throwing in the lit Molotov cocktail. Three then. If his two pistols weren't enough to contend with them all, then he'd goddamn bite the face off the final one if he had to.

He opened his eyes and peered around. Red mist tinted the scene, a result of the intensity with which he'd been squeezing shut his eyes. Ordinarily Pinky's *c'est la vie* nature wouldn't allow him to nurture a grudge over a lost car. But on this occasion he was inordinately angry and he knew it was because the loss of the Mustang wasn't his, but that of his best friend. On behalf of Nicolas he could rage.

Minutes ago Alex Grey, the younger of Tess's two brothers, had left Pinky with a friendly warning not to take matters into his own hands. He was reminded that Portland PD didn't tolerate vigilantism. Alex knew whom he was dealing with, so his instruction was delivered with a wink and nod, and a second reminder that patrol cars would be sweeping the area for suspects in the foreseeable hours. Pinky had promised to uphold the law, but without admitting the law he meant harked back to when taking an eye for an eye was meant literally.

Whenever Tess worked from home it was either from the bedroom Po had converted to an office, or it was from out on the wraparound porch, seated on the swinging chair where Pinky now kept guard. The weather didn't deter her from work; if it was cold she tucked woolen blankets around her and relished the crisp, clear air. Pinky hadn't wrapped himself in the blankets, they could encumber him if he must move fast, and he couldn't risk them snagging his pistols, but it was OK. He was too het up to feel the chill, despite the subzero temperatures.

Tess was a private investigator and in the latter years Nicolas too had become her right-hand man. They tried hard to stay above reproach. Pinky assisted them whenever he could, but had always been uncertain about what best described his role in the threesome. He was a friend, family almost, to both, and he had worked selflessly to help them the way he would for a genuine sister or brother. But he'd also been there as a reformed criminal, rather a criminal on the road to reformation and rebirth. In essence, still a criminal. As with anyone operating outside the law, he had his own ways and means of gaining information, of identifying potential enemies and pinpointing those that might try denying him earning an ill-gotten buck. Keeping his pistols propped on his thighs, he swapped them out for his cell phone and began ringing around.

Within a half hour Pinky had an idea about what, if not who yet, was behind the arson attacks. He set his phone down and sat back in the creaking swing seat. The heat had gone out of him, replaced by seeping ice in his belly. His eyebrows knitted and he stuck out his bottom lip in contemplation. He touched the butts of his pistols, and not even for a second did he consider putting them aside. He picked up his cell phone once more, saw that his battery life had been severely diminished and turned to paw behind him for where he knew Tess had installed a charging lead for when she worked on the porch. He plugged in and brought up Tess's number again, but then discarded it in favour of Po's. Last time he'd called, he had kind of wimped out from ringing Nicolas directly, unsure how his friend would take the news that his car had been destroyed. This time he shouldn't avoid ringing him, because Po should learn straight from the horse's mouth whose fault he believed the attacks were.

Several hundred miles away Po's phone remained silent: Pinky listened as a recorded voice informed him his call could not be connected. He automatically defaulted to ringing Tess's cell phone, but he again received a recorded voice. The weather further north was worse than in Portland, and not only that but his friends were out in the boonies, so it was no major surprise that neither had a valid signal on their cell phones. Last he'd heard they were going out to some backwoods cemetery to collect Joanne. What could go wrong? Pinky had a healthy if not irrational fear of the supernatural, and wouldn't merrily traipse about a graveyard in the dark for fear of being dragged to hell by some fiery-eyed ghoul, even if his logical mind told him the chances of it happening was zero. He doubted there could be anything to cause Tess or Nicolas any trouble while they defrosted the girl and brought her back to Portland. If anything, there was more chance of harm coming to them if they were here and in the firing line because he was certain now that the arsonists weren't finished. Next time they might try burning other than inanimate objects and Pinky wasn't prepared to let it happen.

He again tried ringing his friends but again was unsuccessful, so he put away his phone and concentrated instead on his pistols. He'd been warned not to take the law into his own hands, but every man had the right to defend his life, right?

TWENTY-TWO

The three sharp raps at the door were distractions; the power being cut in the next instant was designed to cause bewilderment; so what followed was the closing of the trap. Somebody had gained entry via another door or window at the rear of the house. They were subtle about their approach, but they were unfamiliar with the layout of the house and the sudden darkness worked against them too; they bumped a shoulder on a doorframe and then a thigh against a counter. Nothing about their attempt at stealth boded well. Tess reached for Joanne's arm and pulled the young woman close behind her and immediately urged her to follow. She neither led her to the front door nor the passage towards the bedroom, but into the corner of the kitchen furthest from the door. Po moved Ellie likewise, and then set himself before the three women. He groped for the first weapon to hand and found the back of a wooden chair. He lifted it and set its seat to his belly, the legs facing out, as if about to tame a lion.

Felicity stood alone, a blur of shadow in the darkness. She must have sensed the danger as easily as the others heard the noises made by the home invader, but she was either fearless or she was as dumb as dirt. 'The power often goes off during storms,' she said, her voice far too loud, 'but don't you worry none, the back-up generator will kick on in seconds.'

Whether or not her announcement was true didn't matter, the fact was it urged the home invader to rush their approach. They entered the room with such haste they collided with Felicity, and a second or two of a scuffle ensued as they first disengaged and then jostled for position.

'He has a gun!' Felicity squealed.

'Shit,' said somebody, but definitely not a man. 'Get over there and don't move, you old bitch!'

Tess sensed rather than saw Po moving to help Felicity. She croaked in warning, because if she sensed him coming the woman might shoot first and determine whom she'd hit later.

'Felicity!' Ellie squawked and Tess felt the woman lunge to assist her sister.

'No, wait,' she said, and grabbed at the woman, but she was already out of reach. Behind her, Joanne also cried out, but Tess was gratified to feel her sink down and stay sheltered behind her. Hands grabbed at Tess's clothing.

Footsteps drummed the floor. Something was knocked flying and crashed to the ground. Voices competed and then Po exhaled sharply and again Tess sensed more than clearly saw him jab the gunwoman with the chair, forcing her back the way she had just entered. In their company he could curse with the worst of men but, surprisingly for Po, he swore savagely at the woman. She swore back and her gun barked. The muzzle flash lit the kitchen for a split-second and left an afterglow in Tess's vision. Thankfully in the moment of clarity she saw the gun was angled towards the ceiling, forced skyward by the chair Po rammed into her, so the bullet didn't find flesh. The gunshot scattered the sisters again, but Tess couldn't say to where they dived for cover.

The generator didn't kick in as Felicity had promised. The house remained in darkness but only for a moment. A fresh shaft of dim light burst inward, along with the door that was almost smashed from its hinges. A huge silhouette blocked the light and lunged inside, snorting and bellowing. If it had carried a horn on its snout, Tess might have been fooled into thinking a rhinoceros had burst inside. Joanne reacted to the new threat by keening in terror, the sound like steam escaping a boiling water cylinder. She sank all the way down and her hands left Tess to cradle herself.

Neither Tess nor Joanne was the immediate target. The huge figure had the benefit of having let in the dim light from outside and in its glow could see Po swinging and jabbing with the chair. The huge man, his head the size and shape of a cinderblock, pounced for him. Tess cried out, and Po reacted, but his attention was snatched towards her rather than the rushing giant. Tess screeched again and Po spun, bringing up the chair to halt the giant's rush. It barely slowed the big man, and in the next instant he had his hands on the chair legs and tore them apart, as easily as anyone else snapping a wishbone. No words passed between the invaders, and none were directed at those previously in the house, but there was no lack of understanding between any of them. The invaders were there to take Joanne from them, and Tess and Po were going to try hard to stop them.

Po hit the big man with the seat of the chair. It landed flat against the man's slab-like chest, with little effect, but then Po jerked upward and this time the edge of the seat struck under the jaw. Any other jawbone would have shattered, but this man had the composition of concrete. He swept the chair out of Po's hands and reached to snare her partner's throat in his thick fingers. Tess was torn between abandoning Joanne to assist her man. She had more faith in Po's ability to defend against the giant than she did in Joanne. She grabbed the young woman and urged her away from the corner and towards the burst open door. Ellie also skirted the battling men, dancing nimbly for her age, to try reaching Felicity. Felicity beckoned her sister to get out and save herself.

The giant's fingers closed on empty space. Po wasn't his match when it came to size or strength, but he had the edge on speed and skill. He ducked and weaved, parrying the man's grasping hands and then drove the heel of his palm under his nose. It didn't matter how powerful his constitution, the man couldn't shake off such a blow. His nasal cartilage concertinaed under the pressure and immediately blood spurted from both nostrils. The giant faltered and Po took the advantage, driving his boot between the man's thick thighs. Air exploded from the man's mouth, spotting Po with droplets of his blood. Po struck several times in succession, punches and elbows battering his body, but the giant took the punishment and slowly raised his head. Po glanced for a second at Tess and she saw a look of resignation in him. He'd avoided it before now, but under the circumstances he changed tack: his hand dipped to his boot where he kept a sheathed knife. Facing the odds of an unstoppable brute and a woman armed with a pistol, and he was forgiven for going for a deadlier weapon than a broken chair.

'Back off you son of a—'

Before he could fully expel the warning, the woman sprang in from behind and she battered the gun down on the base of Po's skull. Tess shouted in dismay as she saw him stagger, and the big man clutch him in hands seemingly the size of pizza boxes. The big fingers entwined Po's throat and within seconds he was struggling for life as the air was sealed from his lungs. His knife dropped from weakened fingers and clattered on the floor. The giant spun around, holding Po inches off the floor and then held him towards

Tess as if he were some kind of trophy. 'If this is your champion then he's severely lacking,' he boasted.

'Get your hands off him,' Tess snapped. She stepped forward, but was conscious of leaving Joanne unprotected. She must make a choice between the two: Po was a warrior in his own right, and he who lived by the sword was expected to die by the sword, but he was also her fiancé and the father of their soon-to-be-born child, and to hell with that bullshit! 'I said let him go, before you choke him to death.'

The giant mocked her with a grin. 'You know, you're right. He doesn't deserve to be strangled like vermin in a snare. For breaking my nose he deserves worse.'

The house erupted into chaos again, voices screeching and hollering and figures swarming. There was little sense of cohesion – too many people had their own agendas and priorities – except from Tess. She rushed forward to try to interject and save Po from further harm, even as the giant swung him aloft and then hurled him down at his feet. Po gasped like a fish plucked from the river, his knees drawn to his chest, neck arched backwards. The impact had both winded him and hurt his spine, Tess realized. He was still seconds – maybe longer – from doing anything to save his life as the giant raised his heel in the air and drove it at Po's exposed throat. Tess grappled the giant's leg. She was barely up to his sternum, and maybe half his weight at most, but her momentum carried his foot past Po's neck and on to the floor. The house shook under the impact.

'Get offa me.' The giant grabbed her hair and shook her. Tess held on to his knee, trying in vain to force him away and earn Po a few seconds of respite. The fingers twisting her hair were too much, sheer agony. He wrenched her head back and then almost tossed her away with the disdain of a toddler dumping a toy it had grown bored with. She scrambled up to press her back flat against a counter.

Tess quickly sought Joanne, but couldn't tell where the woman had gone. Next she checked on Po. He had recovered enough to roll on to his hands and knees, but he was far from out of danger. The red-haired woman who had pistol-whipped him was back at his side, and again had the gun at his head. This time she didn't use brute force, but the promise of a swifter death to control her prisoner.

What could she do, unarmed as she was? Tess understood that diplomacy should trump action, but usually it came before the blood and guts violence could ensue. The situation had progressed far beyond where common sense prevailed, but hopefully she could pull it back from the brink where multiple murders were the violent couple's only recourse.

'Please don't kill him,' she said, beseeching the gunwoman directly, 'we're having a baby. Don't hurt my baby's daddy.'

It was too dim to tell if her words gave the woman pause, but they sure didn't concern the giant. 'I could give a goddamn for your baby or its daddy. He ruined my face and now I'm going to ruin his.'

'No, please. There's no need for you to hurt *anyone*. Don't you see? Things have already gone way too far as it is.'

Tess wondered where the sisters had gone. They weren't in the kitchen: maybe they'd fled with Joanne and led her somewhere safe from these people. For now the invaders were in contention with Tess and Po alone, and if her plan to win them some time worked then it would stay that way long enough for the others to escape; more importantly, time for Po to recover.

'Where's the girl? You'd better tell us, or—' It was the woman who made the demand.

Her question had the affect of stalling the giant from aiming another stamp at Po. He twisted at the knees, his huge torso appearing to be fused at his hips, and his neck too short and thick to allow more movement than a few degrees to either side. The dim glow from outside sparked highlights in the whites of his eyes and on his bloodied teeth. 'Damn it, Siobhan, the rat has gone and bucked out again.'

'Fuck sake,' responded the woman. 'D'you mind not using my goddamn name in front of witnesses?'

'Why are you concerned about them hearing our names, huh? The dead don't carry tales. I was going to do a number on that asshole, but finding Joanne trumps that –' he aimed a nod at Po – 'so just shoot him and get it over. You got qualms about killing a pregnant woman, then give the gun to me and I'll do them both.'

Siobhan shook her head at the instruction. The giant snorted and once more droplets of blood sprayed. He dashed his sleeve across his face, before turning away and heading for the door he'd initially smashed through. Outside, the tracks made by the trio of fleeing women should be easily followed.

Siobhan checked that Po was behaving, reminding him she was in control with a knock of her gun barrel alongside his ear. In the interim of the last few seconds, Tess saw that he'd gotten one foot under him so wasn't as vulnerable as before when on all fours. For her part, she stayed crouching with her back to the kitchen counter, her arms down at her sides, offering no form of imminent threat to the gunwoman.

She said, 'You shouldn't do this, Siobhan. Think about what you're about to do. You will be murdering in cold blood, Siobhan.' Emphasizing the woman's name was deliberate, to remind her that indeed there were witnesses to her crimes and that she couldn't escape the consequences. Sure, she could shoot Tess and Po, but how could she be certain that one of the others hadn't overheard the giant and that they wouldn't escape to alert the authorities.

'Be quiet you,' Siobhan snapped. She scrubbed her fingers through her thick red hair, an unconscious act while thinking furiously for a satisfactory escape from her dilemma.

'You don't want to do this and you don't have to,' Tess asserted. 'I can tell you're not a murderer. Not like that other monster. Is he forcing you to do his bidding? Is that it? Do you need help to escape him, Siobhan?'

Siobhan turned the gun sharply on Tess. 'I told you to be quiet, bitch. Now shut up or I'll damn well shut you up for good.'

Tess averted her face, feigning fear, and not having to try too hard to be convincing. Siobhan wasn't a natural murderer, but circumstances could force even a reluctant killer to pull the trigger out of desperation. 'Please don't shoot me. Don't harm my baby.'

The gun was jerked at her once more, but then Siobhan exhaled in exasperation and she dropped the muzzle so that it touched Po's head again. Siobhan's attention remained on Tess a fraction longer.

Po had gained both feet. He thrust up, parrying the gun aside as he twisted out from under it. Siobhan snapped to attention, but it was too late to drop him cleanly. He wrapped a hand over hers and forced the gun aside and down. His other elbow caromed against the side of Siobhan's skull. She was tough, though, and the situation added to her sense of self-preservation. She shook off the blow and twisted around the pistol, trying to get a bead on

Po. He was still weakened from the beating given by the big man, but thankfully he was still stronger than Siobhan.

The gun fired. Splinters were blasted from the floor. Po shoved the gun further aside and it fired a second time. The bullet punched the ground between Tess's running feet. It didn't slow her charge to help Po. Her right hand, previously hidden in the darkness down by her side rose while Siobhan was unaware, so the redhead made no attempt to avoid the scalding coffee that Tess dashed from the thermos into her face. It was further seconds before the burning agony struck her. By then Po had wrenched around her hand and disarmed her of the pistol. His other hand, flat against her chest jammed her backwards against the kitchen wall as her two hands batted desperately at the liquid pouring down her. She screamed, the sound hellacious within the confines of the little house.

She could expect no pity from Tess. The bitch had threatened her life and therefore that of her unborn child. She had attempted to shoot Po dead too. Both were unforgivable crimes in her current state of mind. Tess grasped the woman's mane of hair and dragged her chin down on to her swiftly rising knee. She wouldn't see it as an act of mercy, but Siobhan was knocked unconscious, and spared any further torment from the scalding. Tess rolled the woman face down on the floor and twisted her arms up her back. She turned to check on Po. In the dimness she caught him kneading his throat with one hand.

'Are you OK?' she asked.

'That sumbitch almost crushed the life outta me,' he admitted. 'Jeez, Tess, he threw me around like I was a bundle of rags.'

'It's nothing to be ashamed of. He's a brute, unnaturally strong.'

'I almost had him, till that bitch cold-cocked me.' His hand transferred to the sore spot at the base of his skull. It reminded him that he still clutched Siobhan's liberated pistol in his other hand. He held it out, butt first, to Tess. She accepted it without comment. Po kicked around in the dimness seeking his knife. When he couldn't find it, he straightened, gave a shudder and was ready to take up the battle. 'You watch her, I'll go stop that asshole.'

'Take the gun,' she said and went to hand it back.

'You need it.'

'You need it more than I do.'

'Y'know I don't mix well with guns.'

'It'll help if you have to face that brute again. Take it, Po.'

'No. You use it. Make sure she doesn't trouble you when she wakes up.' He turned and moved quickly for the door. It was pointless arguing with him: he'd made up his mind and wouldn't be swayed. He was no fool, but there were times when she wished he'd put aside his warrior's sense of honor and instead of defeating his enemies by skill or force, he just pointed a gun at them and made them lie face down in the dirt. After all, she was yet to meet a bad guy willing to fight by the same rules of honor as Po.

TWENTY-THREE

P o had known worse days in his life but they'd been few.
There was the day his father died during a battle to defend
his besmirched honor, after his best friend, Darius Chatard,
stole his wife, but who'd sent out his adult sons to deal with the
fallout. Po had avenged his dad's murder but it ended with him
incarcerated in Louisiana State Penitentiary, also known as Angola,
and there were days inside that he'd rather forget. No less when
another of the Chatard brothers tried avenging their slain sibling
by stabbing out Po's eyes with a shiv; Po carried the scars on his
forearms to this day from defending his sight, before he was able
to return the improvised knife to his would-be killer's flesh. He'd
been injured other times, once almost being gutted by a demented
cartel enforcer, and on plenty of other occasions had taken contusions and broken bones, all in the service or defence of Tess, Pinky
and others. He regretted the deaths of the Chatard brothers; in a
fashion they were no different than he in fighting their fathers'
fight, so how could he hold on to any animosity? Besides, the old
blood feud between Villeres and Chatards had been resolved several
years ago after Po, Tess and the Chatards had united to save their
abducted sister, Emilia.

Having his businesses targeted by arsonists had been hard to
swallow and he'd thought that his classic Mustang being scorched
was the icing on a crappy cake, but that was before having his ass
kicked. He prided himself on being able to tussle with the toughest
of men, and therefore be able to protect his friends and loved ones
from harm. It was a crippling blow to his ego that the big man
had throttled him with disdain. Sure, being cold-cocked from
behind gave him ample excuse for not being on his best form, but
nevertheless, he'd had his ass handed to him on a plate, and it
didn't sit well with him. Not one damn little piece.

Po could be a fatalist. But there were other times when he'd
rage against the inevitable and go down fighting however poor his
chances of victory. This was one of those times. He'd traveled
there with Tess to collect Joanne and deliver her safely into the

hands of her sister, Detective Ratcliffe. He was damned if he was going to allow a beating to stop him. Besides, he might have lost the battle, but the war was far from over. The fatalist in him told him he wouldn't be happy until he'd gone at least another round with the hulk, hopefully this time with a clearer head than before.

He felt that the liberated pistol would've been wasted on him, because he wouldn't shoot the big man. Not unless there was no other possible option. He'd have perhaps used his knife to nick him, maybe draw blood and smear some on his cheeks, before sheathing the blade and meeting the brute man-to-man, fist-to-fist. But that was moot now, because he hadn't discovered where his blade had fallen before chasing after him into the heart of the blizzard.

Snowflakes adhered to Po's eyelashes and they melted on his lips. They accumulated on his shoulders and hair and in the folds in his clothes. Po paid them no mind. He moved, keeping the tracks in his view but also shooting glances high and low and to either side, knowing that the brute could attack from anywhere. For now the huge tracks followed those of several smaller tracks out from the side of the house and towards some outbuildings built in the lea of the trees to the west. Between the house and outbuildings there was a fenced pasture, and Po assumed that the sisters kept horses for when they preferred a more sedate form of transportation than their noisy snowmobile. The horses, if in fact they existed, must have been stabled away from the storm. He wondered briefly if the sisters had led Joanne to the stable with the view of saddling up and skedaddling. No, the big man was too close on their heels for them to try escaping on horseback.

Po darted through the blizzard. He was sore. His spine ached and his throat felt as if it had been wrung out like a dishcloth. Breathing was difficult and his head throbbed with the cold. He wouldn't allow his discomfort to slow him. If anything it galvanized him to regain what credibility the ass-kicking had recently stripped from him.

Ahead loomed one of the sheds. Its roof was peaked, the walls tall. Double doors sat open below a hatch through which a block and tackle could hoist grain and bales of hay on to a loft storage deck. Emanating from within the stable he expected to hear the whickering of nervous steeds, but if any horses were upset their vocalizations were being drowned out. The three women shouted and screeched and the deeper growl of the brute taunted them. Po didn't slow for a beat, he kept running, his footfalls deadened by the thick white carpet. He slowed only on reaching the stable.

He could creep inside and cold-cock the hulk, but that wasn't his way. He slipped inside the dim interior, seeking his target, even as he spotted, checked each woman's location, and decided who was in the most imminent danger. The sisters shielded Joanne from the big man, one of them wielding a shovel and the other with a more practical weapon: a pitchfork. Neither farm implement deterred the man from dancing from foot to foot, arms outstretched in an arc wide enough to encompass the trio. Even as Po lunged forward, the big man swept the shovel aside and then immediately backhanded its bearer aside. The other sister jabbed at him with the fork, but she lacked determination and the man knew it. Her jabs fell short and he was undeterred. He snapped a hand on the shaft of the fork and wrenched it high. The sister – Felicity, Po believed – was hauled off her feet several feet into the air but refused to release her weapon. She was tossed aside with the fork and then the brute charged in, hands grabbing for Joanne.

Po dropped his shoulder and drove into the big man's lower back, using his momentum and body weight to form a battering ram. It was possible that the giant would normally have withstood the attack easily, but he too was on the move and the impact forced him forward. Joanne ducked and he outreached his balance. Po continued to throw his weight into the man's back, pushing with the power in his legs to keep him off balance. The probability that he'd regain his footing in seconds remained, but Po was determined not to allow even a split second's respite. With his arms encircling the other's waist, he threw a leg around the other man's ankle, tripping him. The big man went down, slamming down on his chest. Po had the impression of the trio of women starbursting, each diving for clearance in different directions. He couldn't spare them a fraction of a second more notice than that, and instead shifted so that he mounted the man's back. He rained blows on the nape of his neck and ears. None of the strikes would end the fight, but they were designed to disorient and delay a counter attack. Po made claws of his fingertips and gouged at the man's eyes.

The big man crawled to the nearest wall, used its rough planks to grasp at, and he pulled up to his feet. With an enraged bark he

spun and tried slamming Po against the wall. A nail head gouged
Po's shoulder, but not deep enough to cause internal damage. He
stuck tight, one arm looped about the man's thick throat, riding
him like a rodeo bull. Three times the man spun around, trying to
dislodge Po, and then he went for broke again, throwing himself
back against the wall, crushing and grinding. Po endured the torture
and gave some in return. He stuck his thumb in the man's right
eye, probing deep with the calloused pad to pop the orb from the
socket if possible. The big man screwed his eyelid tight, snarling
as he chewed Po's wrist with his slab-like teeth. He yanked at the
arm around his throat, turned and tossed Po away. Po landed in
an explosion of straw and dust.

He scrambled blindly, making distance between him and the
heel that slammed an inch from the side of his head. Up on his
feet once more, Po spun and bent at the waist, his legs spread
wide, arms crossed before him. His opponent charged and rammed
him backwards, driving him through the litter of loose straw
towards the opposite side of the shed. In the darkness Po couldn't
see the wicked prongs of a thresher machine, but somehow sensed
how close to impalement he was. He broke free and rolled, shoulder
to heel and popped up several yards to the man's left. He'd set
his feet when the giant's ham-sized fist pounded his sternum. His
wind blasted between his teeth and Po emitted an animalistic croak
as he gave ground. He'd fought big men before, but this guy's
power was something else. Po daren't meet him dead on. He
sidestepped and pivotted and returned fire: his fists peppered the
big man's head, and Po was certain that several of the punches
had struck his broken nose. He again sensed danger, but this time
it was for the big man's sake. Po kicked, aiming for the side
of the knee. He employed the tip of his elbow to whip in and
strike the other's ribs. A backhand slash of the arm sent Po dodging
away and he placed an upright support column between them so
his opponent couldn't immediately get at him.

Snapping his head around, Po checked for the women. He
couldn't see them all. Only one of the sisters was in sight and she
was an indistinct silhouette ducking behind a pile of stacked bales.
For now the women were safe from their pursuer, but Po couldn't
let up for a moment to even catch his breath. He jerked one way,
and then went the other and the grasping hands missed him. He
kicked again, once more aiming for the weakest point above the

side of the man's knee. The man buckled, but didn't fall. He spun, grabbing for something in the gloom, and Po was hard put to dodge the pitchfork that speared for his gut. A second time the fork jabbed for him, this time higher to take his throat: Po ducked. The fork was swept sideways. Po understood that the best form of defence was offence. He lunged within the arc of the shank and struck a blow to the man's face. His knuckles felt satisfyingly snug over the mashed cartilage of his nose.

The pitchfork swung and this time Po couldn't dart inside its range. He was forced to leap for safety, and his boots caught in something, a folded tarp or something like it. He stumbled and went down on all fours. His opponent chased him, stabbing with the tines at his lower back. Thankfully the same obstacle that had tripped Po also saved him. The big man's feet got entangled and he also staggered. The pitchfork missed, sinking into the ground beside him. Po darted away.

He gasped for air. The fight must only be into its second minute but it had been taxing. He couldn't compete with the giant's strength, and already winded from their first encounter he would struggle to maintain the advantages of agility and speed.

His opponent had stalled. He too was feeling the strain of combat. He leaned on the fork, using it to support his weight. He gasped and coughed and then spat bloody saliva at his feet. Po could slip away. Avoiding further confrontation was the sensible thing to do. But Po wasn't for retreating. His blood was up and his vision tinged with red. He stood his ground and beckoned the man into round three.

In the gloom, a spark of light flashed off the man's teeth as he grinned in response and straightened. He wrenched the fork out of the ground's embrace and held it across his chest. He was too savvy to allow him to outreach himself again, and to lose balance. He began a slow tread forward and Po matched his steps. With a wordless shout the man lunged, stabbing for Po, but Po was also on the move. He leapt and caught at the floor of the loft overhead and drew his knees tight to his chest. He kicked out with his heels and scored with both. He jumped clear before the fork's trajectory could be altered. The tines stabbed the air Po had just vacated. Po landed beyond the man and he kept moving, scooping up the shovel dropped earlier by one of the sisters. He span, parrying as the prongs were again driven to impale him.

They spilled apart and stood gasping for air, each clenching their impromptu weapons.

'It's no use,' the giant taunted. 'You can't defeat me. I'll spit you on this fork and roast you over a fire like a hog. Then I'll hunt down your woman and do the same to her. But not until after I've scooped your brat out of her belly and thrown it on the fire.'

'I know what you're hoping for, bra. I'm not stupid enough to react to your smack talk.'

'It isn't smack when I mean every goddamn word.'

'If that's the truth, then come on. Sooner you get down to business, sooner you can prove it.'

The big man didn't move. He wasn't about to be drawn into a reckless move the way he'd intended drawing Po. He stood, sucking in lungfuls of air. He was gassed, but still had the strength and ferocity to snap Po in two if he allowed him to get his hands on him again. Po raised the shovel like an axe. The other hefted the pitchfork, but again stayed put. Po sensed that perhaps the man's appetite for the fight was waning slightly.

'Why are you chasing Joanne?' Po asked.

His question came out of left field. The man's eyebrows knitted as he considered it.

'It's obvious now that she isn't responsible for what happened to that family down in Boston,' Po pointed out. 'She's a victim, not . . . oh, you son of a bitch.'

The man's mouth pulled into a tight sneer.

'Catching her's personal to you,' Po growled. 'You need to shut her up, permanently. She's not only a victim; she's also a witness. She saw *you* murder those kids and their mom.'

'Why else would I chase her across the country to this frozen ass-end place?'

'You evil motherfu—'

The pitchfork flew at Po, hurled in a split-second by the killer. Behind it the giant followed, charging to grapple him before he could dodge or regain balance.

As Po sidestepped the flying missile a pistol cracked from the doorway. Bright muzzle flash lit the scene, causing the killer's face to bleach out and grow more grotesque because of the blood smeared over his mouth and chin. He skidded to a halt. The gun fired a second time and the killer snapped a curse of frustration, even as he turned away and bounded for a side exit. He barely slowed to open the door, crashing through it and blasting the door off its hinges. He pounded out into the blizzard.

Po looked at Tess.

'I almost had the sumbitch,' he said. 'If you hadn't frightened him off . . . Tess, what's wrong?'

With her framed by the doorway, he didn't require the muzzle flash to tell that her features were almost as pale as the snow falling beyond her. She still held the pistol aloft, her finger trembling alongside the trigger guard. Her other hand cupped her belly, low down and her fingers appeared to glisten darkly. As he started for her, Tess's knees gave out and she collapsed.

TWENTY-FOUR

Scant minutes earlier, Tess had ordered the scalded woman to get up. At gunpoint she'd ushered her over and made her sit on a sunken couch: it was low enough that the woman would struggle to rise, giving ample warning if she tried to escape. Tess ensured she didn't get too close, but the house was compact enough that she felt as if she loomed over her captive despite being across the room. She could smell the coffee that still dripped from the woman's thick mane and drenched her clothes. She imagined that closer up she would see steam rising. Scalding her was a desperate move, a nasty one too, but Tess couldn't stir an iota of pity for the bitch. She checked her out, but in the dimness the woman was indistinct. She also kept her face averted slightly and from her body language it was through shame.

'I wanted no part of any of this,' she croaked.

'Too late,' said Tess. 'You're up to your neck in it and will be going to jail.'

'I was forced to do his bidding,' the woman went on. 'You saw him, he's a *maniac*. I was terrified of what he'd do to me if I didn't obey him.'

'You were armed with a gun, he wasn't. Who coerced whom?'

'But I didn't use it.'

'You almost cracked my partner's skull with it, you bitch.'

'But I didn't *shoot* him.' The woman's head raised a little, hair hanging in wet ringlets alongside her cheekbones. 'I could have easily shot him and had done. But I didn't. I didn't intend shooting *anyone*, because I'm not like that. I'm not a *killer*.'

Her claims had grown more strident. They washed over Tess without effect. 'That's for the courts to decide.'

'Please, I swear to you, I was forced into coming here. For Christ's sake I'm only a driver. I'm only paid to *drive*.'

'Who is your employer?'

'I can't say.'

'You can and will.'

'No. You don't get it. I can't say because I don't know. My

employer's details are kept anonymous, or at least they're only
known to the man I fetched here.'

'So who is he?'

'I don't know his real name. He told me to call him Bob.'

'That's BS, and you know it. You're not some damn Uber driver
that's been pulled into something out of their control. You had this
pistol, and you damn well know how to use it. You're no stranger
to home invasion or to violence; not judging by the way you first
snuck in and then whacked my partner over the head. So tell me
the truth: you and that monster were hired to find and silence
Joanne, right? Who sent you?'

Her captive grew silent, head down, hands fumbling at her sides
as she tugged at her wet clothing. She was seeking a feasible lie,
something that Tess would accept as near enough to the truth
to see her as a fellow victim.

From beyond the open door Tess heard a throaty roar, and other
sounds, bumps and thuds recognizable in their fashion as the cut
and thrust of battle. She turned briefly to check on her captive and
then leaned away to peer out the door. Snow fell continuously,
and through the shifting curtain she couldn't see the outbuildings,
let alone Po fighting for his life against the giant. For another
second she leaned further, hoping to see Po returning safe and
healthy, and it was a second too long's distraction. She heard the
rustle of clothing, the scrape of the couch and knew the woman
was on the move. Tess had kept the gun trained on her, even while
looking away, but as she spun to confront the woman, her aim
was off. Either her captive had dodged to one side, or her own
arm had strayed slightly. It was only a matter of a split-second for
her to realign the pistol, but it was already too late. With wordless
determination written on her clenched features the woman speared
at Tess, one hand grabbing at the pistol to force it aside and
the other stabbing low.

Time seemed to slow down.

Tess cursed her rookie mistake. She should have frisked the
woman for weapons before allowing her to get up. Her mistake
could be her last. When on the floor, the woman must have discovered Po's knife lying where it had fallen and snuck it into her
pocket. Now her partner's blade – something Tess had never come
to full terms with him carrying – could be what killed her and
their baby.

As a cop she'd practiced weapons discipline and was trained in firearms retention techniques to ensure a perp didn't take her weapon away and turn it on her. So her instinct now was to fight to keep hold of the pistol, while fending off the blade with her other hand. There were few workable techniques for foiling a knife in the gut at such close range, so Tess allowed desperation to guide her hand. The blade pierced her hand, drove completely through flesh and sinew. Its tip scratched her abdomen, but Tess's hand held the knife from going all the way inside her. She gritted her teeth, meeting the other woman's eyes with such hate that she felt the other's resolve wither.

The knife stayed put, but the woman released its handle. Her other arm strove a moment longer to wrench the gun free of Tess, before she shoved and Tess stumbled over something invisible in the gloom and fell backwards. The woman followed her, but Tess fired, screeching at the bitch who would risk harming her unborn baby. The flame from the pistol lit the room, enough for Tess to see her opponent spin and plunge back through the door she'd entered by and race towards the back of the house. Tess scrambled to stand, could feel the metal through her hand grating against her bones. She staggered up and went after the fleeing woman.

She stumbled, and time rushed to catch up. Tess's vision tunneled, and it was as if the cabin tilted wildly from one side to the other. Nausea swam in her gut and she spluttered out a mouthful of acidic saliva. She propped her shoulder against the doorjamb and it was possibly the only thing keeping her upright.

The red-haired woman was nowhere in sight, already outside fleeing through the blizzard, Tess assumed. Either that or she was going again to assist the brute in his fight against Po. Tess pushed away from the door and gave chase. Blood dripped in large ingots from her damaged hand. She looked down and the sight of the knife through her hand shocked her with palpable force; her law enforcement career had ended after almost having her hand severed by a desperate criminal. It had taken several surgical procedures to reattach and then get her hand working once more. To this day she suffered numbness and tingling at times, and her full dexterity hadn't ever returned. It horrified her to think that she might have to go through similar surgical interventions as last time. At the same time she thanked God for ensuring it was only her hand that was injured and not her baby.

She wanted to assist Po, but a knife sticking through her left hand was an encumbrance. She halted and stuffed the pistol in her pocket, so that she could clench the handle and draw the blade free. She'd barely felt the knife plunge through her hand, not so on the way out. She groaned in agony as she slowly withdrew the glistening steel. She should throw the vile thing aside, but didn't. The knife was Po's and he might need it. She slipped the bloody steel into the snow to clean it, then used the hem of her coat to wipe off the residue. She put the knife in her pocket and took out the pistol. As she progressed across the snowfield scarlet dotted her wake.

Almost blinded by snow, it didn't matter. She followed the sounds of conflict, and in a short time a huge barn loomed before her. There was no hint on the ground that the woman had run this way, but she could tell older tracks all converged on the barn. She held the pistol butt jammed against her hip, making it difficult for anyone to disarm her should the woman pounce out of the storm. Her injured hand poured blood, despite the cold's attempt at freezing shut her veins and capillaries. She flicked away blood and then wiped the remainder on her clothing; instantly her hand was awash again. She must already have lost a pint of blood.

Her world tilted again. It was likely that a drop in her blood pressure and not blood loss that caused her weakness. She fought the swoon, feeling a tingling sensation in her face and a buzz in her ears. She exhaled and then sucked in a series of short, sharp breaths. Black floaters swirled in her vision, stark against the white backdrop. Tess halted. She was within a dozen feet of the barn's open door. She had a scant view inside, but within the darkness she detected movement.

She rushed to the door. Previously muffled voices grew clearer and she heard a threat to scoop out of her baby and throw it on a fire.

Tess was both horrified and enraged by the brute's words. She was tempted to empty the entire magazine of the pistol into the scumbag and negate his awful threats. Thankfully Po didn't rise to the bait and rush to his death. The men exchanged words as they gathered strength for the next round.

Stealing herself, Tess leaned around the doorframe.

Her vision was cloudier than ever, a sweeping darkness billowing in from all sides. But it didn't stop her from fixing on the giant and the pitchfork he raised. Po held up a shovel, as if about to use it to hew down a tree. Neither moved.

'Why are you chasing Joanne?' demanded her man an instant before it grew obvious to him.

Tess wasn't as surprised as Po was; she'd already guessed who was responsible for the killings that had initially made Joanne a fugitive. Po said something she found it difficult to understand but more clearly he stressed, 'She saw *you* murder those kids and their mom.'

The brute gloated at the accusation and Po swore.

The pitchfork flew at Po and immediately the giant followed.

She knew her man, knew that his pride had been stung by the earlier beating he'd taken and this was his attempt at evening up his record, but Tess couldn't risk the big man overwhelming him and then turning his violence on her and the other women. She fired, fully intending to bring the big man down, but her aim was off. She fired a second time and caused the giant to spin about and then hurl his weight at an exit door. It was smashed to kindling and then he was gone. Hopefully her second bullet had found his flesh and he'd bleed to death out there in the cold – anyone threatening to rip her baby from her womb and incinerate it could gladly go to hell!

She looked for Po.

In the dimness she couldn't tell if he was injured, but judging by his boastful words he was still game for a fight. All bluster fell from his tone after he took a closer look at her. 'Tess, what's wrong?'

She showed him, lifting up her bloody hand.

That was all she was capable of.

TWENTY-FIVE

T he temptation to strand Harper was strong and had he not suddenly loomed out of the blizzard to slap massive hands down on the hood, Siobhan might have left him to his fate. She hadn't gathered enough speed to run him down, so eased on the brakes instead. He clawed his way around the side of the SUV and momentarily struggled to open the iced-over door handle.

Exhaling in disappointment, Siobhan reached over and popped the handle from within, and he clawed the door wide. He forced his huge frame into the passenger seat, hair brushing the roof, snow-clogged shoes squeezed into the well. His hands made hooks on his lap: they were almost translucent they were so cold and Harper shivered uncontrollably.

'Were you g . . . g . . . going to l . . . leave me?' he demanded.

'Of course not,' said Siobhan with no hint of the lie.

'Y . . . you were d . . . driving off when I st . . . stopped you.'

'I was going to bring the car to collect you. I wish now we'd tried driving up there, instead of hiking through that storm. I'm frozen. Can see you are too.'

He shoved his hands under his opposite armpits. It was the first time in real life that Siobhan had seen somebody so cold his teeth literally chattered. She'd already set the heater to its highest temperature, but she thumbed up the fan to the max. Hot air billowed in their faces but it was a far from comfortable sensation after being chilled to the bone. If she didn't get fresh air, Siobhan felt certain she'd pass out. She stank of coffee and the hot air made the smell more intense, sickening. She could also smell Harper's blood. He'd tried cleaning his face at one point during his return to the SUV, and had removed most of the mess from his lips and chin, but his nostrils were both clogged and rimmed with coagulated blood. Earlier she'd appraised his profile and thought he resembled a granite block. Now that his nose had been smashed, it proved you could get blood from a stone.

'S . . . something funny to you?' Harper snapped.

'I'm only happy we're both alive. Things didn't go exactly to plan up there.'

He rubbed his palms furiously on his thighs and she guessed he was suffering the burning tingle of returning circulation. Good. It was the least discomfort he deserved. He prided himself on using logic. Well, his stupid plan to invade the house and snatch Joanne from her saviors was illogical and had always been destined to fail. In her heart Siobhan genuinely had not wanted to slaughter four innocent people and her reticence to shoot had probably ensured the plan would fall apart. Once the invasion was underway, and her gun taken away, then her views on the matter had altered. She'd not given a second's pause to stabbing Tess in order to facilitate her own escape, whether or not it meant killing her and her unborn child. Siobhan believed that all life was precious, but none was so precious as hers.

He breathed into his cupped palms. Staring over them at her.

'Want me to drive?' she prompted.

'I want you to explain what happened back there.'

He'd stopped chattering, if not shivering. Siobhan started the car rolling, but barely picked up speed.

'How the fuck did you manage to lose your gun?'

'You can't smell me? I didn't put it down for a damn coffee break if that's what you're wondering. That bitch threw the contents of a hot flask all over me and her fella took the pistol away.'

'You were supposed to shoot them.'

'I would've,' she said, 'if my eyes hadn't been burning from boiling coffee.'

'So they got your gun. Explains how that lucky sonofabitch got to come after me. I almost had my hands on Joanne when he intervened. I had to bust him up again and she got away. I would've impaled him and nailed him to a wall if'n you'd kept hold of your weapon.' He paused, wondering. 'How did you get away? If I thought you handed over your pistol willingly—'

'For Christ's sake, Harp! My luck turned, that's all. The woman was distracted by your fight and took her eyes off me. I almost managed to gut her with her fella's knife allowing me to escape.'

'You knifed a pregnant woman in the gut?' He snorted in dark humour. 'Maybe I'll make a decent partner out of you yet, Siobhan.'

'There's no chance of that, Harp. I'm paid to drive.' She tapped the steering wheel. 'That's why it was my first instinct to come get the car and try to find you and get us both the hell outta here. Please tell me you don't want to go back up that hill.'

'Keep rolling.'

'Where?'

'Anywhere else but here. I managed to shut off the power, but they'll soon have it up again and we can't be sure they haven't a direct line to the cops. We don't want to be here when the cavalry arrives.'

'Once the cops have their hands on Joanne it will be impossible to get to her.'

'Nothing's impossible, Siobhan. Never limit your options.'

'So what? Is this a case of discretion being the better part of valor? Are we going to try to get back to Boston?'

'There are few routes out of here, so we'd best put plenty miles behind us before the cops try setting up blockades.'

'This blizzard,' she reminded him. 'We've no idea how heavy it was further south. We can't be sure we'll be able to get through.'

'Folks up here are prepared for inclement weather, they'll have the roads clear.'

'Not like you to replace logical thinking with supposition, Harp.'

'Supposition based on logical historical fact,' he corrected her.

'OK, Dr Spock, you and your logic win.'

'It's "Mr Spock". Dr Spock was a pediatrician.'

'Sorry, I was confusing my pediatrics with pedicide.'

Harper scowled, before his mouth twitched and he said, 'Says the woman who just committed infanticide.'

'Nope. I tried, but I'm sure Tess got her hand in the way. Can't say how badly I hurt her.'

'She was on her feet when she tried shooting me,' he pointed out. 'Still, you tried, so don't come at me calling me names because I've murdered a few snot-nosed brats.'

'I never took you as the sensitive type, Harp.'

'Just shut up and do what you're good at. Get us outta here.'

'Same way we came in?'

'Don't think we have any other option.'

'That means that if Joanne still means to avoid the cops, she'll also be coming the same way. So this is about tactical repositioning rather than a retreat?'

'Now you're thinking. Like I said: maybe I *will* make a decent partner out of you yet.' Harper wiped his red-rimmed nostrils with the back of a wrist. 'And third time should be the charm with that wily son of a bitch that broke my nose.'

TWENTY-SIX

t felt like a dereliction of his duty when the cab took Pinky away from Tess and Po's home, but it was important to him that he check on their other premises: he had taken over Tess's apartment on Cumberland Avenue, rent free, after she'd moved in with Po. The apartment above a curios and antiques shop still belonged to Tess and was as much a target of their arsonist enemies as anywhere else they were associated with. The autoshop, the diner, even Po's muscle car, all were impersonal targets, but to lose Tess's home would be a terrible wrench to her. Earlier in the day Po had collected him from the apartment and he'd willingly come to guard the ranch, but now it was more important he be in situ when the arsonists came for Tess's place, as they surely would.

The cab took him through North Deering on to Forest Avenue, before cutting on to Deering Avenue for the final leg of the journey. It was about a five-mile trip, completed in under a quarter hour, but it felt much further and time-consuming to Pinky. He didn't exchange a word with the driver beyond telling him his destination, but he was damn well tempted to tell the guy to hurry the fuck up on more than one occasion. He kept his lip tightly zipped. The snow in Portland had stopped falling and the roads had been partially plowed, but driving at speed was still not advisable.

Tess's brother Alex had promised to send a patrol car around Po's neighborhood, and had intimated that he would personally keep an eye out on her place on Cumberland Avenue from the handy confines of the Parkside Community Policing Center, but Pinky was under no illusions. The cops had plenty to deal with, and this winter cyclone hadn't lessened their load. It'd be easy for determined firebugs to slip by; case in point, during the cab ride out to North Deering he hadn't spotted a single police patrol. During his previous life in Louisiana he'd have chuckled at the irony of wishing to see the police coming.

He'd brought his pistols along for the cab ride, tucked inside a knapsack so it wasn't obvious he was packing heat. Alex had maybe warned against vigilantism with a barely perceptible wink,

and though Pinky might expect leniency from prosecution, even
Alex Grey couldn't outwardly condone the shooting of the arsonists. His kid sister's property, and perhaps even her life, was under
threat and Alex's loyalty might be tested, but first and foremost
he was a cop.

Pinky directed the driver to stop the cab at the intersection of
Cumberland and Deering Avenues, and paid over the odds with
bills plucked from his jacket pocket; he added a ten-dollar tip,
advising the guy to get a hot drink inside him. He wished he could
take his own advice, because although the snow had mostly stopped
falling, the wind was biting and chilled him the instant he left the
warmth of the cab. He shivered, his shoulders wiggling, and he
stamped his feet for the first few steps, testing the sidewalk for
slipperiness. The treads in his sneakers left a distinct print. He set
off along Cumberland Avenue, approaching the apartment from
several blocks distance in order to reconnoiter its surroundings.
As he drew closer he began taking more interest in the footprints
of other pedestrians using the avenue. Foot traffic was low and
unsurprising given the icy chill, so it was a simple enough task to
check directions and if anyone had made several passes of his
home, or spent any time lurking and observing the place. It was
too late at night for the curios shop to be open, but a security
night-light had been left on, throwing a dim glow on to the sloping
pavement outside. Pinky's, rather Tess's, upper-storey home was
in full darkness, but that was as it should be. Pinky's car sat
unmolested on the sloping drive and there was no sign of tracks
in the virgin snow heaped on the external steps leading up the side
of the building to the apartment.

Adjusting his hold on his knapsack, Pinky slung it so that he
could easily dip a hand inside and hook out one of his pistols.
He bypassed the building a second time, noting that the light
cast on the sidewalk also contained a slow moving shadow: he
wasn't alarmed, because it was not unusual for Anne Ridgeway,
the shop's proprietor to stay late. The elderly lady had nobody
waiting for her at home, so she'd regularly stay on after the six
o'clock closing time if she was engaged in reading a good novel
or adjusting the layout of her stock of trinkets and curios. He
slowed, darting sidelong glances to see if he could spot the tiny,
bird-like old woman inside, but the view inside was distorted by
condensation on the window. At the end of the building, he

paused momentarily, then turned sharply and walked up the service ramp. At the top there was a small yard wherein Mrs Ridgeway kept her trashcans hidden from potential customers by a tall wooden stockade. Pinky checked and found the gate locked from within. He was tall enough to stand on tiptoes and peer over the fence. There was no movement. He continued around the back. Out of sight of the front street, he drew one of his pistols. He padded along, leaving footprints in the virgin snow, noting he was the only person who'd been around the back of the building in hours.

He couldn't relax his guard. As he moved to the opposite side of the house, he was partially obscured from the street by the set of external stairs that gave access to the apartment. There he stood a minute, listening: there was distant traffic noise, but nothing close enough to be of concern. He stepped out and approached his SUV, parked hood out on the sloping drive. He checked once more before popping the locks and getting inside. He turned off the interior light and sat still. The snow piled up on the windshield helped conceal him. He could see enough of the street through clear patches but his shape wouldn't be betrayed within. He set his knapsack down, but only after withdrawing the second pistol and placing it in reach of his left hand.

Then he waited.

His wait lasted more than an hour. So as not to give away his location he'd left off the engine, but the interior of the car was anything but cold. His exhalations had caused steam to build up on the windows; it warped the small areas of visibility spared by the falling snow, and occasionally he'd had to use his sleeve to wipe away the moisture. He shivered, but it was through the slow release of adrenalin, as he prepared for battle that must surely arrive. He wiggled his toes in his boots and regularly shifted his butt so that there was no danger of numb legs once the doo-doo hit the fan.

Cars and a few late-night delivery trucks rolled past, compacted snow crunching under their tires. He heard a distant siren but the emergency vehicle never showed up in his vicinity. There was no movement that he could perceive from the nearby police office. Twice pedestrians ambled past, laughing drunkenly, late night revelers who had not allowed the inclement weather to get in the way of their drinking and dancing. The other distinct sounds he heard came from within Mrs Ridgeway's shop: it sounded as if she was remodeling the entire store by the amount of scraping and thuds going on.

The more he heard the more he realized that it was uncommon for the old antiquarian to make so much noise. He slept directly above her store and never had she disturbed his sleep before. Besides, it sounded as if she was hauling furniture around three times her weight, because she was a tiny, fragile-looking woman who'd occasionally requested he come downstairs and help her shift a bookcase or trinket box. Pinky kept his hair cut short to his scalp. Nevertheless he could feel it writhing as realization hit.

He popped open the door on his SUV and slipped out on to the ramp. The snow was fresh, ankle deep and fluffy and not yet compact enough to be treacherous underfoot. He planted both feet though, while transferring one of his pistols to a holster in the small of his back. He retained the second pistol, but tucked it close to his abdomen while he approached the front street.

He stood near the shop's entrance, without presenting his silhouette against the door glass, and listened. Those inside, because he now understood that Mrs Ridgeway was not behind the noises, spoke without any filter, believing that Pinky was yet to return home. He made out two distinct voices, both male, both gruff. A third voice, meek and high-pitched had to be Anne Ridgeway's.

Earlier he hadn't discovered any evidence that the arsonists had recce'd the building, so he had left things so that it would appear he wasn't home. He thought it might entice the cowards to launch an attack as they had at the autoshop and diner where there was no apparent fear of discovery. He'd made a major error. He was not the only one to try an ambush; only his damn enemies had arrived before him and gotten in place before the last snowfall. How they hadn't noticed him creeping around earlier he couldn't say, but they'd all been fools and had wasted more than an hour.

Hearing the frightened tone of Mrs Ridgeway caused heat to build in Pinky's chest. Anne Ridgeway was normally fearless, a strong person who didn't suffer fools or bullies. To that end, she must've been shown proof of the threat she faced. It was one thing attacking Po, Tess or himself, because they were all capable of defending themselves, quite another for the cowardly bastards to terrorize an elderly lady. He was sorely tempted to go in, both guns blazing. But he held off. He required a clearer head and locations for his enemies, because the last he wanted was to drop the old lady with friendly fire.

He moved away, dodging around the front of the building again, and around the back. He paced along, and came to where a small window indicated the bathroom and tiny kitchenette that Mrs Ridgeway used while at work. The window was closed and locked, and he had no intention of breaking it to gain admittance, but at its base was a small vent through which fresh air was allowed to circulate without compromising the building's security. Through it he could hear the voices clearer than before and it took only a moment to decipher who was where in the shop. Mrs Ridgeway, he deduced, was seated in her usual chair behind the cash register, where she often read novels between serving customers. The two men were in the shop proper and as long as he kept his pistols trained that direction then Mrs Ridgeway should be safe from a stray bullet.

He quickly went around the opposite end of the building to the trashcan compound. He peeked over the top; it was deserted as before. The gate was locked, but being a resident Pinky had a key. Usually he was the one to pull out the trash for Mrs Ridgeway when the municipal garbage collection truck was due. He opened the gate taking extra care to be silent. Once inside the compound it was barely two paces to the side door into the shop. For her ease of access to the trashcans he hoped that Mrs Ridgeway had left the door unlocked. He laid his fingers on the handle and paused a few seconds having second thoughts about breaching the building; perhaps he should back away, call the police and allow them to do their jobs.

Yeah, that's exactly what he should do.

Back off.

Let the cops do *his* job.

Yeah, right!

Pinky tightened his grip on his pistol and with the other hand turned the handle slowly. As the latch cleared the lock, he shouldered inside, bellowing a challenge.

He immediately spotted one of the arsonists, a short stocky man who had concealed his lower face with a neckerchief and a woollen hat pulled down to his ears. He wore a navy blue padded anorak. Pinky couldn't immediately see the second arsonist; in the half minute since moving from the bathroom window to breaching the door the tableau had changed. Pinky covered the first man, a bug's wing of pressure all he required to discharge the pistol, while seeking the second. A moment later and the second man gave away his location by straightening up and holding out a can of lighter fluid; he held a throwaway cigarette lighter in front of the nozzle. This man, Pinky was certain, was the same asshole he'd chased from behind Po's Mustang and down through the woods to the frozen river. He was also masked and wore a baseball cap and a brown coat. Ordinarily Pinky would shoot and be damned, but not while the impromptu flame thrower was aimed directly at Anne Ridgeway. The old lady looked tiny perched atop her chair, eyes huge and moist, lips splayed in disgust. Her curly hair hung in damp ringlets on her forehead and around her ears and the front of her sweater was darkened with fluid. Pinky smelled the accelerant and understood the horrible truth: she had already been doused and it would take only a spark to turn her into a column of flames.

The first he'd spotted backed away, one hand extended, as if he might catch the bullet Pinky promised him. He was wearing leather gloves, but they'd do nothing to deter a bullet. Pinky allowed him to retreat, while advancing a step further inside the shop. He noted the disarrayed stock and where flammable items had been stacked to fuel a bonfire. They'd never intended confronting Pinky directly in his own home, they had planned to wait until he was settled in and then set the shop ablaze and allow the flames to rise and roast him to death; the sick bastards must have considered Anne Ridgeway collateral damage, perhaps even planning on making it appear that she was behind the blaze. He turned the pistol on the second arsonist.

'Think you can strike that lighter before I put a bullet through your head, you?' Pinky demanded.

'Take a sniff,' the arsonist answered, 'it doesn't matter if it's from my lighter or your gun, one spark and this place will go up like it's the fourth of July.'

'You aren't prepared to strike a flame, you, not if it means you and your buddy burning to death. Put down the lighter fluid and let's go outside and sort this once and for all.'

'You presume to know me and what I am or am not prepared to do.'

Pinky noted that the other guy squinted in alarm at his partner and edged further away, angling towards the front street exit. 'Just one more step, you,' Pinky snarled, turning the pistol back on him. The man didn't lower his gloved hand.

'I know you're a cowardly piece of shit,' Pinky said. 'Who else would choose fire as their weapon? Who else would threaten the life of an innocent old lady? Man up, let's go outside and sort this.'

'You'll shoot us the second we walk outside.'

'I'll put down my gun, but not until after you've dropped that lighter.'

'No deal.' The man rolled his thumb over the wheel on the lighter. It'd take no pressure at all to cause it to catch and strike. Above the line of his facemask the man's eyes twinkled with dark promise. Pinky aimed the pistol directly between them.

Anne Ridgeway moaned and shifted slightly in the chair.

The nozzle of the lighter fluid canister threatened her. 'Don't move, Grandma,' snapped her tormentor.

For that split second the coward's attention was on Mrs Ridgeway and Pinky capitalized on it. He couldn't shoot, but he was big enough and bad enough to beat the living crap out of the arsonist. He lunged forward and, rather than rely on speed and momentum, he swept his left hand up and caught the ridge of a trinket display case. He cast the cabinet ahead of him and it struck the arsonist while he was still charging. The man didn't relinquish either fluid canister or lighter, but neither was aimed directly at Anne Ridgeway when Pinky crashed into him. Pinky battered at the man's arm with his pistol, trying to knock the lighter out his hand. The arsonist cried out, and dodged sideways. Already his friend was abandoning the shop, clawing his way through the overturned furniture to reach the exit. Futilely Pinky could only hurl a curse after him. He focussed on the other, the one that was still capable of turning the building into a pyre.

As Pinky swept aside the cabinet, he kicked at the man and sent him staggering. In response, the arsonist barked in disappointment. He turned the canister on Pinky and sprayed a jet of fluid at his chest. Pinky, a big man, was an easy target. But he wouldn't allow the arsonist to light him up without blowing his brains out too. He aimed the pistol and the arsonist backed away. His partner wrenched open the door and skidded out on to the sloping sidewalk, almost going down on his back. He broke his fall on a hip and

elbow and immediately slithered away, clearing space for his pal
to follow. Pinky came after them and would have fired but for the
threat of igniting the fumes, or the fluid now dripping from his
jacket.

He was at the threshold and in the clear when the sound of a
revving engine tore his gaze from the duo to a panel van racing
along Cumberland Avenue. Its driver braked, but the tires had poor
traction. The large van slewed, teetered precariously for a few
seconds before slamming down on all four tires again. It ended
up overshooting the fleeing arsonists, but Pinky was under no
illusion: this was their getaway driver, proving his instinct that
there'd been more than two of them present at Po's ranch. Pinky
ducked back indoors, just as the driver leaned out and fired a
volley of rounds from a silenced pistol. The bullets struck the front
window of the shop, cracking but not shattering it. Pinky couldn't
return fire. He looked back at where Mrs Ridgeway had abandoned
the chair to scuttle into the back room.

When he checked again outside, the first arsonist in blue was
clambering in a side door in the panel van, but he couldn't see
where the one in brown had gotten. It became apparent a few
seconds later when a stream of flaming lighter fluid arched into
the doorway. The flash and heat that followed was terrible and
Pinky moved on instinct rather than clear thought. He retreated,
firing his weapon now that the fear of ignition was moot, while
swiping at the flames on his coat. He could feel his chest burning.
He dropped his gun, spinning and turning, and tore off his coat
and cast it aside. A second bonfire was ignited where his coat fell,
and then flames writhed, racing across the floor and furniture to
light other fires. Grimacing at the burns on his flesh, Pinky hurtled
into the back room. Mrs Ridgeway stood aghast. Still dripping.
He knew that within seconds the flames would reach the room
and she'd be immolated and quite likely he would be too. Pinky
didn't pause. He snatched his second pistol from the small of his
back and fired it several times, blasting the window out. He used
the barrel of the gun to knock out a few resistant shards, and then
cast the gun outside. Without any preamble he caught up Mrs
Ridgeway and helped squeeze her through the aperture. She fell
outside, and he hoped the snow was deep enough to cushion her
fall.

Pinky felt searing heat at his back. The entire sales area was ablaze, and the accelerant caused it to burn inferno hot. He judged the window frame. Mrs Ridgeway had barely made it through; there was no hope for him. There was nothing for it: he charged and kicked the wall under the window, where the vent had been fitted and broke through. A few more kicks and he widened the hole, splintering the wooden siding on the building. He could barely breath, the heat so intense it robbed his lungs of oxygen. Pinky made a final charge and shouldered through the wall. He went down to his hands in the snow, but his backside and legs remained inside. He squirmed out, drawing his thighs over splintered wood, feeling where they gouged his flesh. He ignored the pain. Acquiring some abrasions was preferable to being spit-roasted in his book. He spilled out on to the snow of the rear yard, the soles of his boots smoking. His trousers were on fire. He rolled, using the snow to help extinguish the flames. After gasping a few breaths he ignored his own discomfort, searching instead for Mrs Ridgeway. Thankfully the elderly lady had crawled away and sat in the open yard on her backside, blinking at him in incredulity now that the immediate danger had passed.

'You OK, Anne?' he asked.

She didn't reply. Her gaze slipped past him and upward, and he knew without checking that the blaze had followed him out the hole he'd smashed in the wall and was now crawling up the building to the upper floor.

TWENTY-SEVEN

' 'm OK. Let me up, why don't you?'
Totally out of character, Po fussed over Tess, grim-faced and rocking on his toes. 'Just you stay where you are, gal. Lie there and get your strength back.'

'I'm fine, I'm telling you.' Again Tess attempted to rise and again was gently but firmly held in place by her fiancé.

She looked around, wondering where she was because it sure wasn't the darkened interior of the barn she'd last been conscious of. She guessed she was in the sisters' house but in a room she hadn't been in before. She was on her back, with her feet raised over the arm of a couch, and it took a moment to realize it was the same couch she'd made the red-haired woman sit in, only she was seeing the room from a different perspective than before. This time it was brightly lit for starters. Someone had gotten the back-up generator running. Thinking a tad clearer, Tess acknowledged Po's instruction to stay down by lifting her hand. It had been neatly bandaged, compliments of one of the elderly women, she thought.

'How does your hand feel, honey?' asked Felicity.

'Strangely I feel no pain,' Tess said. 'I don't know if that's a good or bad sign.'

'Knife went all the way through,' said Ellie, 'and you were fortunate it did. None of your major bones or ligaments were damaged . . . not that we could see.'

Tess inspected her bandaged hand again. She could sense some grinding in it when she turned her hand, so she wasn't as certain about having avoided major injury as the women were. She tested her fingers and they wiggled, her index finger felt numb but hopefully it was a temporary symptom of the trauma.

'I can't believe you were stabbed with my knife,' Po said, hanging his head in shame. 'What if you'd failed to block it and—'

She caught him with her good hand. 'I didn't fail to block it. I got a cut hand, end of story, OK. Don't dwell on it.'

'I know but—'

'Our baby is fine, Po,' she promised.

'When I saw all of that blood . . . hell, you musta lost a damn quart at least. No wonder you fainted.'

'You must've carried me here?' she wondered.

Po shook his head, deferring to the old women to explain. 'We brought you here,' said Ellie.

'We're stronger than we look,' added Felicity.

'I'm sure glad we met such resourceful folks,' Po said. 'They know a thing or two about patchin' up wounds.'

Felicity smiled. 'You learn darn quick how to do anything when there's nobody else around to do it for you.'

'They can fight like a pair of wildcats too,' said Po, approvingly. 'They protected Joanne, held off that Frankenstein-headed punk with some farm implements til I got there.'

Tess sat up too fast for any of them to stop her. She checked around in alarm. 'Where is Joanne? Did they take her?'

'I'm right here.'

She twisted awkwardly to see where the young woman sat huddled on another chair. Joanne's coat and several hats bulked her out so she looked fifty pounds heavier than before. She wouldn't meet Tess's eye. Shame was a strong emotion and Joanne was suffering it in bucket loads.

'Nothing has changed,' Tess reassured her. 'We're still going to deliver you safely to your sister.'

'I'm sorry, this is all my fault,' Joanne moaned, and finally looked at Tess with such earnestness she couldn't believe anyone would judge the girl capable of harming anyone, let alone the children under her care. Teardrops shimmered on her cheeks.

'No, Joanne,' said Tess. 'Get that notion out of your head. None of this is your fault.'

'Only a complete fool would fail to see who were the bad guys here,' said Ellie.

Tess glimpsed up at the woman and caught a knowing nod in reply.

'While you were out I explained things to the sisters,' said Po. 'They know that Joanne has been falsely accused of a horrible crime and that we're takin' her to meet with her cop sister, who can help clear her name and keep her safe. They've agreed not to involve the local cops till we're clear, and allow us a head start on getting Joanne safely back to Portland.'

'We are indebted to you both,' said Tess and tried to stand. Instantly blackness edged her vision. 'Woo,' she whistled, and lay back again, pinching the bridge of her nose with her good hand. 'Maybe I will just lie here a little longer.'

'Felicity's going to take me downhill on the snowmobile,' said Po. 'I'll get the car started and warm things up for when Joanne and you join me. For now keep your head down and your feet up, gal.'

'I'll be ready to go, I just need to—'

'You need to regain your strength,' Ellie butted in. 'Have some of that soup we made and I'll put you up a fresh flask of coffee seeing as the last one was wasted.'

'Wasn't wasted, it hit just the right spot,' said Tess with a turn of her lip at the lameness of her joke.

Joanne approached Tess and kneeled down alongside the couch. 'I'm genuinely sorry you got hurt.' She turned her head to the sisters. 'I'm sorry those monsters followed me here and broke in. I'm sorry any of you was put in danger because I hadn't the courage to stay in Boston and face the music. It's just, well, I panicked, and when I saw what they were saying about me on the TV, I was terrified I'd be shot on sight and I ran. I didn't know that Harper was after me, but if I had I would've warned you what he was capable of. It was him, he was the one responsible for murdering *everyone*.'

'Harper?' asked Tess, suddenly feeling a little stronger. She took Joanne's hands in hers and made the young woman look at her. 'How do you know his name?'

'I've heard it before.' Joanne nodded. 'His full name is Bruce Harper. He used to work for my employers, Lacey and Carl Blackhorse. I was never certain what his role was; I guessed he was a bodyguard or something. No, not a bodyguard, that's not right. More like "muscle" to scare away unwanted attention.'

'Why did Carl Blackhorse feel the need to employ somebody like that?'

'Like attracts like, right? Carl was incredibly successful and rich and had this macho image to uphold. He liked to act tough, so he surrounded himself with real tough guys and girls. He was a complete narcissist, and I think he got a buzz out of playing the big man. You ask me, Carl was nothing but a cowardly bully who needed a bigger bully like Harper to do his dirtiest fighting for him.'

'Harper worked at the house with you?'

'He did until he was sent packing by Lacey. She had Carl fire him a few weeks ago. He was unhappy with her and didn't leave quietly.'

'And so he returned to exact revenge by slaughtering the family,'

Tess wondered. There had to be more to the situation than a simple act of a pissed off ex-employee out for retribution. For instance, what would motivate the redhead to help him clean up after his murderous rampage? She had claimed to be 'hired' as his 'driver', but Tess didn't buy the story, not on its simplest of face values. More, she knew, would come to light once she'd had an opportunity to interrogate Joanne further on the drive back to Portland. For now, the horrified faces of the sisters told her it was neither the time nor place to discuss such things.

Po indicated he was ready to go and Felicity appeared grateful for the excuse to leave. The woman pulled on goggles and a Stetson hat that she strapped tightly under her chin: the cowboy hat concealed a safety helmet. Po must go bareheaded, because he'd lost his baseball cap somewhere along the way. He was unperturbed by the idea of going back out in the storm and Tess knew he was eager to return to Portland. Now her injury made it more important than ever that they return home, where she could have her wound professionally tended to by a medic. Probably a visit with her pediatrician was on the cards too. The knife hadn't gone in her womb, but she couldn't swear the baby was unharmed by the scuffle or her subsequent collapse.

Po pulled open the door and Felicity crowded the doorway too while they checked out the blizzard. There was a lull in the snowfall and the air that crept indoors felt crisper than before. Ice formation on top of the snow could make their journey back home treacherous. She smiled at Po and his turquoise eyes gleamed with love for her before he turned and she heard him crunch a path with Felicity to where the snowmobile waited. The engine roared to life and soon diminished as it took them down the hillside.

'Fliss will be back soon and she'll take you down next, Joanne,' said Ellie as she shut out the outside world. 'Fliss' was apparently a pet name for her sister; Tess considered that Ellie might be a shortened version of Eleanor.

'If your Ski-Doo will carry the three of us, I'll be ready to go, and save Felicity having to make the trip again,' Tess promised. She swung her legs off the couch and then sat up, indicating that she'd gotten over her lightheadedness. She hadn't fully, but didn't want to be fussed over again.

Ellie moved to replenish the flask of coffee. Joanne was yet to get up from Tess's side. 'Why are you doing this for me?' she asked.

'To take you back to Karen.'

'No, that's not what I mean. You must've accepted the job long before you knew I was innocent. I was accused of murdering babies, and you—'

'I'm pregnant?'

'I couldn't tell until your partner said so.'

'You just thought I was fat, huh?' Tess joked.

Joanne wasn't in the right frame of mind for humour.

'You must've hated accepting this job.'

'I won't lie, Joanne, when I first heard what Karen wanted, I was conflicted, but I soon figured that you couldn't be responsible for all the murders.'

'But you thought I might still have been an accomplice?'

'It went through my mind, but it was never a serious theory. When I saw other bodies had been found out in the grounds, I guessed they'd been murdered trying to escape, and that the killer was chasing people down. It didn't strike me as the actions of a young woman. I can easily believe it of *Harper* though.'

'He almost caught me at the wall. If not for Toby Hillman he would've . . . Oh, my God . . .' She devolved into tears and hardly surprising having witnessed Harper brutally murder the young man.

Tess drew her into her arms and hugged the woman while she wept. Ellie stayed out of the way, only appearing with the fresh flask of coffee when the sound of the returning snowmobile announced her sister was back. Tess and Joanne assisted each other in rising. Tess accepted the flask and then went to clutch Ellie's forearm and squeeze her thanks. Her bandaged hand reminded her to use her hand sparingly until she could have it looked at by a professional. She smiled her thanks and gave the woman a peck on the cheek.

Ellie blushed, and said, 'Aww, shucks,' like a character from an old 1950s TV show. Before she could wave away any further gratitude, Joanne caught the smaller woman in a hug that enfolded her in her extra layers of coats.

Tess opened the door. It would be foolish to step outside without first checking all was clear; she'd hate to think either of the bad guys had ambushed Felicity on her return trip and it was Harper or the spiteful redhead that was astride the Ski-Doo. Its rider was of slight build, wearing an overly large Stetson hat.

TWENTY-EIGHT

Once she attained a strong and stable signal, Tess called Detective Karen Ratcliffe, informing her that Joanne was safe and well and en route to their planned rendezvous in Portland. Karen, a tough cookie in her role as a cop, wept with relief at the news about her kid sister and promised that she would be in Portland by the time Po got them back. Tess wanted to call the local cops next, to inform them about Bruce Harper and his companion, but knew that in doing so she'd be ordered to go directly to the nearest police station and hand over Joanne to law enforcement. She asked Karen to make the call instead, and also to request for protection to be sent for the elderly sisters at their ranch. Then she urged Po to drive a little faster than she'd normally encourage in these conditions. The blizzard had blown away for now and the sky had gone clear; the Milky Way looked so close and vibrant she felt she could reach out of the Telluride's window and stroke its underbelly. That wasn't to say that the roads were clear. The snow was piled up at the shoulders and down the center of the passage a plow had recently cut along the Old Codyville Road.

They met little oncoming traffic, having only to pull over twice to safely pass larger vans heading for the border crossing. In good time Po had them back across country and approaching Lincoln, a kick in the butt's distance from Interstate 95. Mostly Joanne had been silent during the drive, choosing instead to huddle on the back seat and keep her own counsel. She became agitated as they approached a gas station that was still buzzing with police activity. 'I stopped here on the way to the border,' she announced. 'What happened here after I left. Do you think—'

'I'd say Harper happened,' Po grunted.

'Oh, God,' Joanne moaned. 'That poor old man! I hope he's OK.'

Tess watched with a mild sense of dread clutching her gut as they rolled past. There was no hint of what had gone on inside the convenience store, but police tape had been strung across the door.

'Think we should stop and tell them about him?' Po asked.

'It'll defeat why I asked Karen to inform the cops about Harper for us. We can't get tied up here, Po, not when the cops will probably arrest Joanne and possibly us as accessories.'

'Yeah, my thoughts exactly,' he confirmed and kept going.

'Dear God,' Joanne moaned again, and sank her chin deep into the collar of her super-sized coat. Tess feared that the young woman would buckle under the stress of misguided guilt if she kept taking the weight of Harper's crimes on her shoulders.

They cut around Lincoln and over the Penobscot River and joined the highway. Hopefully Harper and the redhead had abandoned their plan to shut up Joanne, now that covering up his involvement in the Blackhorse murders had become moot. It had concerned Tess to leave the unprotected elderly sisters behind, but speed was of the essence in reuniting Joanne with her sister. All of the others were convinced that Harper and the woman had fled the vicinity, expecting that law enforcement officers would descend on the area any minute. If anything, Po had cautioned, the bad guys had gotten a head start and most assuredly had traveled the same roads they did to get back across to the highway. For all they knew their SUV was a short distance ahead, perhaps around the next sweeping bend in the road. By the hawk-like intensity of his gaze, he was hoping he was right and that a final reckoning might play out right there on the highway. As it were they reached Bangor without catching sight of the SUV, and then there were too many routes for the bad guys to have taken to assume they were on the same road; for all they knew Harper and the woman could've crossed into Canada, seeking onward travel to a country that didn't have an extradition agreement with the US.

Pinky rang them just after they switched outside Gardiner to I-295 to avoid the toll road. Tess put him on speaker. 'Don't know how you guys will feel about getting home,' Pinky said. 'Things took a turn for the worse after we last spoke.'

'Are you hurt?' Tess asked.

'Not physically. Well, that's discounting a few scrapes and bumps and a lungful of smoke. I can't say the same for your apartment, me.' He fell into glum silence.

'What the hell's goin' on, podnuh?' Po prompted.

'I don't know how to break it to you, me, but it was bad enough telling you about your car.'

'Be as blunt as you need. The way my day has gone I'm not sure it could be made much worse.'

'It's more about you, Tess, who'll be upset.' •

'What is it, Pinky? Just tell us.'

'They burned down your apartment,' he said.

'*Your* home?' she asked for clarity, though there was no need. He exhaled into the phone.

'Were you there?' Po asked without recrimination.

'I set a trap, me. It went to shit and those scumbags got the hop on me. They'd already set an ambush downstairs, them, and was holding Anne hostage.'

'Anne Ridgeway? Is she—' Tess jolted with anxiety.

'I saved her. Had to bust through a wall to get her out. Couldn't do much else, me, not without getting my ass lit on fire.'

'Thank God you got to her in time,' Tess said. 'Is she OK?'

'She's hurting, her. Hurting in her heart, cause her beloved shop got burned to ashes.'

'The apartment?'

'Gone, and all your furniture and bits with it.'

Tears stung Tess's eyes, struck in a way all the other news hadn't affected her. She had moved from her apartment a couple of years ago, but it still felt like her place, despite Pinky moving in. To be fair her memories of living there had been tarnished through her medical discharge from the Cumberland County Sheriff's and the subsequent breakdown of her relationship with a previous fiancé, Jim Neely. There were good memories there too. She'd been living there when first meeting Po, and some of their earliest intimate moments had been spent in her bed there. The furniture she'd gathered from several sources, some of her knickknacks and gewgaws purchased from flea markets or from Anne Ridgeway's shop; none of it held sentimental value, but nevertheless it was hers and therefore she felt the loss as she did from the destruction of the building proper. Really, if pushed, she would admit her emotions were probably askew due to the hormone imbalance of pregnancy. Her genuine sadness was for Anne Ridgeway who'd lost the place she loved most in the world, or for Pinky who'd just become homeless; the latter situation could be readily fixed, but not so for the former.

'How bad was the building damaged?' she asked, hopeful that it could be rebuilt.

'When I say the shop got burned to ashes I wasn't exaggerating, me,' said Pinky, 'and that goes for the apartment too.'

Tess chewed her lip, stuck for words. From behind her there came a moan and Joanne said, 'Look at what's happened now! If you hadn't come to fetch me, this wouldn't have happened. Oh God, Tess. I'm so sorry.'

Tess reached back with her bandaged hand, to console the woman, but had second thoughts. She withdrew her hand and held it before her, inspecting it as if it belonged to somebody else. Earlier she'd felt nothing, now her hand throbbed painfully. She could no more blame Joanne for the destruction of the apartment, or for anything else that had occurred since accepting the job from Detective Ratcliffe, than she could the wounding of her hand. In her line of work shit happened on a regular basis and she doubted she'd have simply enjoyed a pleasant snow day cuddling with Po on their porch swing if Ratcliffe hadn't called.

Pinky and Po had been talking while her thoughts drifted elsewhere. She picked up the conversation again.

'I'll go on back to the ranch now Mrs Ridgeway's safely tucked indoors. Cops are going to see her for a statement and Alex asked me to make myself available too. I told him I'll present myself at the station, soon enough, but right now I'm heading back to your place.' As was often the case when the seriousness of a situation took over, Pinky had dropped some of the patois that made his speech so idiosyncratic. 'I should have mentioned before, but this was never about you, either of you, it was about flushing me out. My former life has caught up with me again and this time it isn't a couple of amateur's trying to claim the bounty on my head.'

'I'd've thought by now that they'd have gotten the idea that you aren't goin' to return to your old life,' Po said.

After joining them on several cases, Pinky had enjoyed a paradigm shift in his thinking and had decided to abandon his previous life. Back then he was a criminal, a supplier of illegal arms and armament, and when he'd jumped ship, many of his customers and competitors had jockeyed to fill the void he'd left behind; none of them wanted him to return to Baton Rouge and take back his huge slice of the market. Because they wished him gone for good they had once already sent triggermen after him, and it appeared after the first attempt to kill him had failed, somebody else had accepted the contract. 'Ain't nobody more paranoid than criminals,' Pinky said.

'F'sure,' said Po, 'but they're gettin' beyond the damn joke.'

'Amen to that, Nicolas. I've reached out to DeAndre, see if he can't get those A-holes to accept the truth and back the hell off.'

'Does DeAndre have that much influence?' asked Po.

DeAndre Freeman had been Pinky's confidant, driver and sometimes lover, back before he'd closed up shop for good. DeAndre had gone on to cut out a little slice of the market for himself, and to this day lived in the house, and drove the cars, gifted to him by Pinky when he left for Maine. They'd parted on friendly enough terms, but who knew what could fester in a man's mind after a couple of years. Po's question was loaded and the sub-context wasn't lost on Pinky.

'It isn't DeAndre behind this, but I'd say he knows who has gotten a boner for me again after all this time. Maybe he can mediate and—'

'There won't be any mediatin' goin' on, podnuh. Those sons of bitches burned my businesses and my ride. Those indiscretions I might have been able to turn a cheek to – for the sake of amity – but not after they've gone after my girl's home and burnt it down. Sounds as if they didn't care that Anne Ridgeway would die for the sake of punishing you. I'm surprised you aren't rarin' for vengeance, Pinky.'

'You didn't let me finish, you. I was about to say that maybe DeAndre can warn them that they're literally playing with fire by coming at us.'

'Nah, let them come. They'll deserve what they get.'

Po's teeth clenched, his jaw bunched as if his cheek contained a half-masticated wad of gum.

'Perhaps now isn't the ideal time to invite more trouble,' Tess warned, with a slight tip of her head towards their backseat passenger. 'Let's deal with one problem before we get embroiled in another, yeah?'

'I don't set their agenda, Tess,' he replied. 'They initiated this attack, but I'd like to be the one to finish it.'

'*We*,' Pinky stressed, '*we* intend to finish it.'

'Goes without sayin', podnuh.'

'I'll call DeAndre, me, find out what I can about our firebugs.'

Po mentally clocked up an ETA. 'Should be back in Portland in about fifty minutes. If you're heading to the ranch, look out for Jo's sister, she's going to meet us there and got an early start from Belchertown. Don't go lightin' her up thinking she's one of the arsonists.'

'I remember Detective Ratcliffe. I liked her, for a cop, her.'

'Yeah,' Tess chipped in, 'as hard as it is to imagine, some cops can be likeable. Even some of us retired cops.'

'If you weren't already Nicolas's girl, you know I'd willingly tarnish my gold standard gay medal for you.'

'I'm flattered,' she told him, deadpan, and the men both laughed.

It was a light note to end the call on. Following a promise to return home within the hour, Tess ended the call.

Typically, the snow returned. It blew out of the northwest, fat, wet flakes that stuck to the windshield and windows. The wipers worked overtime trying to clear the windshield, opening cleared arcs that the storm attempted to fill again in an instant. Po didn't slow, but he stretched forward, hands gripping the steering wheel. His gaze was fixed laser-sharp on the highway ahead. He was determined not to let a winter cyclone slow them and break Tess's promise.

TWENTY-NINE

E arlier Siobhan Doyle had suggested renting rooms in Vanceboro but hadn't gotten around to it. But that was OK. They had abandoned the idea of waiting in Vanceboro, and had cut across country as quickly as possible. Alarmingly the gas station where Harper had previously quietened witnesses was still abuzz with police activity. A cop stepped out in front of them and gestured Siobhan to a halt. Her hand had crept for her pistol before recalling that it had been taken away from her. Perhaps it was fortunate that she had lost the gun, because if she was spotted holding it she probably would've attracted a deadly response from the cops. As it were, the chilled officer had no interest in them, only allowing a colleague to safely reverse out of the gas station. Once the patrol car had straightened out and pulled into the curb, the cop waved Siobhan on, even offering her a nod of gratitude for her patience. She smiled and wheezed a curse under her breath.

Once they were through Lincoln and on the highway, Siobhan said, 'I guess the cops aren't looking for us yet.'

'We can't say that.'

'Wouldn't that cop back at the gas station have pulled us over if there was a BOLO out?'

'You put too much faith in the ability of cops. That guy was freezing and probably dying to take a leak. I'd bet that was all that was on his mind, not details he probably only half-heard from a dispatcher an hour earlier.' Harper picked at a scab of dried blood on the back of his opposite wrist. 'Way I see it is those fuckers were there to collect Joanne and take her elsewhere; they weren't going to call the cops because it would've meant handing her over and leaving empty-handed.'

He took out a cellular phone and checked for a signal: it was strong. He began typing. 'If you're wondering, I'm reaching out to the others. See if any of them can't help us. D'you recall the license number on that Telluride?'

Siobhan shook her head. Her hair was coiled tightly into a wad where she'd been doused with coffee. She yanked at the matted strands.

'I remember it clearly.' Harper gave her a sour curl of a lip, to show how little he respected her, and typed in the number.

'I'm only a driver . . . d'you recall that?' She'd lowered her tone and dumbed it up a bit for the latter part of her statement.

Harper stopped composing a text message and glared across at her. She shrugged. 'OK, it wasn't the best impression of you,' she admitted. 'Sorry, Harp.'

He neglected to acknowledge the apology, just turned back to his phone. She cursed internally, calling Harper a nastier name than she'd previously aimed at the cop.

It was a long message that Harper typed. Finally, he stabbed the send icon and then sat back. He closed his eyes. Siobhan stayed silent, hoping he'd fall asleep, but she suspected that he was fully alert, thinking and plotting.

Before, she'd put forward the suggestion that they should relocate and set a trap for when the Telluride appeared. It seemed that he'd given the idea some credence but wasn't fully committed to it. Back on the narrow county roads was where they could have ambushed their prey, but that was forgetting how they no longer had the firepower to force complete compliance, and it would again turn into a brawl. Actually, the woman – Tess – had Siobhan's pistol, and after being stabbed she might not think twice about blowing Siobhan a new butthole. Her man, the tall Southerner, had proved he was unequal to Harper in brute strength, but more than matched him in ability. They couldn't count on taking them out in a face-to-face fight again, and ramming them with the SUV was probably their only recourse, but who wanted to be stranded out in the wild after she'd wrecked their car?

They were nearing Bangor when a ping announced a response to Harper's request for information. He slowly exhaled and his eyelids peeled apart. It took a moment for his vision to focus and his attention to return from wherever it had drifted. He slowly lifted his phone and read the screen. 'The Telluride's registered to an autoshop in Portland, but our contacts have done a little more digging and have found a specific name: Nicolas Villere.'

'Our southern friend?'

'Apparently he's well known around Portland. Folks say he's a badass, a Cajun nicknamed Po'boy. Works alongside a local private investigator called Teresa Grey.'

'Teresa . . . Tess? Yeah, that sounds right to me.'

'Hear this,' said Harper, with a note of self-satisfaction. 'A case they famously closed involved a pervert abducting women and keeping them as sex slaves before murdering them. The lead investigator on the case was a detective outta Belchertown PD called Ratcliffe.' He paused for dramatic effect.

'Go on, Harp, you've earned your moment.'

'Ratcliffe, formerly Karen Mason, is the elder sister of Joanne Mason.'

'You gotta be kidding me?' said Siobhan. 'No, you aren't kidding, are you? This Po'boy and Tess are connected to Joanne's big sis?'

'Could be they intend having a family reunion,' Harper suggested.

'So it's back to Massachusetts and Belchertown?'

'I doubt it. Those fuckers are from Portland; I'd say they'll head there first. I wanted to avoid involving the others before, but after reaching out to them they can help us now that shutting up Joanne's only part of the problem. They're still poking around, looking for clues down near that motel in New Hampshire, I'll have them rendezvous with us in Portland.'

'Thought you fully intended on claiming the bounty on her, you certain you want to share it with the others?'

'Claiming the entire bounty would be nice, but avoiding a death penalty is preferable.'

'There's no capital punishment in Massachusetts,' she reminded him.

'Not officially,' he remarked, and she understood what he meant. If they didn't clear up the mess they'd made then a bounty would be placed on their heads, and death sentences that didn't require the approval of a state governor would be carried out.

'Was going to ask . . .' Siobhan left her question hanging.

'Ask about what?'

She'd caught herself before committing to voicing the suggestion that, once they were back in Portland, she could pass him off to one of the others and she'd make herself scarce. After all he kept on reminding her that she was only a driver and already she had gone above and beyond what was expected from her. But she also realized that to suggest such might invite a death sentence if she was no longer of value to him, or to their actual employer. Harper turned and appraised her, waiting for her to speak.

'Was going to ask if you needed to stop anywhere and get

cleaned up,' she lied. 'Don't know about you washing that dried blood off your face, but I sure could do with getting this muck out of my hair.'

'Keep driving,' he told her, 'there'll be time for vanity once we're in Portland.'

'It's not about vanity, Harp. It's about not attracting attention. Sheesh, I stink like a garbage can outside of Starbucks.'

He gently touched his misshapen nose. His mouth quirked in an uncommon show of humor. 'To be fair, you might, but I'll be damned if I can smell you.'

She wasn't that bothered about her odor. But when she took a closer look at him, Harper was dotted with his blood and there was a half-moon of it gathered at his collar and upper chest. 'Anyone gets as much as a glimpse of you and they'll ask questions about all of that blood. You certain you don't want to get cleaned up?'

He tugged at his collar, felt how tacky and stiff it was. 'Maybe you've got a point. Pull over at the next service station.'

She stayed silent for the next few minutes, concentrating on driving and what she'd do once she found an applicable stop. The snow came off and on, off and on.

'There's one coming up in a hot mile,' she finally announced, having noted the roadside signage.

Harper squinted through the windshield. The wipers swept icy flakes to and fro, leaving a wet smear on the glass. Through it the neon of a twenty-four-hours service station was fragmented, sending daggers into his eyes. He sat back. 'Yeah, this will do. Park outta sight of the gas pumps.'

'We need gas.'

'We've enough to get us to Portland. Unless you want me to go inside and do a number on another clerk or two.'

She checked her fuel dial again. 'We've enough to get us to Portland,' she repeated in monotone.

On the highway the traffic had grown steadily heavier between the bigger towns and cities, but the service station wasn't busy. There were a few cars in the adjacent parking lot and one currently at the gas pumps. A couple of truck drivers had pulled off the highway and parked their vehicles at the hinter edge of the lot, possibly with a view to staying put all night. In one of the cabs a light shone dully, behind drapes that the driver had pulled for his or her privacy. The other truck was in complete darkness and snow had piled on its cab and trailer; it had been there awhile. Harper flicked a gesture towards the latter truck. 'Park up behind that and turn off our lights.'

Siobhan did as instructed.

Harper nodded. He peered out the side window, checking for a bathroom and spotted signage half concealed behind a layer of ice. The conveniences were situated in a separate wooden structure from the main store and café. It suited his plan to wash up and leave again without attracting attention.

'OK,' he instructed Siobhan. 'We spend as little time here as possible. Women's washroom's there and I'll be next door. Five minutes and I want to be back on the road again, you hear?'

'Sure.'

'Good, then let's go.'

Siobhan turned off the engine and they got out. Immediately the chill struck her again after spending time in the warmth of the car. The coffee had dried in her hair, but her clothing was mildly damp and therefore colder. She was about to trot to the washroom when Harper grabbed her elbow. His grip was painful and she was convinced he'd deliberately probed for the nerve with his calloused fingertip. She winced, her hips making an involuntary sashay.

'The keys,' Harper said.

'What?'

'Give me the car keys. I don't want to come back outside and find you gone.'

'Sure, Harp. Hell, d'you think I was planning on abandoning you?'

'I'm still not convinced you weren't about to leave me back there on that hillside.' He snapped his other fingers and jutted out his palm. 'Give them up, Siobhan. Don't make me ask again.'

She handed over the keys, but before releasing her, he gave her elbow an extra squeeze, eliciting another wince of pain. He let her go, but aimed a pat of his hand at her backside. There was nothing sexual about his gesture, more like he was commanding a dog. 'Off you go, and don't keep me waiting. Five minutes.'

'No problem,' she assured him, but as soon as her back was turned her face contorted in a series of oaths and curses aimed under her breath at him and at her inability to give him the slip.

THIRTY

The taint of smoke smudged the otherwise crisp air as Tess stepped out of the Telluride outside Po's ranch house. His classic American muscle car sat in a doughnut of filthy slush, a burnt-out husk of its former glory. Its windows were blackened and cracked and its tires had blown so that the car had sunk down and settled on the crushed seashell hardstand. Small explosions had cast metal and rubber shrapnel several yards around the wreckage and even near to the steps on to the front porch. She felt sick and it had nothing to do with her condition.

She looked from the unidentifiable piece of metal to where Pinky and Karen Ratcliffe waited on the porch. Ratcliffe, a dark-haired woman wearing spectacles and a fur-lined parka, jeans and boots against the cold, looked diminutive alongside Pinky. He was a big guy still, despite taking up a fitness regime to fight off the debilitation of a condition that had blighted him since his late twenties: it was a rare condition of male lipedema, and though exercise and diet couldn't get rid of the painful fat disorder, it had slimmed him out quite a lot since first she'd met him. Either that or the evening had been severely taxing on him, leaving his usually jolly features worn and lined. He didn't meet her gaze at first – she knew that he'd be mortified at having failed to prevent the attack on the car, and more so on her apartment. She stung from distress but would never lay the blame on Pinky; hell, she could only praise him for saving Anne Ridgeway from certain death.

Before Tess could greet them, Ratcliffe swept down from the porch and Tess thought for a second she was the detective's target. But no. With barely a split-second's acknowledgment given to Tess, the detective hurried to reach her sister. She enfolded the younger woman in a hug and once more displayed that to her family trumped duty. Tess couldn't hear exactly what was said between the women, but Joanne apologized repeatedly while Karen assured her that everything was going to work out. Joanne's innocence was no longer in question, but she would have to answer many tough allegations before this was over. So too now must

Tess and her friends, and this could see an end to Ratcliffe's career as a police officer. Right now, while the sisters consoled each other, the future didn't matter.

Pinky stood with his bottom lip and his arms hanging and his eyes were rheumy. Normally his skin was a rosy brown but it appeared ashen and the crinkles of skin under his eyes were purple. He'd endured a hard time, but he showed he didn't care about his discomfort. His attention fell on her bandaged hand she held clutched to her chest and she saw his yellowed sclera sparkle on the verge of tears. She had neglected to tell him how close she'd come to having her womb sliced open, or how badly her hand had been pierced in fending off the knife.

'Aww, Tess,' he moaned as he came down the steps and hugged her.

'I'm OK, Pinky. I need to have this checked out thoroughly but it can wait. I'm more concerned about Po. He took some heavy hits and I'm not convinced he's unhurt.'

'Hard-headed Neanderthal,' Pinky called him, 'never would admit when he was in pain, him.'

She touched the back of her skull. 'He was pistol-whipped and then beaten by a guy that'd make you look tiny.'

Pinky searched for his best friend. Po was still in the Telluride, apparently making a call on his cell phone.

'Must've been up against Goliath, him,' said Pinky. 'I know him well enough, me, to know that his pride will've been stung. Being defeated by this giant musta put the turd-topping on a crappy day, what with all these fires and all.'

'Can't say it's all been bad.' She looked to where the reunited sisters were now talking animatedly, nose to nose, hands clutching each other in mutual support.

'You haven't seen your apartment yet, you,' Pinky cautioned.

'No time for regrets,' she said. They took on the task of rescuing Joanne from an icy tomb in the knowledge that Po's property was being targeted. She'd take saving an innocent woman's life over the loss of inanimate stuff any day of the week, and the way in which all their day had ended was with the saving of two women's lives. In effect that made it an almost perfect day.

Po had left the Telluride to stand near his Mustang. He kicked lightly at a crumpled piece of metal, melancholy etching lines in his cheeks and forehead. She watched him shake his head and turn his back on the wreckage. 'Would never look right with a booster seat in the back,' he commented, making light of his loss. Po was usually the type so laid back he could double as a draft excluder; his flippancy didn't fool Tess for a second, not when a tic danced in his jaw and murder brooded in his turquoise eyes.

'I got suckered, me,' Pinky told him. 'While I was chasing shadows, another of the sons of bitches snuck in behind me and lit up your ride.'

Pinky had already gone over how he'd been fooled, several times now, but it appeared that he felt he owed Po an explanation again. He added, 'I called DeAndre like I said I would, and it's the damnedest thing. He swears he's heard nothing of a new plot to kill me, and he's got his ear firmly to the ground. I don't get it, they're after me, but I don't know who or why.'

Po said, 'This is on me, Pinky, not you. I shouldn't have left you to deal with this crud alone. I was wrong.'

'You accompanied Tess, that was the right thing to do.'

'Not disputin' that, podnuh, I only wish I'd arranged back-up for you before those bastards came callin'. You could've been killed.'

Pinky shrugged. 'I'm OK, me, just a bit singed at the edges. Tess said there's no time for regrets . . . applies to you too, Nicolas.'

The men clapped hands on each other's shoulder. It was all that was necessary.

Joanne and Detective Ratcliffe moved to join the huddle at the foot of the porch steps.

'Let's go inside,' Tess suggested, 'and get warmed up.'

Pinky gave way for them all. 'I'll be outside, keeping watch, me.'

Inside, Po greeted Detective Ratcliffe by way of a nod and she whispered her thanks. Her spectacles were stained from the tears on her eyelashes. For now the woman put aside emotion and got back to business. 'I'm taking Jo into protective custody. Tess, your brother's with Portland PD, right? Could do with some assistance from him to organize protection.'

'Alex will help,' Tess promised. 'Come inside and I'll call him. You're right, I think it's best we get Joanne out of here before her hunters catch up.'

'There's no way that this Harper could know where you've brought her, right?'

'Couldn't say. He chased and found her all the way up at the Canadian border, so we have to assume he's more intelligent than he looks. Plus, we don't know what other resources he has at his disposal.'

'True. I've contacted both the homicide investigation team in Boston and also the local police and FBI office and alerted them. They'll be on the look out for him and the redhead you told me about. But we can't assume that they won't slip past and come after Jo again.' She squeezed her sister's hand reassuringly. 'I have to keep Jo safe, she's my sister and I love her. She's also the only living witness to what happened at the Blackhorse house, whose testimony can prove who was behind the murders.'

'There's the possibility that Harper and his girlfriend have realized they're cooked and have made a run for it. But it isn't a chance we should take.'

Po had remained silent while they spoke. Tess would swear she could feel the buzz of anticipation off him. She looked over and saw that he had found a bag of frozen peas from the freezer and was holding them to his neck. 'We all know he isn't going to stop. Joanne isn't the only living witness now to his crimes. There's us and there are the sisters up in Vanceboro. Mark my words, if he has his way Harper will try shutting us all up. Probably you too, detective, now that you're involved.'

'He can't avoid jail, not now,' said Ratcliffe. 'What could he gain from trying to murder anyone else?'

'Satisfaction,' said Po. 'I looked him in the eye, fought him with everything I had. I hurt him, but he was unfazed. He got off on the violence and wanted more. I might sound dramatic, but I'd swear he was born to kill.'

'Let's get things moving and get Joanne safely out of harm's way.' Tess sought her cell phone, dipping her bandaged hand into a pocket before remembering that it hurt like hell to do so. She called herself stupid under her breath. Took her phone out the opposite pocket and brought up Alex's personal number. Even making the few clumsy taps with her finger showed that some healing was in order.

From outside there was a snapped-out curse and the drumming of feet as Pinky charged across the porch. Tess aborted calling her brother and instead followed Po as he lunged towards the door. But for the knife he'd reluctantly returned to its boot-sheathe, he was unarmed. Tess on the other hand still had the redhead's pistol.

Ratcliffe drew her sidearm, but rather than follow them she forced her sister to take cover below the kitchen counter and she knelt down to shield her. Surely, Tess thought, it was impossible that Harper had found them as quickly? But that was assuming that Joanne was the target and not Pinky. She went to the door, but didn't offer up an open target the way in which Po did. He darted on to the porch, seeking their friend and enemies alike. Then without pause he vaulted over the railing on to the unmarked blanket of snow beyond. Peering around the jamb, Tess saw another person's footprints cutting across the yard and going around the far side of the Telluride. Pinky's SUV, and a car belonging to Ratcliffe, was parked before it, and hid the trail in the snow. Pinky was already beyond the cars too, jogging towards the perimeter of the yard, to where another figure rushed into the woods. She understood then that Po fully intended on blazing another route and cutting off the figure's escape to the river. Pinky had earlier chased an arsonist in a similar fashion and it had been a ruse in order to draw him away and allow an attack on Po's car; Tess wouldn't be drawn into the chase. If left unprotected Joanne could die to flame as easily she could the brute force of Harper.

THIRTY-ONE

Pinky set his feet, aimed and fired. In the dimness under the trees it was difficult to see if the bullet struck, but he was rewarded by the fleeing figure going down in the snow and then struggling to rise. Pinky ran once more, closing down on his quarry. Before he could snatch at the downed figure's clothes and force him to the ground again, the man scrambled away and rolled over an embankment. The churned snow was dotted darkly with blood, a pleasing sight. But there wasn't enough of it to pay for the damage done to Po and Tess's property. Pinky chased after the fleeing man again and was gratified to see another figure dart from the gloom and block the man's path. The guy scrambled again, but couldn't escape Po who was fleeter than Pinky expected, despite him carrying injuries from his previous encounters with Harper.

Pinky was ten yards away when Po's boot connected with the man's stomach, doubling him over, then a flashing right cross almost spun the man's head around one hundred and eighty degrees. The guy toppled sideways, his wounded left leg buckling and he fell and rolled in the snow a second time in the past minute. He didn't rise this time. Po knelt on him, frisking him for weapons as Pinky crunched through an icy drift and stood over them. Pinky aimed one of his two pistols at dead center and was prepared to blow a hole in the arsonist's spine. Po held out a hand to stall any stupidity. Pinky was sorely tempted but he wasn't a murderer. Po dragged the unconscious man over and stretched him out in the drift. The man writhed, flapped his arms and made a snow angel. Pinky exchanged grins with Po. Po loomed closer, grabbed the man's battered jaw in his left hand and squeezed. The pain wakened him with an involuntary yelp. He peered up at them, terrified by their proximity. Pinky didn't recognize the face, but he could smell the waft of gasoline fumes rising off him.

'Time to answer some questions, you,' Pinky growled.

'Let go of me, let me up,' the guy wailed at Po.

'Try gettin' up. Go on. Try.'

'I can't breathe.'

'Don't start that shit with me,' warned Po.

'I mean it. I can't breathe. Your knee . . .'

'My knee's stayin' put.' If anything Po leaned in, adding weight to the point of his knee in the man's solar plexus. 'Sooner you answer our questions, the sooner you get to breathe again.'

The man wheezed. Po had kicked him sorely and probably winded him, but they weren't prepared to show pity. Po fixed the man with a promise of death in his gaze. 'Who are you and who sent you after Pinky?'

The man gasped and wheezed, but it was obvious to Pinky that he was largely acting, attempting to gain some leeway, perhaps find a route through which he might still escape.

Po slapped the man's cheek. It was a sharp, stinging reminder who was in charge. 'Speak,' Po snapped.

'Pinky? Who the fuck is Pinky, man?'

Pinky neglected to reply.

Po said, 'If not Pinky then who sent you after me?'

'This isn't about you, man. Shit, until a few days ago I'd never even heard your name.'

'I'd say you ain't going to forget it, punk.' Po slapped him again, and this time tears started from the man's eyes. 'Why are you targeting my businesses, and why target my fucking car?'

'Payback, man.'

'Payback? Payback for what exactly?'

'That's all I'm saying. What you going to do? Kill me? I don't think so.' The man laughed, though it sounded strained.

'Not going to kill you outright,' Po promised. 'I'm gonna hurt you first and then keep on hurtin' you til you beg me to kill you.'

'Bullshit.'

'Let me gut shoot him,' said Pinky.

'Too easy,' replied Po. He reached back, grabbed the man's testicles and squeezed.

The arsonist yowled. His hands clutched for his genitals, but Po held on tight. He gave them a twist before releasing them. He rested his knee heavier than before on the man's gut. A wheeze of relief turned into a heavier wheeze as air was forced from the man's lungs. Instantly Po lessened the pressure, so that his prisoner could suck in oxygen. He ground his knee down into the man's solar plexus and the pain must have been tortuous. The man howled, almost sounding like a plea.

'You said this was about payback. Who'd I piss off enough that they sent you and your asshole buddies after me?'

'Told you already . . . I ain't saying anything more.'

'Nope. That's the wrong answer.' Po grabbed his genitals again, despite the man attempting to shield them with a cupped palm. Po merely enfolded the hand and squeezed it, transferring the pressure to his testicles. The guy tried pushing Po away with his other hand.

Pinky moved in, forced his foot over the man's upper arm and flattened it into the snow. With his other foot he tapped the bullet wound in the man's thigh and a bloodstain blossomed in his pants, agony flared anew in his already contorted face.

Po commanded, 'You'd better think about how you want your day to end, bra. Talk or start screaming, it's your choice.'

'It's payback for sending her down.'

'Sending who down? Who are you talking about?'

'Our mother,' said the arsonist.

Po was at a loss and so was Pinky. They exchanged confused glances.

The guy stared up from his position in the snow, eyes blazing as fiery as any he'd helped start with gasoline. 'I'm talking about our mom, you bastards. She was sent back to jail for breeching her parole.'

'You've tried burning everythin' important to me because your goddamn momma couldn't behave?' It was Po's turn to aim a fiery stare.

'If she hadn't been sent back to jail she'd be OK,' the guy snapped. His fear had diminished in the face of fresh hatred. 'Instead she's barely alive, burned so badly the doctors are talking about amputation. You bastards did this to her, you and that fucking bitch. You sent her back and they were waiting for her. She got burned, so we're gonna burn you!'

'No, you son of a bitch. You're done. You aren't burning another thing.'

'You've got me, but it won't make a goddamn difference. My brothers won't stop, not until we take everything away and she's burned the way our mom was burned.'

While Pinky stepped aside, Po's fist bunched in the front of the man's jacket. He dragged him to his feet. It was so he could strike him down again. His fist smashed the guy's jaw, knocking him on his ass. Po's grasp transferred to the man's hair. He twisted, contorting his neck sideways. The edge of his other hand made a blade. 'You punk, I should take your goddamn head off.'

Literally he wouldn't decapitate the arsonist's head, but a knife-edge blow delivered with force to the carotid sinus could kill. Pinky could tell that Po was on the verge of dealing the punishment and he understood why: these brothers, sons of a woman sent back to prison meant to harm the person they deemed responsible for handing her in. Their target wasn't Po, and it wasn't Pinky. It had always been Tess.

Pinky observed, then after a moment he reached and laid his hand on Po's shoulder. He would intervene if his friend couldn't control the rage, but for the moment it was apt that the arsonist fear he was about to die. It was small payback in return for what the asshole and his brothers had put them through. There was once a time when Po's need for revenge had gone too far and he'd spent years behind bars as a result. Pinky wouldn't allow him to make the same mistake again. Under his hand, Po shivered, and then the tautness melted from him and he shoved the arsonist back down into the snow.

Po and Pinky again exchanged glances. This time there was no confusion.

'I've got him covered, me,' said Pinky. 'You should go and check that Tess is safe.'

Without uttering a reply Po set off at a dash, racing again through falling snow as the blizzard returned.

'Can you walk?' Pinky asked.

The arsonist groaned and reached to touch his sore face. Before his tentative fingers had completed probing his swollen jaw, he hissed and reached instead for his thigh. Pinky's bullet had barely creased him, but the wound bled profusely and probably stung like a bitch. 'You shot me,' the man accused.

'Yep, I did that, me. Call it payback for shooting at me outta that car down on Cumberland Avenue. That was you, right, cause you aren't either of the assholes I caught troubling that innocent old lady.' Pinky wasn't totally soulless. No, he understood why the siblings might have a need for vengeance against those they thought had lead to their mother's injuries. In a fashion he could respect them fulfilling their family duty. But they'd overstepped a line by involving Anne Ridgeway, and for that reason he saw them as worse than dirt.

'How'd you expect me to walk with a shot leg?'

'With a limp?' Pinky countered. 'The thing is, I'm taking you back, me, and if I must carry you I'm going to knock you the hell out first. Will be easier on the two of us if you can haul your own ass out of the woods.'

As expected, the arsonist found his feet.

'OK, off you trot, you,' said Pinky, with a gesture of a pistol. 'Try anything funny, the next bullet goes in your spine.'

THIRTY-TWO

'What's going on out there?' Detective Ratcliffe asked from within the house.

'Hold on, I'm still figuring things out,' said Tess. She'd gotten no further than the porch before halting. She swept the yard with her gaze, seeking anything out of place. The Mustang was an ugly blot, but she'd already taken in its appearance so it didn't stand out as it had before. The Telluride, Pinky's SUV and Ratcliffe's car formed a partial wall so she'd no clear view to the woods where her fiancé and Pinky had disappeared minutes ago. She allowed her gaze to track to the left and right, watching for movement in her periphery as Po had once taught her to do. The falling snow made noting other movement more difficult, but she thought that any shadows or colors moving against the tumbling flakes would be conspicuous.

Nothing alarming pricked at her senses.

She put some faith in her senses, but more so in tactics and strategy. She treated the scoping of the yard as if it were a crime scene she'd just rolled up to in her sheriff's cruiser. She kept the pistol trained wherever she looked, holding it in both hands: her bandaged hand made supporting the gun awkward but not too much. Her index finger lay alongside the trigger guard.

She should check the entire perimeter, especially her blind spots to the sides and behind the house; anyone could be lurking there. But that would leave the front door unguarded, so for now her presence was more valuable there. Ratcliffe was the final line of defence, making Tess the first, if Harper made a play to get at Joanne again.

'See anything?' asked Ratcliffe.

'The guys chased an intruder into the woods,' Tess replied. 'I think it's connected to these darn fires and not with Joanne being here. I heard gunfire, a single shot, but nothing since. We can't lower our guard just yet.'

'I should drive Jo to the nearest police station,' Ratcliffe announced.

'You're probably right, but let's hold on til the guys come back. We can form a convoy with our vehicles, put you guys at the center and protect Joanne that way.'

Tess had fully intended calling Alex and arranging a police escort for the women, but that was before Pinky and Po had gone hurtling off like hounds chasing a jackrabbit. She couldn't allow the distraction of making a phone call until somebody else was on guard outside. Time was precious and the sooner they could move Joanne the better; however they must do it safely and not while other intruders could be in the vicinity. If the sisters drove away without support, they could be heading directly into a trap.

It wasn't surprising that their strategy had changed from avoiding the cops to intending rushing directly to them. Now that Joanne was under her sister's personal protection, nothing untoward should happen to her. Before then Joanne had feared that she'd be gunned down as a despised fugitive, or that she'd be ripped to pieces by a wrongly informed baying mob, but things had grown clearer and the general consensus now held that Joanne was probably not a coconspirator and was instead running terrified for her life from those responsible for the violent incursion of the Blackhorse house. Of course, there'd always be someone with a gripe, a chip on their shoulder, or simply a vile piece of work who'd swear there was no smoke without fire and that Joanne should be strung up for what had happened to the children in her care.

There had been previous cases when Tess had avoided alerting the authorities until after the dust had settled, but each time believed her reasons had been valid. It was usually in hindsight where she'd scolded herself for waiting. This time she didn't think that trying to handle the murderous Harper was a sensible course of action, not in her condition, with a wounded hand and with a partner aching more from perceived shame than he was physically. Harper was the bad guy in all of this, and it should be he who was sent to prison for the remainder of his days, and not good people forced into unlawful actions.

Movement caught her eye, a shifting of the shadows under the trees to her right corner. She aimed the pistol, but immediately lowered it when the tall figure ducked out from under a bough laden with snow and into the yard. Po appeared unhurt as he scanned each side and then moved forward at a lope. She knew without him indicating that he'd spotted her on the porch, because she'd seen his shoulders lower an inch or two in relief. He was midway across the yard, and turned so that he could retreat backwards to her without losing sight of any potential enemies. Tess was already reasonably assured that the arsonist was a single interloper on this occasion, otherwise why hadn't the others capitalized on the situation when Po and Pinky chased their pal?

'Tess, I need you to go back inside,' Po called.

'We're clear, Po, there's nobody here.'

'That's not a chance I'm willing to take.' He darted up on to the porch, took a brief glance at the pistol she held. 'You should keep that close at all times, seein' as it's you those firebugs are after.'

'What's that? I'm the one the arsonists are attacking? I thought they went after my apartment because of Pinky living there?'

'Yeah. So did we. But that was before we got it straight from the horse's mouth.'

She looked at his scorched car. Bile flooded her throat. 'Who'd I piss off enough for them to do that? Jeez, Po, everything we've been involved in for months has been low-key stuff.'

'Has something to do with you sendin' a woman to jail for breakin' the terms of her parole.'

'That isn't on me,' she said. 'I don't—'

She halted. Po knew she had zero involvement in returning a parole violator to jail, that was down to several hearings and the final decision of the Board of Parole. However, her services were often called on to locate absconded parolees and bail jumpers. She would find and detain them, and then hand them over to the relevant law enforcement authorities, so she supposed she was one small link in a chain. Sadly she couldn't say who might be behind the arsonists' rampage, because as she'd just said all their cases had been low-key. Why would anyone hate her so much that they'd have everything dear to her razed to the ground?

Po ushered her towards the entrance. 'Let's talk inside. There's more to it than being responsible for sending this woman back, it's what happened to her after that's gotten her sons riled up.'

'Carol Wolsey,' Tess sighed.

'Truth be told, I didn't push to get a name only a motive. You can ask him directly. Pinky's bringing in the firebug.'

'I'm pretty certain it's Wolsey. Don't you recall, she was the one hiding out in one of her son's trailers? We served the warrant on her for parole violation and took her to jail.'

'Yeah, I recall she wasn't a happy gal. Spittin' and kickin' the entire time, making wild threats.'

'That's the one. I didn't give those threats any credence at the time. You know how some people react when you take away their liberty. She was screaming that we'd killed her by sending her back to jail, and we just ignored her and allowed her to let off steam. Seems maybe we should've listened after all.'

'She wasn't kiddin' about us killing her. Not literally, but we apparently put her back in reach of some enemies in prison, and they set her ablaze. She survived, but barely. There's enough life left in the mad bitch to sic her boys on you.'

'Jeez, Po, how can we be judgmental about her after what happened to her?'

'You don't have to be. Just know that she's still got a couple boys out there intent on lightin' you up the same as happened to their momma. I've done the judgin' and found them guilty of tryin' to harm you and our babe and for that I've damned them all the way to hell.'

'Maybe now you've captured one of them the others will back down.'

'Why would they when they'll be joinin' their momma in prison before long? The one we caught swore his brothers aren't the type for stopping, and I believe him.'

'First it's Harper and now these pyromaniacs. What is it about us that attracts monsters, Po?'

'Pinky swears you're on the side of the angels, so it stands to reason your enemies will be devils.'

She snorted at the absurdity.

Ratcliffe rose up from behind the kitchen counter. She'd lowered her pistol but wasn't ready to holster it yet. 'I take it we're safe to come out of hiding?'

'For now,' Tess said, 'but we'd best think about getting you out of here.'

Joanne raised her head above the counter. She said, 'I just listened to what Po said about angels and devils, it isn't the first time I've thought of Harper as a monster. If you are the type to attract them, then so must I.'

'I'm a private investigator,' said Tess, 'so it kind of goes with the job, but a nanny shouldn't have to worry about the kind of maniacs I often have to deal with. In fact, you've had enough to worry about these past few days and have suffered enough. Let's get you somewhere safer.'

Po said, 'We can't go anywhere yet. Not until Pinky and his prisoner arrive. If you plan on taking Joanne to Alex, we should also give him the arsonist we caught.'

'What's keeping them?' Tess wondered.

'Beats me. I expected them to be right behind me.' Po abruptly turned and headed for the door.

Tess darted to intercept him. 'Take this.'

He eyed the pistol with distaste. 'No thanks, it's bad enough you were stabbed with my knife. If I lose the gun, who's to say it won't be used against you?'

'Pardon the pun, but that's a bit of a long shot.'

'But not impossible.'

She had to concur, watching as he again slipped out of the door with only a knife in his boot. She followed, again posting up against the doorjamb. Po hadn't gotten much further than she had earlier. He stood at the edge of the porch, one foot on the upper-most step. Beyond him, Pinky jabbed a reluctant prisoner to keep walking. The young man shambled, knees knocking.

'What was the hold up?' Po asked.

Tess checked, concerned that Pinky might have been injured. Pinky grinned without humor, nodded at the arsonist. 'Apparently his leg is sore, him. Told him he'd better start strutting or I'd bust his ass with a kick. I only had to do it the once, me.'

He was one of the men responsible for causing the fires and yet he showed no remorse when he spotted Tess in the doorway. His mouth contorted in a snarl of hatred and his head jutted forward on a neck suddenly as taut as steel wire. 'You're the one,' he hollered. 'This is all on you, you stinking bitch.'

Taken aback by his vitriol Tess had no ready reply. It was for Po to protect her. He jumped down from the porch and grasped the man's coat and yanked him towards the house. 'You'd better keep a civil tongue in your mouth or else I'll cut it out.'

Making such threats was pointless; in no shape or form was Po the type of man to mutilate another human being, regardless of the nature of the man's crimes against them. However the arsonist must've understood he was on shaky ground, because he didn't backchat Po. He turned aside his face, unable to meet Tess's searching gaze. He looked like a kid. She moved so Po could push him indoors.

'What are we going to do with him?' she whispered as Po moved past.

'Just keepin' him in sight til we're ready to leave.'

'I was planning on using all our cars in a rolling convoy,' she said, 'but we can't if we have to watch a captive.'

'We don't have to treat him with kid gloves. I'll knock him out and he can ride to the police station in the trunk. That way we can all concentrate on what's goin' on outside.'

Detective Ratcliffe offered a solution. She held up a set of handcuffs unclipped from her hip. She'd finally holstered her service weapon. Pinky was reluctant to put away his guns and so was Tess. Po accepted the cuffs. At Po's threat the young man had faltered in the open space between the kitchen and family room.

'You mind not drippin' blood all over the place?' Po grasped the man and forced him to turn around and present his wrists to the cuffs. Once restrained, Po handed him a wad of paper towels and told him to get down on his knees. 'You may as well mop the floor while you're down there.'

It was a needlessly humiliating and cruel instruction, but Tess felt no sympathy. She, like Po before her, saw the youth as nothing other than a threat to their unborn baby.

Once the droplets of blood had been wiped, Po shoved the youth over on to his rump, and indicated that he should use the same wad to staunch his wound. Pinky menaced him from a few yards away. Ratcliffe must have gotten some of the story about the arson attacks from Pinky before they'd returned with Joanne. She was largely unfazed by them bringing inside a bleeding prisoner with no involvement in her sister's trouble. She glanced down at the youth dispassionately, then looked at Tess without speaking. It was clear what she asked though, how soon would they be leaving?

'If we're all good to go, we should do it now.'

'I'm good, me,' said Pinky. 'Want me to take this pukeball?'

'No, we'll take him with us. That way I can watch while Po drives. You can have pole position, Karen and Joanne next, then we'll cover from the back. We should go to the main midtown office and I'll have Alex meet us there.'

'You heard the lady,' Pinky told the arsonist. 'Up you get, you, and it's off to a cell.'

Seated on his butt, hands locked in front, the young man struggled to rise on his injured leg. Pinky clucked his tongue, reached in and lent a hand; he grabbed the man by his hair and dragged him to his feet.

'There's no need for that,' the man croaked.

'There was no need for shooting at me when I was trying to save an innocent old grandma,' Pinky countered. 'Now move it.'

Joanne was tentative following Pinky and his captive. She exchanged glances with her sister and Ratcliffe nodded in reassurance. 'This will all soon be over,' she promised.

Tess, trying not to be pessimistic, thought that this was actually the beginning of a long and troubling time ahead for the young woman. Even in protective custody she could remain a target of Harper and others of his ilk, because it had become apparent that this was not about a disgruntled employee taking out his revenge on his boss's wife and kids. Case in point, the redhead swore she was 'only Harper's driver', but had proved the lie when pistol-whipping Po and later trying to gut Tess, as those were the actions of somebody that knew what they were doing and had few qualms about hurting another person. In all good conscience she couldn't work with a mass murderer – a child-killer – unless she was of a similar disposition. Tess feared that Harper and the redhead weren't the only ones that Joanne might need to fear in the coming months or years until this was finally resolved.

'How's your hand?' asked Po.

It twinged with each beat of her heart. 'Can barely feel a thing,' she lied. 'I'll have it checked later, I promise, but for now we should concentrate on Joanne.'

'Keep that pistol ready, anyone comes near us with as much as a lit cigarette, put a few holes in them.'

Ratcliffe and Joanne waited inside until Tess and Po were ready to leave. After securing the door behind him, Po joined the women on the porch, then acted in the phalanx of bodies steering Joanne towards Ratcliffe's car. Once the young woman had been deposited on the back seat and instructed to stay down, Tess and Po backed towards the Telluride. Pinky held his prisoner with one hand on his collar and a pistol jammed into the small of his back. Po popped the locks. Pinky yanked the young man aside in order to lift the tailgate.

'Put him on the back seat,' Tess said.

'You sure, pretty Tess, he could cause trouble?'

'Only if he wants to be shot. Besides –' she loomed in close to the arsonist – 'he'll be cuffed to the door handle, so won't be able to do much.'

'If that's the way you want it?' said Pinky, and he couldn't resist an almost undetectable check with Po that he was in agreement. Po's eyebrows lifted a fraction, and it was the only assurance Pinky required. He dragged the man to the back door, made him sit inside, then told him to present his wrists. Po had already shackled him, but Tess went to the detective and was given the key. In a matter of less than a minute the arsonist was secured once more and unable to physically assault Tess without lying on his back and kicking, by which point she was confidant she would be able to deter any nonsense by aiming the pistol at his thighs. She went around and got in the car at the opposite end of the seat. Po sat cater-corner to their captive in the driving seat. He swung the Telluride around, ensuring that the young punk saw what had become of his prized muscle car and how little tolerance he had for those responsible for its destruction.

Ratcliffe followed close behind, and latterly Pinky fell into line. They drove with less than a car's length between them, their progress slow at first as they followed the unplowed suburban streets towards the highway. Any of those practically deserted streets were ideal locations for an ambush, but they made it to the intersection of Allen Avenue with Ledgewood Drive and the road there was treated and the going a little faster. Once Pinky completed the turn a van previously tucked away on the grounds of a private residence pulled out and raced to follow them.

THIRTY-THREE

L ogic and intuition could work hand in hand, but chance could also be fickle. This time he must put trust in facts. Harper was unfamiliar with the layout of Portland, Maine, and the others he'd drafted in to join the hunt were no less strangers in town. However, those that had driven up from New Hampshire had arrived in town before them and had conducted recon on his behalf. Due to their inclusion, he had three extra hands and two extra vehicles, and also an address for Nicolas Villere and Teresa Grey in a Falmouth neighborhood next to the Presumpscot River. During an initial reconnaissance of the Villere home, Jaycee Monk, an unscrupulous ex-detective out of Boston had his cop radar on high alert and spotted the prowling Portland PD cruiser before fully committing to driving into Villere's front yard. Monk backed off to a safer distance and from there relayed what was going on – including news that the patrol car had driven off, summoned elsewhere with its light flashing. He'd watched an SUV approach, a huge black man at the wheel, followed shortly by a bespectacled woman so twitchy with anxiety she appeared ready to self-combust and lastly the Telluride he'd been posted to watch for. Some time after he watched a man on foot flitting from the well of shadows between trees at the edge of Villere's property and correctly concluded he was up to no good. He didn't observe the foot chase through the woods, but was close enough to hear the single pistol shot that must've heralded the end of the race. It couldn't have been more than a quarter hour before the three vehicles exited and drove away in convoy. He waited until they were out of sight before falling into line: all the while he spoke over a group chat line on his car's Bluetooth system, giving directional updates whenever the convoy took a turn. Debbie Lyman and Mallory Carson – lovers, and perhaps the most dangerous pair of bitches that Harper had ever worked alongside – used GPS technology to map the convoy's route and set up in their van to take over close surveillance once it was in range. Once they followed the convoy, Monk flanked them via another route past Pleasant Hill Cemetery.

Harper and Doyle, their car probably recognizable to Villere or Grey, stayed ahead, seeking a place where they could close the noose. Lyman and Carson had earlier pinpointed a likely location on Ocean Avenue at the entrance to a derelict quarry and landfill site. There were no houses within several hundred yards, and this late in the evening there was little chance of witnesses if they acted with shock and aggression: Harper had always been about the latter. The convoy had almost reached the end of Ledgewood Drive and would turn on to Ocean Avenue within a minute. Harper thought that within ninety seconds he would have his hands around Joanne Mason's throat and her protectors would be taking their last breaths, shedding their final drops of blood.

'Head's up! Looks like we have other players in town,' Jaycee Monk announced.

Harper's initial thought was that more of those seeking to claim the bounty on Joanne Mason's head had decided to snatch her from under his nose.

Monk said, 'I don't recognize these cats. We have two Caucasian males in a ten-year-old red Toyota Corolla and they're coming fast.'

His description of the car was typical of an ex-cop. Harper was surprised that Monk didn't give them the license number.

'Where are they?'

'I'd say they intend crashing the party at the next intersection.'

'Yeah? Well, we can't allow that to happen, can we,' said Harper. 'Close the gap, Monk, and run those fools off the road.'

'Say what?' Monk said.

'You heard me.'

'Harp, if I get locked in with them I can't be there to help you.'

'Don't worry about us,' Debbie Lyman chimed in, 'we'll manage with you.'

'I still get my cut, whether or not I'm on the scene when you take her. You got it, Harp?'

'You get your cut,' Harp agreed, 'but only if you do what the hell I told you to do. Stop those fools from meddling in my business.'

'We don't know who they are, you sure you want me to hit them?'

'Did I stutter?'

'OK, I'm with you. Consider them stopped.'

Harper checked with Siobhan Doyle and saw her chewing furiously at her bottom lip. She had made it clear to him before that there were many places on earth where she'd rather be, but she hadn't tried running, not yet, and for that reason she'd earned his respect. Not that she had any respect for him whatsoever, because though she'd never voiced her feelings about him, she couldn't hide it when their eyes met or in the subtext of her comments. Perhaps he had pressed her into acting beyond her original remit, as he hoped she'd step up again if required, but what could she complain about: she'd been hired to drive him and it was what she was doing.

'Turn around when you get there. Don't let them get further than the entrance to the quarry,' he commanded.

It was hours ago that she'd been scorched by hot coffee. In the bathroom at the gas station near Bangor where they stopped she'd managed to wash and also detangle her hair. Her ablutions hadn't really helped. It had been a long day, and even longer evening, and she was growing ragged around the edges. He'd accepted earlier that as the female form went she'd probably be attractive, but right then there was ugliness in her, something foul, and he wondered if the darkness in his soul had somehow infected hers. Harper was under no illusions about his nature. He had murdered and it had mattered not to him the age, gender or infirmity of his many victims; all that mattered was that he dominated and crushed them. He killed dispassionately, but wallowed in the warmth of his memories when replaying the scenes in his mind later. If he could claim any erotic satisfaction it was while replaying the murders in his head and touching himself was unnecessary to encourage orgasm. He was psychopathic. Rather, he was a sociopath because he fully understood the consequences of his actions, he just didn't care. In civilized society he'd be labeled a predatory beast, but that was fine by him, because a predator showed no pity to its victims, it killed to live and savored the taste of its victim's flesh between its fangs. He was a force of nature, there to cull the weak and helpless.

Siobhan caught him studying her profile and snapped a frown at him before returning her attention to the road.

Harper continued to appraise her. 'I was once told to choose a job I enjoyed and I'd never work another day in my life. I don't think you chose well when deciding to be a driver.'

'I'm a good chauffer, but there's driving a client and then there's this type of driving,' she said. 'I never signed on for this when Carl Blackhorse employed me.'

'You can't fool me, Siobhan. You play the innocent at times, but you're anything but naïve. You knew exactly what type of person Carl was, and that your job wasn't to ferry around the nanny and kids on the school run.'

She didn't reply; she began chewing her lip again making a confession unnecessary.

'Just think,' he said, 'after this is over, we're guaranteed money for life. Carl can't afford to let either of us go unrewarded, not knowing what we know and what we've done for him.'

'Like you just pointed out, Harp, I'm not freaking naïve.'

'What do you mean by that?'

'You know.'

He smiled.

Jaycee Monk's voice blasted through the car's speakers. He was breathless. 'Shots fired! Shots fired!'

'Fuckwit still thinks he's a cop,' said Mallory Carson and behind her voice her partner giggled. 'Thinks the cavalry are coming to save him. Harper, we're sticking with you guys, don't expect us to go and pull that limp dick out of trouble.'

'If he's under fire, it means he has slowed down these new players. Monk has my gratitude, but yeah, you girls stick to the plan.'

Monk cut in once more. 'Who are these sons of bitches? They have Molotov cocktails. Holy sh—'

Monk said no more.

The atmosphere was palpable within the SUV while they waited. After a moment Harper grunted. 'I guess Monk won't be getting his cut after all.'

Mallory Carson and Debbie Lyman sounded unperturbed by Harper's dispassionate announcement. 'More for the rest of us,' said Mallory.

Debbie crowed, 'Yesssss!'

In his peripheral vision, Harper spotted Siobhan's disbelieving headshake.

'Another perk of the job,' said Harper sarcastically, 'is working with such trustworthy partners.'

This time Siobhan couldn't conceal the look of sheer hatred she cast him.

He ignored her. 'Here's the quarry. Do as I said and turn around. Face the oncoming traffic and prepare to flick up your high beams. By my reckoning we should see that Telluride again any time now.'

After completing his instructions, Siobhan turned down her lights but left the engine running. She reached down and caressed the butt of a pistol secreted between her thighs. It was a weapon supplied to her by the women in the van, who'd also offered Harper a revolver. He had at first sneered at the gun, but recalling that Tess Grey was still probably armed with Siobhan's pistol, it didn't go against his creed to tip the balance in his favor. He'd put the gun in his coat pocket; it could be useful as a blunt instrument if he chose to bludgeon rather than shoot anybody.

'We're off Ledgewood and on to Ocean Avenue,' Debbie announced.

'They should show any second,' Harper told Siobhan and changed his pre-arranged plan. He said, 'Watch me. You see me raise this revolver –' he took the gun out – 'flick on your high beams and then start shooting. I want them in there.' He switched tone, his next words for the women in the van. 'Move in and push them towards us.'

Alongside the SUV there was a low wall, the remnants of a demolished building. The site next to the road was dominated by similar demolished and collapsing workshops, some overgrown by shrubs and vines. The snow in the entrance to the site was unmarred by tire tracks and footprints, so it was probably currently deserted and therefore a good place to carry out the hit. Harper left Siobhan and jogged across to the opposite sidewalk and kept going, aiming for where the road met another, forming a V-shaped intersection. It was imperative Villere wasn't allowed to lead the others down the wrong street.

He posted at the point of the V. Dug the revolver from the pocket where he'd pushed it while jogging across the icy road and made a rapid check of it. It was a reliable six-shooter, fully loaded. He thumbed back the hammer, even as lights approached. He stepped sideways on splayed legs, moving to block entrance to the second street, and brought up the revolver. Those in the convoy of vehicles got little warning, and less time to react as he began firing. At the rear of the close-knit trio of vehicles, the van loomed, coming at speed, and the driver took Harper's instruction literally, ramming the rear of a black SUV and shoving it forcefully into the back of a smaller car. Harper concentrated firing on the Telluride, and watched it sweep by, taking the road towards Siobhan. Already her high beams were blinding the driver, evidenced by how Villere had thrown an elbow across his face to shield his vision. His arm would do little to slow a bullet. Siobhan's bullets smacked holes in the windshield, and in all likelihood Villere would get struck. Harper ensured that was the case by firing at the side of the Cajun's head from less than ten feet away.

THIRTY-FOUR

Joanne had apologized to her sister more times than was necessary, and Karen had asked her to please quit it. Except she felt she should continue apologizing, because by running away she'd caused more trouble than enough. If she'd stayed behind in Boston to face her accusers, all of this would have taken a different shape than the messy bundle of trouble it had ended up. It was possible that by helping her in this way, her sister had ended her career, for which Joanne was truly sorry. Tess Grey could lose her private investigator's license and perhaps even face prosecution for abetting a murder suspect. Po Villere and their friend Pinky, they might not escape prosecution either. It wouldn't matter that Joanne had taken no part in the Blackhorse murders; she was wanted in connection with the crimes and therefore a fugitive in the eyes of the law. Knowingly assisting or harboring a fugitive from justice was illegal under both state and federal law, and could incur serious criminal charges. Would the fact that all involved had purely good intentions, and their involvement was to protect her from the actual killer, sway a judge at trial? It was true that ignorance was no defence in law, but at the beginning both her sister and Tess Grey had taken her side before the events had shown her to be the terrified victim rather than the child murderer. In effect they'd conspired, aided and abetted with Joanne before establishing her innocence, so would a jury be sympathetic towards them or damning?

Even after Harper's acts had proven him capable of the killings, it was still to be proved. Her innocence had to be proved too. She had no idea how much evidence detectives had gathered, but surely by now they'd ruled her out of their investigation: the bludgeoning of the victims would have surely pointed them at a brute like Bruce Harper rather than the kids' nanny. Surely, by now, anyone with a brain would've concluded that Harper hadn't acted out of revenge for losing his job. He'd killed the Blackhorse family on the instructions of somebody who'd truly wished them dead. There should have been a lower body count. He had entered the house and sought Lacey and the children, and beaten them with a hammer.

There, under the illusion of a home invasion/robbery gone wrong, the killings should've ended. Evidently Harper had gone over the top. After murdering the actual target – Lacey Blackhorse – he'd taken his murderous spree to the children, and then to the few in-house retainers and staff. He had murdered the cook, Toby Hillman, and a security guard and had chased but failed to finish her. Had he managed to beat her brains in too, he would probably be high and dry, and the likelihood of his employer coming under suspicion was slim. Carl Blackhorse could play the grieving husband and father, while secretly congratulating himself for ridding his life of the parasites set to leach him of half his wealth.

From the outside looking in, Lacey Blackhorse had the perfect life. She had a handsome, rich, successful husband, who had taken her as his wife despite her coming with the baggage of another man's children. Her life was one of dinners at fancy restaurants, glamorous vacations, private tennis lessons and shopping sprees, and a retinue of staff to take on burdensome housework and child-care. On the inside things were different. Her shiny façade no longer glistened. She was totally domineered and controlled. Her husband despised her and her bastards – his words, not Joanne's. Lacey had confided in Joanne that Carl was a sadistic lover and that he left her feeling worthless and violated after practically raping her whenever it was his pleasure. She claimed that he believed he owned her, and that he owed her nothing. She planned on leaving him, and thank God for the prenuptial agreement that they'd signed, otherwise she would have endured living under his control for nothing. She had begged Joanne to keep her plans of divorcing Carl a secret, and Joanne had been true to her word. Alas, somebody else must have gotten a sniff of her plan and related it to her husband.

He was never going to let her go, not on her terms. He was never going to allow her to benefit from a pre-agreed divorce settlement. Not while he had a monster like Bruce Harper on his payroll. That he was willing to also sacrifice the children, even Joanne couldn't say, but she'd bet that their deaths hadn't troubled him too much. Toby Hillman, the security man and Joanne herself had all been collateral damage, and if she'd gotten it right, then she'd think Carl hadn't given any of them a second's thought either. Harper had reason to continue chasing her. She was an eyewitness to the crime, and couldn't be allowed to live if he or

Carl was going to get away with the slaughter. But she also thought he had other reasons to chase her and it was because he was being rewarded for his faithful service, and also that he damn well got a kick out of it. By involving Karen and the others she had placed them in the killer's sights, for which she was truly sorry.

She said so again, and on that occasion, Ratcliffe had elbowed her driving seat with mock frustration. 'Jeez, Jo, if you don't shut up I'm going to boot you out the car at the next intersection.'

Joanne raised her head, peeking out the window. Portland was a remarkably wooded town, even in the depths of winter, and each bough was laden with several inches of snow. The backwash of the car's headlights, and also from Pinky's following close behind, lit the scene with almost antiseptic starkness, causing the shadows to appear darker and sharp-edged. There was little color in the monochrome world they passed through.

'You must keep your head down, Jo,' Ratcliffe insisted.

'I was only trying to see where we are.'

'Do you know Portland?'

'No. I've never been here before.'

'Ditto. I haven't any idea where we are, but Tess and Po do and I need to stick close to them or I'll get lost.'

'All I see is trees and snow.'

'Yeah, well all that's coming up is more of the same, so you may as well keep down.'

Joanne took a lingering look out through the window, before twisting in the chair and peering out the rear window. Condensation misted the glass and all she could see was the glare of Pinky's headlights and a suggestion of the large SUV behind. Unsure whether Pinky could see her or not, she raised her hand and gave a tentative wave. She wondered if he was the type to wave back, or if he'd scowl at her childlike naivety. From what she'd gathered he was an ex-con, an ex-gangster, but also a trusted and loyal friend of Tess and Po. She'd only met Pinky briefly, and from what she'd witnessed there was a hard side to him, evidenced when threatening the arsonist earlier. But he'd also just come from saving a helpless old lady from a burning building so his gruff behavior could be explained, and it could be excused.

'Jo, for crying out loud!'

'There's nobody but Pinky going to see me,' Jo retorted, but ducked down all the same.

No sooner was she below the level of the window when Ratcliffe croaked in dismay, and Joanne was thrown sideways against the door as her sister tried to avoid a collision. The car jounced on its chassis and the back end began to slew sideways, throwing her forcefully against the door again. She feared it would pop open and spill her out on the hard-packed ice. Next instant, forces yanked her aside and across the seat again. The car was struck from behind, the noise horrendous as the trunk buckled. Their tires lost traction, and the car went airborne it seemed, and then they struck another larger vehicle in front – Po's Telluride – and then it was as if the trio of vehicles were all melded into one writhing snake. Ratcliffe cursed, fighting the forces being exerted on her body. Joanne had no recourse other than throw out her hands and grab at the back of her sister's chair. It didn't help. She was thrown once more against the door, this time her head caroming off the padded armrest. The noise hadn't abated. It had swollen and the cracking of handguns added punctuation to it. Bullets struck metal and glass, and horribly, she thought, flesh too. At such close quarters how could they not get shot?

The cars came to a juddering halt. She heard the squeal of tires as one or the other was freed from the metal sandwich and pulled away. Bullets struck their windshield and glass littered the interior of the car. Ratcliffe grunted in pain.

Joanne cried out for her sister.

'Stay down, Jo,' Ratcliffe commanded. 'Stay down.'

'Are you hurt?' Joanne tried to claw a way between the front seats.

'Goddamnit, will you do as I ask?' A hand batted at her, forcing her to remain in the back seat. There was blood on it.

'You're bleeding.'

'It's just a small cut. From the flying glass. Stay down.'

Icy wind rushed inside the car. Ratcliffe had her service pistol out. She hollered a command at the unseen shooters, a habitual response that was flatly ignored. Warning given, Ratcliffe fired. Joanne was deafened by the report. She clapped her palms over her ears, cringing with each shot fired.

Something shunted them again. This time there was no attempt at stopping by the vehicle ramming them. Ratcliffe's car was spun a quarter moon in the road and its rear tires butted up against a curb heaped with hard-packed snow. It juddered to a halt.

Whomever her sister had shot at was now out of her line of fire. When Joanne looked up a larger vehicle again than Pinky's SUV hove into view, some kind of dark grey colored van. A woman wearing a half-face mask leaned out of the passenger window and fired almost point blank at the car with a shotgun. Ratcliffe yelled and twisted to return fire. The next blast of the shotgun lit up the cab. Ratcliffe fell silent.

Joanne screamed.

THIRTY-FIVE

I t was lucky that Tess's injured hand was her left and she was right-handed, otherwise mounting a defence would have proven almost impossible. In the intervening hours since it had been taken from the redhead, the feel of her pistol had grown familiar to Tess and shooting it came natural. The magazine was partially depleted from previous usage, but there were enough bullets left to drop Harper and the woman. That was if one or two bullets would be enough to stop the big man, and a small part of her dwindled in unholy terror at the thought that he was invincible, and no number of bullets would even mark his skin. However, a much larger portion of her knew she was thinking ridiculously and shot in the heart or head, he'd die as easily as anyone else. Case in point, Po had smashed Harper's nose to pulp, so he wasn't as impregnable as he looked.

Po gave the impression that he was tougher than whalebone and gristle, but she knew that he was hurt. Harper had shot at the Telluride from barely twenty feet away, and the bullets had all found their way inside the car, one or maybe two of them nicking Po, but for the time being he didn't let on how badly he'd been injured. It was only sheer luck, and a miscount by Harper, that had saved Po from an even closer shot to his skull. Six bullets had been spent rapidly, so it was a seventh time that Harper pulled the trigger and the hammer had fallen on an empty casing. Now that Harper was out of ammunition he wasn't Tess's priority.

Ahead of them, looming closer with each second, came a car with its high beams glaring. The driver fired with an arm hanging out of the window, making accuracy difficult, but most of the bullets struck the Telluride, busting the windshield and caroming off the hood and roof. Tess didn't waste time leaning out of her window, she fired directly through the broken windshield and her hand was steadier than she would've believed possible following the bout of weakness that struck her earlier. Her eyesight was clear, and once she'd pushed Harper beyond her concern, her mind was focussed. Each of her shots was grouped in a small batch not much larger than a baseball. Allowing for the woman leaning out the side window to shoot, Tess had fired marginally further to the left than she might otherwise have, each shot intended for the redhead's heart.

Maybe it wasn't Harper who was indestructible, perhaps it was the redhead instead, because the car never wavered, kept on coming, and if anything picked up speed. Po sawed the steering, first jinking left, and then right, and then spun the wheels as he lost traction on the ice. A moment later and the tires bit down and the Telluride jumped forward. The SUV speeding towards them didn't deviate. It struck the back end of the Telluride, smashing a path through and Tess heard rather than witnessed it crash into Ratcliffe's car. Tess craned about seeking the women, and also wondering what had become of Pinky in the past few crazy seconds. Instead of Pinky's black SUV, she spotted a grey van and wondered how in hell it had managed to approach so stealthily as to avoid detection. Of course, they had the storm to blame for that. Any moving vehicle beyond fifty yards was totally masked by the whirling snow. It must have hurtled in the instant that Harper sprung his trap, intending forcing them into what Tess recognized as the entrance to the old landfill site, now a field dotted with solar panels. Before reaching the defunct garbage tip, they must pass through some barren ground where only the foundations of buildings remained from when it was an operational quarry.

It was apparent that Po had also recognized Harper's intention and wasn't for playing the man's game. He hit reverse and sent the Telluride hurtling into the center of the road, using its momentum and a stamp to the brake to assist the skid that set it between the van and where they'd last seen Harper at the V in the roads. There was no sign of the hulking killer, though Tess searched for him, leaving the driving to Po. Po hit the gas. He rammed the van, buckling it almost in two as he kept the gas pedal on the floor. The same instant as the collision, somebody within the van had unloaded a shotgun on Ratcliffe's car. Hopefully he hadn't been too late and had thrown off the shooter's aim. Before the van had settled on its tires again, PO reversed, then powered forward, striking the van a second time and jamming it against a mound of packed snow at roadside. The van's engine squealed like a dying thing. The driver tried to get it moving, but the van refused to budge. Doors spilled open and two women – strangers to Tess –

leapt free. One of them carried the shotgun. She turned it on the Telluride with an angry shout.

A pistol cracked. Not Tess's, because she was poorly positioned to return fire at the woman. Ratcliffe, still alive thankfully, fired from within her car and blood puffed from high on the shotgun wielder's shoulder. The gunwoman bent almost double, racing for cover. Tess understood that she'd already spent the two cartridges loaded in her gun. The second woman pulled a handgun out her waistband. Tess leaned past Po and fired at her. She too darted for cover, using the van for concealment.

Out of imminent danger from that duo, Tess's attention snapped to where Harper was last seen, then on the car his driver had employed to ram them. The door of the SUV hung open, but there was no sign of the redhead who must've scrambled out while Tess was otherwise engaged. There were dark splotches on the snow, but Tess couldn't possibly tell if it was blood; surely her shots had hit the murderous bitch?

Po's head almost torqued off as he twisted to take in his surroundings. 'There's Pinky,' he said, making a roll call of their numbers. 'Ratcliffe and Joanne. We've all made it, but things can still change.'

Tess thought that they were missing one person. She clawed around in her seat and checked for the arsonist. He lay across the back seat, hands locked to the door handle. Blood dotted his clothes. At first she feared that he was dead, but then she saw that his eyes were stretched wide, his mouth in a tight grimace. He shivered with anxiety. He'd survived, but might require a change of underwear.

'Are you hit?' she asked him.

His head barely shook in the negative.

She checked with Po.

The blood dotting the arsonist had sprayed from him. He was bleeding from the side of his neck, and also, on closer examination, from a wound on his thigh and another on his left arm. 'You've been shot,' she said, alarmed, 'three times!'

'Not shot, just skimmed. I think the cut on my neck was from flying glass, not a bullet.' He ignored her a moment, while gesturing to Pinky. His instruction required no words: Ratcliffe's car was done; get the women safely into his SUV. Pinky drove forward to comply. Po swung the Telluride around to block them from those hiding behind the van. Tess covered with her pistol, aware she had only a couple of rounds left, if that.

Pinky called to them, waving in the direction of the decommissioned quarry. 'Those witches, they took off with their tails tucked between their legs.'

'Did you see what became of Harper?' asked Po.

'Saw a woman stumble away, me, but nothing of Harper since he unloaded on us. You hit, Nicolas?'

'I'm good, podnuh. You?'

'Pissed, man. I didn't even get off a shot.'

'Don't worry,' Po said, 'you'll get your opportunity, f'sure.'

Ratcliffe looked pained as she got out of her car. She clutched at the side of her head with one hand, but her grip on her service weapon was firm as she guided her sister out the back and to Pinky's waiting car.

A car approached too fast for the road conditions. Tess aimed her pistol at it, trying to identify if the occupants were friends or foes. She'd gotten off the promised call to her brother Alex, who had assured her he'd greet them with a protection detail when they arrived at the station. She guessed he'd also have alerted the patrols in the area to be on the look out for them. The older model Toyota Corolla speeding towards them wasn't a Portland PD cruiser, but Tess couldn't discount that it could belong to undercover officers. She didn't lower her pistol though, thinking that Pinky might get his chance to fire a shot after all.

Po powered the Telluride across the road, then swung the front around to intercept the Toyota, should the driver intend using it as they had the other vehicles. The Toyota decelerated, but the snow made stopping a more difficult task than usual. It skidded, the noise like a shriek of fright, and Tess braced for impact. It stopped with bare feet to spare. Tess peered back at two furious faces glowering at her through the Toyota's streaked windshield. Even contorted in hatred, she recognized the familial likeness with their sibling currently gasping from fright behind her.

She turned to briefly appraise their captive. 'If you care that your brothers survive this, you'd better warn them from doing anything stupid.'

Learning his brothers were close by, the young man reared up, trying to see where they were. He opened his mouth, and Tess was certain he was about to holler for help. That would surely bring his brothers running, and cause a second violent confrontation in only a few minutes.

'We are armed and ready for them,' Tess warned, 'and this time they won't have a chance. If you want to shout anything to them, it should be advice to put aside this stupid vendetta against me.'

'I told you already they won't stop,' the captive retorted. 'You deserve the same as happened to our mom.'

'Let them come,' Po growled. 'Pinky will drop them before they get more than a couple of steps. If not, I'll snap their damn necks.'

Po was rightfully angry with the siblings. So was Tess, but she couldn't raise the same amount of ire she had for Harper and his henna-haired whore. Just then she hoped to find remedy with the arsonists, one of mutual forgiveness; she couldn't help protect Joanne when trying to stave off a bunch of misguided firebugs. Who was she kidding? They might be poorly informed amateurs, but they were no less potential killers than Harper or any of his cronies. Their fires had already put several of Po's employees out of work, burned Po's muscle car, and worse, they had destroyed Anne Ridgeway's treasured curios shop and Tess's apartment, and almost killed Anne and Pinky in the process. There could be no peaceful resolution.

The driver of the Toyota rode the gas pedal up and down, making the engine noise rise and fall. It was a pitiful attempt at intimidation. The car suddenly backed away and swerved into the opposite lane. It came to rest within spitting distance of where Harper had launched the ambush. The passenger alighted and stood with a bottle held out from his side. It contained gasoline and a wad of paper as a makeshift fuse. Unlit, it wasn't threatening, but striking a match would take no time whatsoever.

'What you going to do with that, you?' Pinky challenged. He ensured that the brother could see his pistols. 'I'll shoot that outta your hand before you can throw it. Might even put a coupla rounds in your face while I'm at it, me.'

'You have Jake,' the man called, giving a name to their captive. 'Let him go or I swear to God—'

'You've no business swearing to God, you evil son of a bitch,' Pinky snapped. 'I see you, and I know you. You're the one squirted lighter fuel all over me, and I'd say you were the one to soak Anne Ridgeway too. You've got the devil in you.'

The arsonist took out a plastic disposable cigarette lighter. He held it up and then gestured at the paper fuse with it. 'Let Jake go or you'll see how evil I can be. I'll burn you, I'll fucking burn you all.'

Po was itching to get out the Telluride and deal man to man with the threat, but Tess stalled him with a hand on his shoulder. 'He's bluffing,' she whispered with an almost imperceptible nod towards their passenger. 'He can't use that firebomb without hurting his brother Jake.'

'Shoot that piece of crap and have done, Pinky,' Po called to their friend.

'I'm sorely tempted, me,' said Pinky.

'You aren't going to shoot me. You're supposed to be the good guys. Well, that's bullshit! Your good deeds almost killed our mother. D'you know how badly she's burned? Do you have any fucking idea? They're going to amputate her hands, and her face is burned right down to the bone in places.'

'Think about what you're saying,' Tess responded. 'Why target me for your mother's misery? Why not anyone else in the long chain that led to this moment? How am I responsible for your mom's injuries, because I was the one to send her back for breaking her parole? She was the one who broke it, and you probably helped her do it. Your actions are equally responsible for what sent her back to jail. Are you going to burn yourself to ashes, are you going to burn your brothers along with you?'

'I will if I have to.'

Tess coughed in scorn. 'Now you're just being ridiculous.'

The driver must have said something, because the firebug suddenly jerked his head and they spoke coarsely but Tess couldn't hear what was said.

From a distance, the sound of sirens arose.

'The police are coming,' Tess said. 'If you're going to do anything you'd best do it now, otherwise you'll never get another chance.'

He wavered, holding the cigarette lighter an inch from the impromptu wick.

'Think you'll get a flame in this storm, you?' asked Pinky. 'I know that my pistols won't fail me.'

The sirens grew louder.

The driver again gave warning and frustration replaced the cold rage in the man's features. He lunged back into the Toyota and the driver backed away at speed.

Po didn't relax for a second. If the brothers decided to go for broke and change direction, he was ready to intercept them. As the Toyota completed a turn in the road, Pinky rushed to get back in the SUV and get the sisters out of harm's way. 'Let's roll,' Po called to him.

The sirens continued to wail and gumball lights occasionally tinted the falling snow ahead. Po maneuvered around the abandoned van and SUV and Pinky followed. They'd gone several hundred yards when the first responders whipped by – a fire truck rather than a patrol car. Unbeknown to them at the time, the firefighters were en route to a flaming car several blocks north of where Harper's attempted ambush had failed. Jaycee Monk had survived the confrontation with the Wolsey brothers, but not without injury; his burns were so severe he'd require skin grafts and amputations.

THIRTY-SIX

Harper squatted under the low boughs of a fir tree, his hulking form amorphous among the shadows. His hair and shoulders were dusted with clumps of snow. To anyone passing by they'd take him for another shrub among many shrubs at roadside. He watched while the confrontation disintegrated to one of bluff and counter bluff, and then the guy with the Molotov cocktail backed down and scrambled to escape. Harper didn't move, he remained exactly where he'd squatted in the snow and the Toyota passed him and then took the sharp bend on to Presumpscot Street. Neither man had given him a split-second's notice. He was as invisible to them as he had been to Tess Grey when she'd sought him minutes ago, and to the eyes of her Cajun beau and his black friend. His vision was untroubled and he'd seen everything with stark clarity. He watched as whom he took to be Joanne's sister guided her into the rear seat of the black man's SUV. He recalled her name – Detective Ratcliffe – and even without the benefit of foreknowledge he'd have recognized the familial likeness between the sisters. For trying to protect her kid sister, Ratcliffe had taken wounds, either from Mallory Carson's shotgun or the shattering window. The black gunman he'd overheard called Pinky. What kind of name was Pinky for somebody almost as husky as Harper? He was unharmed from the encounter, but Harper had noticed a weakness in his reticence to shoot the punk threatening to burn him when he had the opportunity. Harper thought he could use that hesitancy to kill against him if necessary. Tess Grey had escaped injury from her second joust with Siobhan Doyle. Villere though, seemed pained, and even from a distance Harper saw that the Cajun carried a flesh wound to his neck and probably had been hit elsewhere. He was momentarily disappointed that the revolver hadn't held a seventh round, but not really. When death arrived for the Cajun, Harper wanted it to be delivered more up close and personal than at the end of a gun barrel.

Villere led and Pinky followed.

Harper weighed the possibility of using either the van or Doyle's

SUV to give pursuit, but neither vehicle was roadworthy. He wondered what had become of Carson and Lyman. They'd swiftly booked out the instant the fight had turned against them. It didn't surprise him. They were full of shit and had shown they were as little use to him as Jaycee Monk, and he'd proved useless. Siobhan had won kudos for the way in which she'd followed his instructions to the letter; the manner in which she'd launched the attack was as fearless as any he could have hoped for. It was such a pity that she'd shown her bravery was fleeting and that she'd slunk off like a broken-backed dog the instant the opportunity arose. She had been hit by Tess Grey's return fire and had been almost bent double with pain when she bugged out of the SUV. He supposed he couldn't criticize her for following her survival instinct. He wondered, as in his crippled dog analogy, she'd crawled somewhere to die.

A fire truck hurtled into view, sirens and lights and a blatting of horns. It slowed marginally as the crew spotted the vehicles at curbside, but it was apparent to them that they – a road hazard – weren't their priority. They were headed someplace else, probably to where Monk had failed miserably in his attempt at running the Toyota off the road.

Those in the Toyota were an interesting addition to the night's goings-on. When Monk first reported the car speeding to intercept the convoy, Harper had assumed the occupants to be allies of Grey and Villere. Not so, it appeared, and quite the opposite. He hadn't gotten a look at Grey and Villere's captive, but had overheard enough to learn he was a brother to the duo in the Toyota. All three were pissed at Grey, for some tenuous slight the private investigator had supposedly dealt their mother. They'd chased after their sibling, hoping to rescue him, but after showing they were serious against Monk, they could only champ their teeth and make baseless threats when confronting their true enemies. At first Harper had wondered if he could use them and their hatred of Grey as a distraction. He'd willingly have sent them as fodder to the slaughter to allow him to get to Joanne Mason, but decided against it when he considered how they'd dithered and then retreated the second there was a hint of a siren on the wind. They were punks, useless to him, unless . . .

Once the fire truck regained speed and disappeared along Ocean Avenue, Harper rose up from his hiding place, turned on his heel

and pushed through the shrubs separating the roads. He stepped
out on to Presumpscot Street, noting the fresh tire tracks in the
latest fall of snow and followed them towards where the brothers
had taken cover in the parking lot of a marine supplies store. The
Toyota was one of around a dozen cars, vans and trailers parked
overnight, and the only one currently without a covering of snow
on its roof and hood. About a hundred yards ahead and to his
right, Harper spotted a taxicab depot and fleetingly wondered if
he should dispense entirely with his new idea and try comman-
deering a yellow taxi instead. He decided against the taxi without
using the logical decision-making process he prided himself on
and instead went with the irrational buzz of anticipation, heading
directly towards the Toyota.

The driver had reversed between a couple of trucks, concealing
the Toyota from the road, but also obscuring their view of anyone
approaching. Harper went steadily, mindless of the snow gathering
on his blocky head and wide shoulders; but mindful of his footing.
He carried the empty revolver, holding it down by his right
thigh. He breathed, feeling the icy sting in his abused nostrils. He
spat a thick clot of blood on the ground.

Movements inside the car were sharp and jerky and there was
a rumble of conversation. Harper couldn't decipher one voice from
the other, those inside were arguing and frustrated and – like
Harper was – trying to come up with a contingency after their
original plan to rescue their brother had fallen to pieces. Absurdly
they whispered so that their voices didn't carry: Harper doubted
that they'd be heard by anyone else but him even if they shouted
and screamed. He contemplated the possibility that they were
armed, and decided if they had access to guns then why try to
threaten Grey and Villere with a jerry-rigged firebomb? He tapped
the barrel of the revolver against his leg. He hadn't dumped the
empty shell casings yet. He'd no fresh ammo. But the amateurs
in the Toyota could have no way of knowing. He adjusted his
direction and flanked the nearest truck and approached the car
from its back left corner. His silhouette was blocked by a group
of trees behind him. He moved further, and once he was adjacent
to the car he strode without pause and grabbed the driver's door
handle. He yanked open the door and jammed the revolver under
the man's chin as he spun in alarm to confront him.

'Police,' said Harper. 'Don't move.'

The second brother, as stunned as the first, dropped a cell phone he'd been working on. It slipped between his knees. His hand moved to the side. Going for a gun?

'*You no speakee Inglis*?' Harper mocked him. 'Did I not just order you to keep still?'

For good measure Harper screwed the barrel of the revolver into the soft flesh of the driver's throat. His brother raised his empty hands in surrender.

The driver's eyes darted at Harper, and then at what he could see of the gun, then back to Harper again. 'You're no cop.'

'Damn, I didn't fool you long. But you know what that means, don't you? I'm not a cop, so there's not a fucking thing stopping me from blowing your goddamn head off.'

The other brother, the same as tried forcing Grey and Villere to release a third brother called Jake, scowled up at Harper. 'You're one of that bunch that tried ambushing Tess and Po'boy back there.'

'What of it?'

'The enemy of my enemy is my friend, right?' he asked hopefully.

'I don't go in for any of that bullshit. Don't get any ideas. Just cause you've got a boner for the private eyes you're not my friend. No way, no how.' Harper tilted his large head to one side. 'In fact, from this angle you look exactly like a piece of dirt.' He straightened up. 'Still the same from this angle too.'

'Buddy,' said the driver, his bottom lip trembling, 'what is it you want from us?'

'I want your car.' Harper reached and snatched out the ignition key and pushed it in a pocket. 'See, my usual ride's been trashed along with a van I might've used, and you two fuckwits are responsible for putting the only car left to me out of commission. What did you do with Monk?'

'We don't know who Monk is?'

'I'm sure you can figure it out. Guy that tried driving you off the road earlier, and you repaid him with one or two of your Molotov cocktails?'

'He got out the car, on fire,' the driver admitted, 'and started rolling in the snow. We didn't hang around to see if he survived.'

'Don't blame you,' Harper said. 'Don't worry, he means nothing to me. On the other hand, his car was my ride outta here, so now you've gotta make recompense.'

'C'mon, man, give us a break, whydon'tcha?' said the passenger.

'We have something in common here. You want somebody, and we want our brother Jake back. We both want Tess and Po'boy out of the way and we can help each other. Yeah?'

'OK, let me consider your proposal. No. I've thought about it and you still remind me only of a piece of dirt.'

Without warning Harper grabbed the driver and yanked him out of the car, crushing him bodily against the door column. He shoved the revolver harder into the flesh of his throat. 'Tell your bro to get out without any fuss, or I will kill you.'

'A-Aaron,' the driver stuttered. 'He means what he says.'

'You'd better believe it, Aaron,' Harper said.

Aaron got out, holding his empty hands aloft.

'OK, come on around here where I can see you.' Harper didn't release the driver, but motioned for Aaron to join them with the barrel of the revolver. When he transferred it back to his captive, he placed the barrel in the driver's eye socket. Aaron hurried to comply.

'Jeez,' Harper said, 'you guys stink like gasoline. Maybe I shouldn't use this gun to shoot you or we might all go up like Hiroshima. What you got in the back there?'

'Couple cans of gas,' said Aaron.

'I'd better drive with the windows down or someone in the back might get high on those fumes, eh?' said Harper, and he offered Aaron a conspiratorial grin. Aaron wasn't amused.

'Let Jim go, man. You can have the car, but let my brother go.'

'I don't intend taking either of you with me. Least of all Jimmy-Bob. Come here. Closer.' He wagged the gun at Aaron. 'Don't make me tell you twice.'

'Why? What you gonna—'

Before Aaron could finish his question, Harper hammered the gun butt down on the top of his head. He felt the skull fracture under the terrific weight of the blow, and Aaron dropped as if the tendons in his skeleton had all been cut simultaneously. Jim, the driver, squawked in alarm, and Harper had to give the man his due: he tried to fight. Harper's left hand was at the nape of Jim's neck, and immediately after striking Aaron with it, he stabbed the gun back into Jim's eye socket. He shoved both hands inwards, twisting and screwing with the gun as if attempting to manually force a coupling together. It was a savage and terrible and uncalled for act, but Harper relished every second of the man's agony. Within no time the pleasure diminished as Jim diminished also. Shock as much as pain robbed him of his senses and he went limp in Harper's grasp. Harper dropped him and both brothers lay with their heads touching.

They made easy targets for Harper's heels.

THIRTY-SEVEN

S ergeant Alex Grey met them at the midtown police headquarters with a handful of patrol officers and a couple of plain-clothes detectives looking on. Usually officers accessed the building via Newbury Street, while the public entered via a paved plaza adjacent to a multi-storey parking lot. Alex had told Tess to bring Joanne to the short flight of steps off the street, as it was less exposed to witnesses. There was a moment of confusion after Po drew the Telluride to a halt and Pinky drove past and swung the hood of his SUV into the curb as if blocking Po's further progress. The officers were unsure which car carried Joanne Mason, until it became obvious they'd formed a blockade with the cars to cover the girl while she left the SUV and into the phalanx of officers who could then gather about her. Detective Ratcliffe shielded her sister too and Pinky filled a void in the formation as Joanne was ushered off the sidewalk and up the concrete steps to the entrance. After handing over Jake Wolsey for official arrest and processing, Tess and Po also joined the rush to get Joanne inside and out of reach of a drive-by shooter. Harper and his group had shown they were capable of such rash attacks so she wasn't safe until Joanne was fully behind the station walls. Even then, Tess wasn't fully convinced of her safety and was pleased when Alex directed them beyond the reach of the public into a more secure area deeper in the building.

Tess used to be a sheriff's deputy and had worked out of the Cumberland County Sheriff's office rather than here, but she was familiar with the Portland PD offices too. In her current role as a private investigator she'd had plenty of reasons to attend the station, no less than to visit with her brother on occasion. Most of the cops in attendance recognized her and Po, some of them were on first name terms. As was sometimes the case, Pinky drew glances that had little to do with his skin color, or his impressive bulk, and more to do with his rap sheet. He'd probably only convinced fifty per cent of the officers there that he was reborn, and not the notorious criminal from Baton Rouge he used to be. For Tess fifty

per cent was enough, because they made up those Alex had desig-
nated as Joanne's protective detail. She was taken with Detective
Ratcliffe to a private office, whereas Wolsey was hustled towards
lock up; none of them were in a hurry to deal with the arsonist
yet. Tess even smiled at the pun that the firebug should be left to
cool his heels in a cell.

Alex led Tess, Po and Pinky into his office.

'I've had to deploy officers to several crime scenes throughout
Portland. How is it every time you take on a case, I end up having
to go over budget on staffing levels?' Alex asked wryly. He gave
Tess a discreet hug to show he was happy she'd made it to the
building safely, then frowned in concern at her bandaged hand.
The elderly spinsters had done a neat job of bandaging her wound,
but hours had past since and Tess had used her hand where it
should have been rested. Blood had seeped through and stained
the dressing. 'You need to have that looked at.'

'It looks worse than it is,' she assured him.

'Seriously, Tess?'

'OK, you're right. It's beginning to hurt like hell.'

'What about . . .' He nodded at her abdomen.

'Baby's fine.'

'That's good. But let's see to that hand. I'll have one of my
team fetch the first-aid kit.' Alex turned to Po. 'For Christ's sakes,
you're bleeding all over too.'

Po shrugged non-plussed. 'They're only scratches.'

'You're bleeding from your side worse than a stuck pig. Go sit
down over there before you fall down.'

Po shook his head at the proffered seat. 'I'm good. You might
want to have somebody check Ratcliffe over, from the way things
went down I'm pretty sure she got a face full of buckshot.'

Ratcliffe was nowhere to be seen, having accompanied Joanne.
She was determined to chaperone her sister until she was totally
convinced of Joanne's safety. There were still some that might
doubt her innocence in the murders of the Blackhorse children
and treat her accordingly.

'Been a helluva night for you too, Pinky?' Alex pointed out. It
wasn't the first time the men had met that evening. 'Pleased to
see you look no worse for wear than before.'

'I carry off the singed pants look, me,' said Pinky with a sassy
wink. Alex was a confirmed heterosexual and was currently in a

relationship with Tess's occasional employer, Emma Clancy, but
it didn't stop Pinky from flirting shamelessly with him. 'But I look
even better in my birthday suit.'

Alex leaned his knuckles on his desk and shook his head. He
looked at all three in succession, before returning his attention
solely to Tess. He exuded incredulity. 'My superiors want answers.
They want to know what the hell is going on. From what you've
told me already you've managed to piss off two separate parties
this time. We've had buildings torched, cars and vans wrecked,
and who knows how many people have been injured or how many
bad guys we still have running loose? I've got to say it, Tess, but
you've gone and exceled yourself this time.'

'Six,' said Po.

Alex shot him a look. 'Six?'

'You've got six bad guys on the loose. Harper and his girlfriend;
two female shooters from the van; and two more Wolsey brothers,
seeing as you already have one of them locked up. Six.'

Alex nodded in agreement. 'You don't know it yet but another
guy was picked up and taken to hospital. Seems he somehow got
in the way of the Wolseys before they tried breaking their brother
loose, and got burned almost to a crisp.'

'Jeez.' Visions of the terribly burned man invaded Tess's mind
and she shivered at the horrible punishment the Wolsey brothers
had intended for her. She was yet to learn John Corbett Monk's
name, or see a photo of him before his horrific disfigurement, but
it didn't matter; she pictured an anonymous face writhing in flaming
agony. She sat in the chair previously declined by Po.

'Tess, are you OK?'

'As well as I could be.' She told him about the gas station they'd
passed up near Lincoln and how they believed Harper was responsible for whatever crime had happened there during his hunt for
Joanne. She told him about Harper and the redhead's attack on
the farm where Ellie and Felicity had taken Joanne in. 'He's irrational in his determination to shut her up. By now he must realize
that he's the number one suspect in the Blackhorse murders, and
anything he tries here will change nothing.'

'Wouldn't be the first time a murderer has gone for broke,' Alex
pointed out. 'You've heard the saying, you're as well being hanged
for stealing a sheep as for a lamb, right?'

'You watch too much British TV,' she said.

'Yeah, maybe, but you get what I mean, right?'

'The way he's acting it's as if he doesn't care about the consequences of his actions.'

'So he's nuts. Probably believes he's unstoppable.'

Po kneaded the base of his skull. 'He's pretty convincing.'

Alex tapped the gun holstered on his belt. 'Nobody is unstoppable.'

'Don't make the mistake of underestimatin' him.'

'I won't.' Alex returned his attention to Tess. 'What about this woman, the one who stabbed you? What do you know about her?'

'She tried claiming innocence, that she was employed by Harper to drive him and got drawn into his trouble, but her actions proved otherwise. She looked fit, strong, but not like a gym bunny, more like she's a vet, ex-army if I'd to guess. I overheard her name . . . Siobhan, but that's all I got. Perhaps Joanne can enlighten us. She knew Harper before all of this, maybe she knew Siobhan too.'

'I've put out BOLOS for this Siobhan, based on the description you gave, and for the two gunwomen you described that booked outta the van. My trouble is the lack of manpower. I've requested assistance from our partner agencies, and the sheriff and state police and they are going to assist in the hunt. We have liaised with the local FBI office and have agents on route. Multiple murders, cross state crimes being committed, this has fallen into the jurisdiction of the feds. Until everyone else gets their act together, you have us; all my usual available patrols are tied up at the other crime scenes.' Alex rested his knuckles on his desk again. His forearms trembled. Tess and Alex looked so much alike that some people assumed they were twins. It wasn't the case, because Alex was older. They had another brother, older again. Except right then, to Tess, he looked like a nervous kid, while she felt as if she carried a century of tough years on her shoulders. Perhaps her fatigue was reflected in his posture because Alex changed tack. 'Hey, Po, why don't you take Tess to the bathroom and see if you can't get you both cleaned up? I'll have the Med-Kit fetched so you can dress your wounds. Then there's a couch in the lieutenant's office where Tess can stretch out and get some rest. You too, if you like, cause you both look set to drop.'

Po didn't argue, he didn't say anything, which was as good as agreement from him.

Pinky stirred, said, 'There a couch that I can share with somebody?'

Alex snorted, but wasn't in the mood for Pinky's teasing. 'Would be best for you to keep those pistols holstered while you're in here, Pinky. Don't want anyone seeing you and getting the wrong idea.'

'A black man with a gun? Yeah, I'd just have to be the bad guy, me.'

'Don't make this about race,' Alex said. 'There are a lot of twitchy gun fingers amongst my officers tonight. They all know you're one of us. Any of the others soon to arrive won't know you from a hole in the wall.'

'Fair enough. Where can I fill my hands with a strong coffee instead? I'm parched, me.'

Alex led the way, directing Tess and Po to the washroom and Pinky towards a recreation room where the cops and civilian staff took their breaks. A jug of coffee as black as oil simmered on a hot plate.

'Now that's what I'm talking about,' Pinky announced.

THIRTY-EIGHT

Harper left the brothers where he'd stomped them into the snow. If any life existed within them it wouldn't matter, because the cold would finish the job and kill them in no time. By morning, and the arrival of workers at the marine supply store, they'd probably be encased in a layer of ice. Now that he'd assuaged some of his frustration at failing to catch Joanne Mason again, he put the brothers out of his mind, concentrating on what he must do next.

His first notion was to check the car for weapons, because this had gone beyond the use of blunt force trauma: if he was going to accomplish his mission, he required better weapons than the butt of an empty revolver. Within seconds he discovered where the brothers had secreted a pistol. He didn't enjoy the impersonal killing method of using a pistol, but was also a pragmatist, so was thankful to find it fully loaded. It wasn't the brothers' first choice of weapon either. Whatever had gone down between them to make enemies of the brothers and the private investigator, he couldn't fully say, but they had wished Tess Grey harm almost as fervently as he wished Joanne dead. In the trunk he spotted the gasoline cans. A quick check of them showed that they were mostly full. There were other items he didn't immediately recognize, but deduced they must be jerry-built fuses and timers so that the brothers could be clear of the flames when they ignited. He found the Molotov cocktail that Aaron had threatened Grey and Villere with, as well as several capped bottles primed with accelerant seated inside a cooler box on the back seat.

Lastly he dug for the cell phone that Aaron had been playing with on his arrival, and found it where it had slipped from between the man's knees into the footwell. Harper checked and found that it had gone to sleep, but a simple press of the home button wakened it again. He depressed the home button twice more in quick succession and brought up the web pages and apps that Aaron had recently used, and was rewarded instantly when the latest showed an app for locating another person's phone.

Obviously, the brothers had been monitoring Jake's cell phone from a safe distance and after he got himself captured, had used it to locate him: it explained how they were able to take a different route to intersect with the convoy, and had run into Jaycee Monk as a result. Harper checked on Jake's current location. Logic said that wherever he'd ended up, so too had his captors, and Joanne with them. He didn't know how to react when he saw that the cell phone had come to rest. It was good that he now had a target, bad that it happened to be a police station. In the grand scheme of things, he decided it was good. Thinking they were secure behind a police station wall, their guard would drop making her protectors more vulnerable to attack than they'd been while out in the open.

He had to shift the driver's seat all the way back to make room in the Toyota Corolla. He preferred not to but he could drive, but was out of practice, more so when it had a stick shift and a clutch pedal. He put the cell phone on the dash and got the Toyota moving, finding his big feet cumbersome and unresponsive on the pedals, and had to make adjustments before he stalled the engine. He crept the car towards the exit. No traffic had passed in the last few minutes. On the intersecting road, over near the abandoned quarry, fire trucks and cops had converged on Siobhan Doyle's SUV and Lyman and Carson's van. For the moment he was safe from discovery, but the likelihood was that the cops would begin expanding their search radius. He had to accept they were probably aware of the brothers' involvement and on the look out for their Toyota. Yeah, well, the last place anyone would think to look for him was heading directly to the police station.

He checked, saw the road was clear, and began a left turn. It took him across the carriageway towards the taxicab depot, so he kept his face averted as he drove past. If anyone were working that late in the evening it would be a cab dispatcher who might also have been sent a 'be on the lookout' notice from the local PD. Once past, he stared directly ahead, concentrating on staying in the ruts already dug in the snow by other vehicles. His nerve endings prickled at the thought of losing control of the car in a manner they never did approaching a life or death showdown with Joanne's protectors.

A figure stumbled out ahead of him. Bent over at the waist, one arm thrust out, forcing him to stop. For a second he considered speeding up and running the figure down, rather than deal with her, but decided that she'd kind of proven her value so Siobhan Doyle deserved more. He applied the brake and felt the tires slide. He pumped the pedal and brought the car to a grinding halt inches from crushing Siobhan's shinbones with the fender. She buckled forward, her palm going flat on the hood. She exhaled and even through a misted windshield, he spotted a smear of blood on her top lip. When she exhaled a string of bloody drool swung from her chin.

'H-help me, please!' she croaked. One knee gave way and she sank down, her torso only held up by the hood.

He got out and loomed over her. Siobhan's face lifted slowly and it took long seconds for it to dawn that she wasn't looking at a savior but the last person she'd hoped to see.

'So you went and got yourself shot, huh?' he asked needlessly.

Tess Grey's bullets had found her, striking her twice in the upper chest. One wound was near her collarbone, the other lower down and far more troubling. The blood bubbling in the corners of her mouth hinted at a punctured lung.

'I need . . . the closest ER,' she said.

'You aren't kidding,' he said. He offered a hand, which she blinked at, dazed. 'Come on, let me get you inside.'

'You . . . you're driving?'

'You thought I couldn't?'

'I . . . just thought your skills lay . . . elsewhere.' For the briefest moment her lips pulled up into a snarky smile, reminding him of the woman who'd sat alongside him throughout the trip. In the next moment she shivered and what little color was left in her complexion drained. Her pale skin was almost translucent in the gleam of the Toyota's headlights. 'Harp, it's over now. If I don't get help I'll die.'

'I'm here for you,' he said.

When she didn't rise, or even reach for his proffered hand he ignored her mild resistance when bending and picking her up, one arm around her back, the other under her knees. Her head lolled against his shoulder. He heard her groan and then weep, and knew it was because she thought she'd escaped him, only to fall directly into his hands once more. He moved the crate of firebombs and laid her across the back seat. He had to fold her knees up towards her belly in order to shut the door. She cringed in agony.

He said, 'Try and stay still or you'll bleed more.'

'It stinks in here . . . what is it? Gasoline?'

'It's only exhaust fumes,' he lied. 'I had to open a window to keep the windshield from misting over.'

'So what's in the bottles?'

'Could be piss for all I know. When I was looking for a car to get out of Portland in, I couldn't pick and choose.'

'Why you lying to me, Harp? Now that I've thought about it, this is the car you told Monk to run off the road.' She sounded stronger, but that was through the strength of accusation. 'What are you planning next, Harp?'

'Taking you to a hospital.'

'That's bullshit. Let me out, Harp. Whatever you have in mind it's probably insane, and I want no part of it. I've done my bit, so do the right thing and let me go.'

'I couldn't possibly abandon an injured woman in this cold. You won't survive more than a few minutes.' Harper closed her door and quickly settled in the driver's seat. This time he didn't feel as awkward at the wheel. He set off driving, despite further protestations from the back. Before she could try opening the door with the idea of sliding out on to the road, he engaged the child locks. She swore at him and he smiled and ignored her completely. His attention was once more on Aaron's cellular phone and the location it showed for his brother Jake's phone. He drove on, taking US-1 over Tukey's Bridge at the entrance to Back Cove and into downtown Portland. By the time he left the highway and found Franklin Street, Siobhan had fallen silent in the back: dead or only unconscious he couldn't tell and wasn't really that bothered either way.

For a second back there, when she'd stumbled out and he recognized her flaming red hair he'd felt something akin to a warm flash of happiness. Monk had proven worthless to him, and Lyman and Carson were cowards who'd ran away the second the fight turned against them. Throughout the mission, Siobhan Doyle had blown hot and cold in his estimation but latterly he'd come to distrust her and expected she'd try to book out at the first opportunity. After her abandoning the SUV he thought she'd skipped, and was literally in the wind by now. The last he expected was for her to stumble into his path and stop him. But her actions had been guided by desperation and mistaken identity: she'd thought him a Good Samaritan, and couldn't be further from the truth. He owed her nothing, not even a dignified ending.

It was the early hours and the snowfall had forced home even the most determined of revelers, so it was quiet downtown. Harper didn't see another person while scouting the area several blocks to each side of the police station. Being in one of the few moving vehicles in the vicinity he ran the risk of discovery, but other than a single PD cruiser parked with its wheels on the sidewalk, he saw no other indication of police activity. As he rolled by the cruiser he found it abandoned, the patrol officer obviously else-where on foot. He looped around the adjacent blocks and found some roads were one-way and contrary to his direction of travel. He took one of them anyhow, driving slowly and steadily towards what appeared to be an open-air parking lot used by the cops. On his right there was also a multi-storey car park. It was unlit between the levels, so he'd no idea how many vehicles were inside. He doubted that during a nightshift a police force in a town the size of Portland could call on dozens of reinforcements. He must account for civilian staff, but all told it would be surprising to find more than a dozen people inside and a good third of them would be non-combatants. Eight armed officers was not a number to be sneezed at, but he wouldn't confront them all in one concerted defence. Faced with a couple of cops at a time he felt easily their match, one on one, he was their better.

He was always one that preferred taking direct action. There was no pussyfooting around with him. Once a decision was made to act, then he acted and the devil could take the losers. He parked the Toyota out of sight of the entrance to the police station, concealed by other parked cars. If inspected, the lack of snow on his car, compared to those in the lot would give him away, but for now nobody was outside. He twisted round to check on Siobhan and found her huddled on the back seat. Her side barely rose and fell: she was breathing easier than before, so perhaps her lung hadn't collapsed, only been nicked. It was too dark to tell for sure, but he thought she'd bled a couple of quarts or more, and wasn't long for this world without immediate medical intervention. He'd lied about taking her to hospital and she'd known it; he wouldn't bother trying to convince her with any other lies. He ignored her; instead he checked the pistol he'd found. As with driving, he could use a firearm, he simply preferred not to. However, logic and

pragmatism sometimes trumped his preferences. The gun was a
Glock 19. He'd fired one before and knew that with a standard
magazine he could expect fifteen rounds. He didn't know if the
brothers had used the gun during what he took was some kind of
feud with Grey and Villere. He ejected the mag and saw it was
full. A controlled working of the slide also showed a bullet nestled
in the chamber. Good enough: if he'd estimated correctly, then it
allowed for two shots apiece to those that might join in the fight.
The others he was happy to beat down with whatever impromptu
weapon came to hand. Speaking of which . . .

He got out of the car, and stayed a moment hunched over at
the open door. From there he reached in and snagged the crate of
bottles. He uncapped one and a brief sniff told him all he needed
to know about the liquid's combustibility. He emptied one bottle
over the passenger seat and another on the floor. Next he drew
open the back door and manhandled Siobhan out: he set her down
in the snow. She murmured her thanks, misunderstanding his
intentions. He felt at her waist and found her belt. He unclipped
it and worked it free from under her clothes. She mewled slightly,
trying to push his hands away, as if he was some sicko trying to
cop a feel. She didn't fully wake, delirious now from blood loss.
He picked her up as he had before, one arm under her knees, one
around her back. Her hair got in his mouth and he spat it out. He
set her in the car, in the driver's seat he'd vacated. He placed her
hands together and then cinched them to the steering wheel
with her belt. The seat belt held her upright, but her head lolled
between her forearms.

He set aside a couple of the Molotov cocktails, but then emptied
more of them in the back and even over Siobhan. Her hair dripped
gasoline. She choked on the fumes, but without reviving from her
swoon. He leaned in again and knocked the car out of gear. He
turned on the ignition and the engine grumbled. He placed
Siobhan's foot on the clutch, and shoved the stick shift into first
gear. It was all he'd need. Gently he lifted her foot clear and set
it instead so her toe barely rested on the gas pedal. The car began
a faster than expected crawl forward. He wrenched at the steering
wheel, turning the car as it emerged from hiding and he aimed it
towards the open entrance to the multi-storey parking garage.
Siobhan murmured and her head rose slightly. If she understood
what was going on she didn't possess the strength to fight back.

Harper grabbed what he needed, then strode alongside the moving car. He'd discovered cigarette lighters in the crate and now lit one. He aimed it at the fuse inserted in the neck of one of the bottles he'd set aside and immediately that it caught he tossed it inside the car. He kicked the door shut and darted aside. He could no longer see Siobhan for the boiling flames.

THIRTY-NINE

Tess wanted to tend Po's wounds before seeing to hers. She had benefitted from the administrations of Felicity and Ellie, and although some blood had seeped through the bandage, she didn't believe the injury had grown worse. On the other hand, her man's wounds were fresher and hadn't as much as seen the lick of a damp cloth. When Harper launched his ambush outside the decommissioned quarry he'd fired through the body of the car at Po, and though he hadn't scored a direct hit, some shrapnel had torn furrows in his flesh. He bled and would probably go on bleeding for a while yet if she didn't staunch the flow and get it to coagulate.

'I'm fine, stop your fussin' will ya, gal?'

'Alex wasn't exaggerating when he said you're bleeding worse than a stuck pig. Come on over here and let me take a closer look at you.' Tess was beside a washbasin, running lukewarm water from the faucet. She had collected a wad of paper towels from a wall dispenser, which she ran under the trickle until they were dampened. 'Drop your pants,' she instructed.

'Ha! Any excuse to get me naked, huh?'

'Don't flatter yourself. Seeing your naked butt covered in cuts and blood doesn't get me amorous.'

'Dang, it never stopped you before.'

She shoved him playfully.

'Hey, one minute I'm being treated like the walking dead, next a sexual plaything, and now I'm to be pushed around?'

'Don't say I'm ever predictable,' she quipped. 'Come on, Po, lift up your shirt.'

He finally conceded. He doffed his leather jacket, laying it down on the floor. She pulled up his shirt, checking with an expert eye. By now his body was as familiar to her as it could get. She spotted abrasions, contusions and cuts. Some of the injuries were old enough that the surrounding skin had discolored; others were fresher. By the look of things, his fights with Bruce Harper had been seriously bruising. She dabbed at some of the bloody scrapes

with the towels, cleaning them, but almost immediately fresh beads
of blood seeped from the scratches. In his side there was a deep
groove from which blood had trickled down his hip and upper
thigh. His jeans were sopping.

'Looks as if you're going to need stitches,' she commented,
even as she leaned in and pressed the towels to his side.

He hissed and moved aside. 'Let it be, Tess. It hurts like a
sumbitch.'

'I don't believe it, my man actually admitting that he's in pain.'

'I never claimed to be indestructible.'

'How's your head?'

He cupped the back of his skull. 'Worse than my side.'

'Sit down.'

'Where? On the can?' He nodded at a row of stalls. There wasn't
room for them to maneuver if he sat on one of the toilets.

'At least prop your butt against the sink. I'd hate for you to get
light headed and fall over.'

'I ain't light headed.'

'You might be when I get you to bend forward.'

'Oh, right.' He did as asked, using the sink for support. Gripping
the edge with his left hand, he propped his other hand against his
right knee and then leaned down so that Tess could check the
damage to the base of his skull. The redhead, Siobhan, had given
him quite a hefty smack with the barrel of her pistol. Po kept his
hair cut short at the back. The flesh at his nape was swollen and
raw. A gouge from just behind his right ear extended past where
his skull met his spinal column. She delicately probed at the
damaged area, feeling him wince to each touch, but he didn't
vocalize his discomfort.

'I don't think you have any fractures, but I'm no expert. You'll
probably need an X-ray along with those stitches.'

He stood again and she studied him for any sign of wooziness.
He returned her perusal with a steady gaze. 'If my skull is fractured
and I'm bleeding on the brain, I think I'd know it by now.'

'Not necessarily.'

'It's been hours,' he reminded her, 'and I've had no hint of a
concussion. It hurts worse than a sumbitch, but I ain't out of the
game yet. I asked Alex to check on Ratcliffe. She took some
buckshot in the face, she probably needs a medic more than I do.'

'You know,' she said, 'the presence of all those other shooters proves there's more going on than we first thought. There's the guy Jake's brothers allegedly attacked and burned, and then those two women in the van that shot at Ratcliffe. Harper isn't just a murderer chasing a witness to stop her identifying him; he's one of several cleaning up shop to protect somebody else.'

'Yeah,' he agreed. 'I figured that the minute he showed up with that redheaded bitch, and I'm betting you did too. He's the killer, no doubt about it, but that motive for killing the family sounds like bullshit. Does he strike you as the disgruntled employee type? Even without a living witness, he was certain to be identified as the killer. Y'ask me, Tess, he's being paid richly for his services, enough for him to agree to take his earnings and skedaddle once the deed was done.'

'And the reason he chased Joanne so assiduously was because she could finger the one rewarding Harper,' Tess finished for him. 'If he goes to jail Harper doesn't get paid, and all of this will have been for nothing. Can only be one person, right?'

'Carl Blackhorse,' they said simultaneously.

'The grieving father and husband,' Tess said scornfully.

'If we're right, he's even more of a dirt bag than Harper. Let alone his wife, how could any man wish harm on his own babies? I swear to you, Tess, I'd kill myself sooner than lay a finger on you or my kids.'

'It's hard to fathom,' she agreed. 'And not something a decent person like you could ever contemplate.'

'Joanne's been fixated on Harper, but we could do with hearin' from her if we're on the right track before I shift all of my hatred off him and on to Blackhorse.'

'I've enough hatred for the both of them. In fact, count that bitch Siobhan in with them too.' She worked her hand inside its bandage. It was painful but nothing compared to the alternative if she'd failed to stop the knife intended for her womb.

Po tucked in the tail of his shirt and then stooped to retrieve his jacket.

'Your other wounds still need cleaning.'

'Later. For now, let's go confirm things with Joanne before the feds whisk her outta here.'

He'd made up his mind and from past experience she knew that haranguing him was pointless. She dumped the damp towels in a trashcan and followed as he exited the washroom into the police station. She spotted Pinky, standing in an open doorway with a large paper cup poised under his chin. She smelled strong coffee from across the hall, and was reminded how thirsty she was. She opened her mouth to ask where she could grab a cup, but her words were drowned under the high-pitched warble of an alarm. As did everyone in her vicinity, Tess stood, unsure what to do or where to go. A klaxon joined in, followed almost instantly by the ringing of an old-fashioned alarm bell. Lights flashed in warning. Then she was under no illusion: the building was on fire and they must evacuate.

'What the hell is this, man?' Po asked of nobody in particular.

Pinky said, 'Too timely to be a coincidence.'

'Don't tell me those stupid Wolsey brothers have chased us here? This is a police station, are they insane?' Tess's questions were rhetoric, but whom else would she associate a sudden fire with but the arsonists targeting her?

'I don't like this one bit,' said Po. Unconsciously he took Tess by her elbow and began steering her towards where they'd last seen Ratcliffe and Joanne. Tess worked out of his grip, capable of walking unassisted.

Pinky aimed a nod at nearby signage. 'Says the fire exits are over there.'

'We need to check on the others,' Po told him, 'then we'll leave together.'

'Nicolas, I get you, me, but Joanne's the cops' problem now. Our priority's getting out before we end up burned to ashes. Don't know about you, but I don't like the idea of a police station for my final resting place.'

Portland PD had taken charge of Joanne Mason, and protecting her was now their responsibility until she was handed over to the feds, or the cops traveling up from Massachusetts. But that was beside the point; until she was safely transported out of Portland Tess still felt a personal duty of care towards the young woman. Plus there was Detective Ratcliffe, and also her brother Alex to consider, both of whom Tess cared for. She'd hate to later find either had become trapped by a blaze that she could have helped them escape.

'You smell that?' Po asked.

'You don't mean this slop masquerading as coffee, do you?' asked Pinky as he set aside his cup.

'Smoke,' said Po.

'So this isn't a false alarm,' said Tess, equally needlessly.

'Couldn't say where it's originating. I think it's being carried in and coming through the air vents.'

Perhaps he was right. If the fire alarms had been tripped, she assumed that the doors were primed to close automatically to slow down the spread of a blaze. The fire doors would slow the smoke, but some would still find a way to them via ceiling voids and conduit and vent routes.

A police officer entered the corridor, heading towards them. He had a look of grim purpose on his face. Tess recognized him as one of the party that had met them outside. He signaled them to turn around. 'We have to evacuate,' he said, and ushered them to go back the way they'd just come.

'We need to check on the others,' Po said.

'No. You need to evacuate. Right now, sir.'

The cop continued to direct them towards the exit, arms out to his sides as if they might rush him and attempt to squeeze past. None of them was about to disobey him, besides, his demeanor left no room for argument.

'Where's Alex?' Tess asked the cop.

'Sergeant Grey's your brother, right?' The cop asked for confirmation. 'He's with that out-of-town officer and her sister.'

'The suspect we brought in,' said Po, meaning Jake Wolsey. 'It's probably his brothers who're responsible for this fire. They're the ones been setting half of Portland alight in the past twenty-four hours, stands to reason it's them again this time.'

The cop tapped the microphone clipped to his shirt, indicating from where he'd gotten his information. 'From what I heard, the fire's down in the parking garage. Car was driven inside on fire. Sounds like it was a suicide mission.'

'How's that?' asked Tess, though it was obvious. 'They're dead?'

'One unsub is. Can't be certain there isn't a second person, nobody can get close enough to confirm for the heat and smoke.'

'Jeez,' Tess wheezed. The length the Wolsey brothers were seemingly prepared to go for revenge was beyond madness. So much so that it felt *wrong*.

They passed under the sign that Pinky had previously pointed out. They found a space of about ten feet, faced by another door. This one led into a stairway with a short flight of steps to a final door secured by a push bar. Pinky was at the door first, so did the honors. He poked his head out, then glanced back. 'Takes us into a public plaza.'

'Yeah,' the cop confirmed, as they bustled out, 'whenever there's an evacuation we rally on the far side of the square.' He aimed a finger, as if it wasn't obvious where he meant. Already a couple of civilian staff had made their way to the prearranged fire point.

Tess asked, 'Where do other exits let out? Specifically, where will any detainees be brought out during an evacuation?'

'Usually into the parking garage and from there taken in a secure vehicle to another station.'

'And if that option isn't available to them because of where the fire is?'

'Then they'd use the side exit where we greeted you earlier, or through the main entrance on to this square.'

Tess looked for where she knew the entrance was and saw a uniformed officer emerge. They were unaccompanied. The officer moved across the plaza, heading to the rendezvous site. He was an older copy, carrying a paunch and silver hair. He spoke into his radio as he walked. She couldn't hear his words through the other cop's radio as he was wearing an earpiece to ensure communications were discreet. The cop answered, and the older one acknowledged them with a raised hand. Instantly Tess noted a change in the cop's demeanor. His face was pale to begin with, but all color drained out of him. She noted a look of consternation pass between the two cops and then the older, heftier man was jogging towards an access door into the parking garage.

'Go and wait over there,' the younger cop instructed and stabbed a hand at the rally point. 'Somebody will be there to check on you soon.'

Without another word to them, he ran a bit swifter than his colleague for the same access door.

Tess exchanged quizzical glances with Po and Pinky and saw that they'd even less intention of following evacuation protocol as she. Pinky, who'd put away his pistols drew one and offered it to Tess. She shook her head: she was still armed with Siobhan's pistol, having failed to turn it over as evidence yet. He didn't bother making the same offer to Po because he already knew the answer. Po had put aside his earlier hatred of his knife, and by instinct had dipped his knees and drawn it from his boot sheath.

There was muffled gunfire. They again glanced at each other, then in mutual agreement galloped across the plaza, in the opposite direction to the door the cops had just gone through.

A concrete arch gave access to a shadow-filled underpass, which opened on to a set of steps. On one side there was a steel-covered access door and another shorter flight of steps. These gave access to the road and also on to a ramp at the bottom of which was a roller shutter. Tess recognized the location where they'd first drawn up their vehicles to hand over Joanne and Jake Wolsey to the PD welcome party. The steel door had been open then and gave access to the station, but now it was resolutely shut having recently disgorged a mixed group of cops and civilians on to the street. Anyone evacuating under normal circumstances would have gone through the underpass and joined their colleagues on the plaza. But these were not normal circumstances.

Tess saw Detective Ratcliffe kneeling, her sidearm raised, but without a clear target because of a police van partially blocking the road. Ratcliffe shouted wordlessly, as did somebody beyond Tess's view. Another figure was on the ground, curled in a fetal position in snow that had been trodden to brown slush by many boots. They wore a helmet and Kevlar vest emblazoned with the POLICE logo, but Tess recognized the layers of clothing underneath and realized that the unthinkable had happened.

After everything they'd done to keep Joanne safe from Harper, his fiery diversion tactics had worked to lure her from safety and he'd gunned her down.

FORTY

S cant minutes earlier, Joanne would have sworn her ears were still ringing from the shotgun blasts fired from the van into her sister's car. She considered that she was lucky getting off so lightly, whereas Karen had been cut first by flying glass and then seconds later by buckshot. They'd both since thanked God that Karen ducked away at the opportune time to save her skull from being blown apart, and only gotten a few ricocheted balls of lead shot in her cheek. One or two had also skimmed her jaw and some her scalp. The thick lenses of Karen's glasses had saved her eyesight. Joanne had heard guns before but never as close as they'd been discharged from the van, and was surprised by how compressed her hearing had been since. She'd tried pinching her nose and blowing out her cheeks, but had failed to equalize the pressure. There was an underlying ringtone, one that suddenly warbled, and several seconds later began to ring like a turn-of-the-twentieth-century fire engine. It took several more seconds before clarity struck and she separated her enforced tinnitus from the alarms wailing throughout the police station.

Ratcliffe stood slowly from the chair she'd sank into on entering the room. She gripped the arms of the chair for stability, knuckles pronounced and stark white beneath her skin. She looked to Sergeant Alex Grey for answers, even as Joanne grabbed for her sister's arm. 'Please tell me you have a fire drill scheduled?'

She was being sarcastic and Alex knew it. He didn't reply, only rushed to the door and opened it. He looked into the corridor. The two officers guarding the room turned to him for direction, but he was as lost as anyone else.

Ceiling warning lights began to strobe.

'This is *not* a drill,' he emphasized.

Joanne didn't hear the instructions he gave his men, because she was too intent on begging answers from her sister, who, under those circumstances she thought of as Detective Ratcliffe. Surely her sister knew what was going on and what they should do during a dilemma such as this one.

'I don't know, Jo, so give me a break, for God's sake!' Karen responded. She sounded angry, but Jo knew her big sister was stressed, so she didn't pay her tone any mind.

Together they moved towards Alex. He hadn't gone beyond the threshold of the room yet. Joanne heard the two officers rush away, probably with instructions to help with an evacuation of station personnel. They too should leave but Alex blocked their passage.

'Let me confirm what's going on first,' Alex asked. 'This could be a false alarm.'

'We both know it isn't,' said Karen.

'Just give me a minute to find out. Don't worry, you're safe here for now.'

Alex had previously explained that the room he'd chosen to keep Joanne safe was an excellent choice. It had no windows and only one door, on which he'd doubled the guard. To get to the room, any intruder must first pass through the front public areas, and into the office block used exclusively by PD staff. The station wasn't designed to hold prisoners, and only had the minimum two cells required for male and female detainees, and those were very rarely used. He didn't deem the lockups suitable accommodation for her, not now he knew she was innocent of the horrible crimes she'd originally been accused. She dreaded to think where she'd have been held had he not had his mind changed. The room was comfortable enough, though airless. It was warm, and at first she'd been thankful, but then it had grown stuffy. She couldn't wait to leave it, but not exactly under these circumstances.

'Come with me,' said Alex.

'We're right behind you,' said Karen, and Joanne was alarmed when her sister drew her sidearm. She'd claimed not to have any answers, but her cop intuition must've been working on overdrive.

Alex took them along the corridor and through a door. Immediately they turned right and into a squad room. Jo pictured all those movies where a gruff desk sergeant and even gruffer captain snapped orders and instructions to a bunch of laconic or sarcastic patrol officers. In those movies, cops sprawled in chairs or sat on the edges of desks eating last night's pizza. Here she found a neat, ordered room. At one corner there was an array of computers. In the opposite corner there was a door. It accessed an adjacent equipment storage room. Alex went to a rack and pulled free vests for both his wards.

'Here,' he said, 'put these on.'

Karen nodded at the idea and took one from him, but she turned to Joanne with it and began helping her into the unfamiliar vest. Joanne had seen cops wearing identical vests since arriving there, but without considering how heavy and cumbersome they were. Modern cops wore armor that had to be both stab and ballistic proof. Without asking for approval first, Karen also reached for a helmet and settled it on Joanne's head. 'Kevlar,' she explained. 'It will stop a bullet to your skull but not so much your face. So keep your chin down, sis, and let me lead you out.'

Once Joanne was suitably attired, Karen took the second vest and pulled into it. She cinched the Velcro straps tightly, but the vest looked bulky and ill-fitting compared to Joanne's, due to a combination of Karen's slighter frame and a vest built for a stockier person. She didn't bother with a helmet. Alex, it dawned on Joanne, was already equipped with a lightweight version of their vests, worn under his uniform shirt.

While they had been dressing, Alex had been communicating via his radio to officers elsewhere in the building. Using the briefest description possible he relayed that a person unknown had driven a burning car inside the building. Officers were fighting the flames, but were poorly equipped for the job. They must evacuate in case the entire building caught fire. He had already instructed Joanne's guards to go and evacuate Tess and her friends and also the detainee, Jake Wolsey, from lockup.

Joanne had reached a point where the sirens and klaxons were on the verge of melting her brain. She couldn't think straight, and gave in to Karen when her sister grasped her by the collar of her vest and bent her over at the waist. Alex led the way, while Karen sandwiched Joanne between them. Joanne stumbled along, eyes on the floor, keeping her chin tucked as Karen had warned.

Alex spoke into his radio, but Joanne couldn't hear the responses that went directly into his ear: even if she could have heard each word clearly, her mind was too frazzled to have made much sense of them. She put her entire trust in Karen and Alex, as she had earlier in the evening in Felicity and Ellie, and then in Tess and Po.

At one point she grew aware that other people had joined the exodus and she was clear enough in thought for a moment to take

in those moving in tandem with her. Two armed officers similarly
sandwiched the detainee, Jake, controlling him more roughly than
either of her protectors did her. Joanne thought she possibly wasn't
the only one who thought his siblings must have something to do
with the attack.

They came to a halt.

'You OK, sis?' Karen asked.

'I think so,' Joanne croaked. 'What's going on?'

'I've ordered a van to be brought around,' Alex explained. 'I'm
having you taken across town to the sheriff's office. They have a
fully secure jail facility, with deputies and corrections officers who
can ensure your safety. I'll make arrangements for the feds to meet
us there instead.'

'You understand this move is designed to force us out into the
open, right?' said Karen.

'I know, but the alternative is succumbing to smoke inhalation
or the fire. I don't know about you, detective, but I'd rather we
try to get Joanne out of here than get barbecued.'

'Let me assure you, I'm all for leaving,' said Karen. Next she
leaned close to Joanne, speaking loud enough for her to hear
despite the padded helmet muffling her words. 'Next bit is going
to be the scariest bit, sis. Just do as I say, move when I tell you
and don't look up. Got it?'

'Got it,' Joanne agreed, although there was nowhere else she'd
rather be than going outside the station and into the reach of Harper
again.

They waited, uneasy. Jake must have said something unpopular
to his guards because one of the cops shouldered him into a wall,
warning him gruffly about making any more stupid threats.

'It isn't a threat,' Jake snapped in return. 'It's the truth. My
brothers won't abandon me, they'll burn down this entire city
before they'll let you take me in. Look at what they've done here,
to a fucking police station.' He laughed, a cackle tinged with
insanity.

'I hope it is your pathetic brothers waiting for us when we go
outside,' said Alex Grey. 'They're far preferable to the alternative,
I've heard.'

'You don't know who you're messing with,' Jake crowed. 'We
stick together, us Wolsey brothers. You mess with one, you mess
with us all.'

'That right? Well, there's three of you but I've got the bigger gang,' said Alex with a smirk. After that he ignored Jake completely and concentrated on protecting Joanne. He made them move to a set of double doors. When the fire alarms had activated, a magnetic sensor had flipped and the doors had shut, a barrier against smoke and flame. On the far side the corridor was filled with wreaths of smoke. 'We can't go that way, back up. Take the side exit.'

He slipped past Karen, then put a comforting hand on Joanne's shoulder, helping to guide her. 'I was going to take you out through the basement with the roller shutter doors and directly into the back of the van. We can't do that now. We have to use the door we originally brought you in. Do you remember, there are some steps down to the road? That's where you'll be most vulnerable, so trust in us and just keep moving.'

'I trust you all,' she confirmed.

'I think you're a bunch of losers,' said Jake Wolsey, to a snapped response from one of his guards. He jeered at the cop.

'We should leave you behind to roast, see if you appreciate it then,' the cop growled.

'That's enough of that talk,' said Alex.

He had a duty of care for his detainee as much as he had for her, Joanne assumed.

He pointed the way for Joanne and Karen, then moved forward a body length to a door. It had a rocker switch that opened the locks. He held the door until the women were through, then handed over to the cops leading Wolsey. A steel door with a push handle release faced them.

'OK,' said Alex and placed his fist against her vest over her sternum, so that Joanne could move no further forward. Behind her the others bustled in the tight space. He checked over his radio that the van was waiting and must've received confirmation. 'Once I open the door, we move quickly and silently. Down the steps and into the van, we got it?'

'I understand,' Joanne confirmed. Except her legs had suddenly turned to water and she doubted she would traverse the steps without them giving under her. Maybe Karen sensed her sudden fear because she leaned in and hugged her around the shoulder: there was more about physical support than affection in the gesture.

'A few more seconds is all,' Karen said. 'You're being very brave, sis. I love you.'

'Love you, too,' Joanne said and couldn't help the awful sense that they were saying their final goodbyes.

'OK, head down and don't stop,' said Alex.

He pushed open the groaning door and checked outside. He must have been given the all clear, because he drew his sidearm and then proceeded further; he waved the women out after him. Karen guided Joanne again, with one hand on her vest's stiff collar. She held her pistol in her other hand. Joanne's feet skimmed the concrete surface, barely feeling it underfoot. Then she stumbled down the steps, heels bumping on the edges of the risers: she was never in any danger of falling, being fully supported by Alex in front and Karen behind. Ahead, in the surprisingly bright glare of halogen light the police van waited. Its back doors were open, bench seats set to accommodate both her and the detainee. Its driver watched their approach, his weapon drawn. Another cop had his back to them, watching the street. Joanne was seconds at most from the safety of the van and there was no hint of outside trouble, but each second also felt so elongated they each could last a lifetime.

One second.

Two seconds.

Three. And Alex stepped aside to allow her to clamber on the step into the van, Karen assisting.

She felt the impacts before she heard the gunfire.

She was punched in the chest and abdomen and then the world span away from her and she crashed down on the sidewalk, slushy snow invading her helmet, getting in her eyes. Karen screeched something, her voice sounding alien due to heightened anxiety. Her sister knelt on her, forcing her down.

In the next few seconds Joanne had no sense of who went where, or did what. All she knew was that she was hit, possibly dying and there was nothing anyone could do to change that. Voices melded together in a cacophony, gunfire was at once incredibly loud and then muffled by distance. Earlier her hearing had been affected by the gunfire, now it was affected once more. Conversely it undid whatever had compressed her eardrums earlier, and now it was as if explosions resounded within the confines of the Kevlar helmet. It didn't occur that those were bullets ricocheting off it.

FORTY-ONE

I t was one thing being licensed to carry a firearm, quite another to use it to kill another human being. As a sheriff's deputy, firearms discipline had been drummed into Tess to a point where she was sometimes reluctant to draw her service weapon if another option presented first. Not shooting when confronted by a deranged gas station robber had almost cost her a hand and Tess had not fully learned her lesson. There had been times on cases with Po and Pinky where she should have shot a perp before the situation escalated to where it had, placing herself in needless peril. But how could she act beyond the line that she'd morally drawn in the sand? It was one thing claiming in hindsight that shooting somebody was the correct course; another when it meant their deaths would rest uneasily in her dreams forever. Tess didn't deem killing anyone lightly, however heinous the enemy. Perhaps it was a personal failing, but it was one she'd gladly accept because it showed she wasn't a cold, emotionless person. However, when her loved ones were threatened she had no qualms about defending them with lethal force.

When she saw Joanne Mason on the ground, Detective Ratcliffe kneeling over her, trying to save her sister, a similar instinct washed over Tess. Alex was a cop, but first and foremost he was her brother, and she'd be damned if she'd let anyone hurt him if she could stop them. She ignored Po's request for her to stay clear of the fight, and immediately went after him and Pinky as they rushed to assist the downed women. Tess danced down the slick steps, and then jogged, bent over at the waist for where Alex had gone down to his knees in the slush. He had one hand clutched to his side, while his other hand groped for his pistol where he'd dropped it. His face was pale in the wash of a halogen light. Two more cops struggled with Jake Wolsey, who had taken the opportunity of the ambush to break free from his captors. He was cuffed, but it didn't seem to occur to him that he was struggling against the inevitable. They dragged him backwards, intent on taking him back up the stairs and maybe into the plaza. Another cop lay face down on the sidewalk, shot from behind by a psychopath and coward. One last officer hollered instructions from beside the van at an unknown assailant. They exchanged gunfire. The cop had nowhere to go but crouch beside the van's wheel, but Tess was horrified to hear that the return fire was from an angle where the van couldn't protect him.

Tess grasped Alex's shirt and pulled him down. He was stunned, face strained by a grimace of pain. He immediately grabbed his gun. His hand came away from his side, slick with blood, but he worked the pistol perfunctorily, checking it wasn't compromised from falling in the snow.

'Tess,' he acknowledged, 'thanks.'

'Thank me after I've saved your flabby ass.'

She hooked her arms under his armpits, taking care where she placed the pistol, and then crabbed sideways with him. She grunted at the effort. Alex helped, butt-walking and digging in with his heels. She pulled him on to the sloping ramp, and out of the immediate line of fire.

She helped him gain a knee once more.

'Flabby ass?' he asked.

'OK, I was out of order, but you are heavier than me.'

'Tell me that again in a few more months when your ass is bigger than two beach balls.'

They dropped the teasing. She pressed fingers to his side and they came away bloody. 'You're hit.'

'Yes. Don't know how bad, but I ain't dead yet.'

'Jeez,' she said, 'you're beginning to sound as pithy as Po can.'

Gunfire came in a slow tattoo.

Pinky was firing in tit-for-tat response to whoever had sprung the ambush. Whoever? Who was she kidding? There was only one scenario and it had nothing to do with the Wolsey brothers.

'Where's Harper. Have you had eyes on him?'

'No. He fired at Joanne, then dropped Desoto and Billings. He's taken cover across the street, but I couldn't swear where.'

'There's only one shooter, right?'

'Appears so. I don't think you need worry about that redhead anymore, cause they're pretty sure it's her sitting behind the wheel of the burning car.' He tapped his earpiece to indicate where he'd gotten that fresh information. 'Before you ask, I couldn't swear if any of the others are with Harper, but for now I'd guess he's alone.'

'He's dangerous enough alone. Are Desoto and Billings dead?'
He squeezed his eyelids tight. 'I sure hope not.'

'But we have to assume they're out of action. That leaves how many?'

'There's Collins, but I don't think he's in much better shape than the rest of us.' Collins, she thought, was the cop taking cover by the van. Alex grabbed for his radio and pressed a button. Throughout Portland an 'officer in need of assistance' alarm would sound out to all available police. 'Officers down, officers down,' he transmitted and gave the street location. Everyone available would drop whatever they were doing and respond on lights and sirens. Unfortunately before reinforcements could join them, there could be more casualties. It wasn't in her nature to sit on her thumb and wait for somebody else to come and save them.

Boots scuffed through the slushy snow. Tess knew it was Pinky helping Ratcliffe drag Joanne to the relative safety the slope offered. His broad back was bent, his backside shuddering with each step. Joanne was a dead weight even for Pinky.

'Where's Po?' she asked.

'Out there,' said Pinky as he helped Ratcliffe set Joanne down. 'I'm going after him.'

'Not alone, you're not.'

'Tess, are you in a fit state, you? I mean . . .'

'I know exactly what you mean, but if Po's going after Harper, then he needs me. Jeez, Pinky, is he even armed?'

'Only with that toothpick knife of his.'

A pang shot through her bandaged hand at the memory of what damage that toothpick could do, but she also knew it was wholly ineffective against a gunman, let alone one as physically powerful as Harper.

She hoisted up Siobhan's pistol. Whatever had brought the woman to her fiery end must've been awful, and still Tess could find no pity for her. Still, she thanked the redhead for the gift of the gun. She checked on Joanne, found her blinking up from the ground through startled eyes, and trusted her into the keeping of Ratcliffe and Alex. Her brother, bleeding from his side, was back in control of his body and determined to protect the young woman. From the ramp, he and Ratcliffe could drop Harper if he tried anything as stupid as charging across the open street.

It struck Tess that the gunfire had ceased.

It wasn't necessarily a good sign, but it gave a window through which she and Pinky could go to help her man.

Alex shouted at her to stop, but she didn't. She'd helped one loved one, now she must do the same for another. She followed Pinky, but they moved apart so that they didn't form a single target. While they covered for him, Officer Collins retreated from the van, joining the others on the ramp. Tess spotted a splash of blood where the cop had initially taken cover. The other two cops had disappeared with Jake Wolsey, and anyone else in uniform was down, perhaps permanently. A boom sounded from the direction of the parking garage, the car's fuel tank exploding. Instinctively she ducked, even though there was scant reason.

Pinky moved obliquely to her. He'd taken out both pistols. One of them she assumed was on the verge of depletion by now, and the other was held in reserve. As one magazine emptied, he'd swap the pistols around so there was no break in his rhythm.

Opposite the station there were several buildings housing banks and other services. They were arranged about a horseshoe-shaped plaza not unlike the one the police station was built around, though smaller. A series of wide steps gave access to the plaza, and to each side there were terraced flowerbeds currently devoid of flora but still containing hardier shrubs and trees. The snow had blanketed them and made them a formidable barricade from where the gunman had shot from concealment. Things had changed since he'd launched his sneak attack on Joanne and the others, Harper abandoning his position in favour of flight now that he believed Joanne dead. He hadn't gotten far before Po had caught him and launched on to the big man's back.

Tess had no idea how long they'd been fighting, but it appeared again that Po's knife wasn't as ineffective as Pinky had made it sound, because Harper was bleeding from several wounds on his shoulders and upper chest. His gun was still in hand, but he wasn't trying to shoot Po, he used it to hammer backwards at Po's face, trying to knock her man loose. Po gritted his bloody lips and held on tightly, stabbing down again with his knife into the giant's flesh.

Harper went down, skidding in the blood-flecked snow, but it saved him a final stab to the neck. Po spilled loose and rolled in the snow. Harper scrambled, grasping at the edge of a raised flowerbed for stability. He used it to haul forward on his knees, until momentum helped him find his feet once more. Po too had gotten his feet under him and twisted around to confront the brute. Harper aimed a kick at him with a tombstone-sized boot. It found Po's midriff. Po gasped, clutched at his belly, and in that moment Harper raised the gun and this time did point it at her fiancé's head. During the other ambush, he'd aimed similarly at Po with a revolver, not a Glock, and the hammer had fallen on an empty shell casing; this time there'd be no mistake, considering he must've been saving a bullet for such an opportunity.

Back in the barn, when Harper was likewise on the verge of maiming or killing Po, she'd been unsteady and weak, and her shots had flown astray. Her hand was steady this time, and she didn't flinch from killing the man about to kill Po. She fired the gun, hearing an echo as Pinky also unloaded on the giant. Neither of them missed.

But the damned giant stayed upright.

The bullets striking him had done more immediate damage mentally than to his flesh. Po capitalized on the moment while the giant stood in shocked silence. He grabbed Harper's pistol with one hand, yanking it aside, even as he plunged in with his blade. It slid through the soft skin under Harper's chin and, once in deep enough, Po wrenched with a bent elbow and opened his windpipe. Blood gouted from Harper's throat. He let go of the pistol, now firmly gripped by its barrel by Po, and stumbled backwards. Both his hands cupped his wound, but couldn't contain the volume of blood pouring from him. He turned, shocked that he was not as indestructible as his exploits had fooled him into thinking, and stared wide-eyed at where Tess and Pinky stood with their pistols raised still.

He mouthed something, but there was no way of hearing what he said as Tess again fired a volley of bullets, this time dead center to his exposed heart. Harper sat down abruptly. His hands fell from his throat. This time she was confident he was dead.

AFTER . . .

Months passed before Po fully recovered from his battles with Bruce Harper. The third time was often the charm, and it had proven true again that it was during their third physical confrontation that he'd finally beaten his nemesis, but it had come at a price paid in broken bones, contusions and smashed teeth. After Harper's ambush outside the decommissioned quarry, Po hadn't confessed to how hurt he was from the shrapnel and bullet wounds, so he'd gone into that final battle at only about sixty per cent his norm. He'd fought tooth and nail, and it was perhaps a blessing that Harper's madness had convinced him he could kill Po without resorting to shooting him as he had the police and Joanne. He'd kept one bullet in reserve, but Tess and Pinky had thwarted him from executing Po at the end. After taking a hellacious beating to his head with the gun barrel, and a kick to the gut he was certain had burst something important inside, Po had opened Harper's throat, admittedly a horrible deed, but one he didn't regret. After Tess finally slew the brute with the heart shots, Po had sunk down into the dirty snow and lain there gasping like a landed trout until an ambulance arrived to whisk him to hospital. He didn't recall what had happened in the hours afterwards, but he'd wakened the following day and discovered he'd undergone surgery to fix a broken arm and several other wounds, but thankfully his spleen hadn't been ruptured as initially feared. He'd peed blood for a couple of days afterwards. His lips were split, and five of his teeth broken, two of them unable to be saved. The wound to his side had severed a tendon and made walking without limping nigh on impossible for a while, but he'd gotten over it and walked with his usual languid gait after many weeks.

As he'd gotten more mobile, Tess had grown rounder and less nimble. She was glad. Her wounded hand required minor surgery, but it was nowhere near as bad as the injury that had ended her career with the sheriff's office, and healed without any complications within a few weeks. Siobhan had come close to murdering her child in her womb, but failed. Her final trimester had passed without any major hitch, the baby growing and getting stronger day by day, and in the end was eager to meet her parents. Their baby girl was born three days earlier than originally expected, and she'd the pale skin and white blonde hair of her mother, but her dad's expressive turquoise eye colouring.

Alex Grey survived the gunshot wound to his side. He got married to Emma Clancy, Tess's sometimes boss, and now, sister-in-law, and they would become a wonderful uncle and aunt to Felicity Ellie-Jo Villere.

Those she was named after had all kept in touch with Tess, the two elderly sisters acting as if they might be ideal fairy godmothers, and if ever she required a nanny then Joanne Mason would be her go to. Joanne had survived being shot by Harper, the anti-ballistic quality of the vest given to her by Alex doing its job. She'd been winded, and shocked, and overwhelmed by the ambush she had fainted, but had fully recovered in the days following. Her sister Karen Ratcliffe's injuries required medical attention, but she hadn't left Joanne's side until she was safely in the protection of the FBI. Joanne's testimony had gone on to help prove Carl Blackhorse was the architect of Bruce Harper's murder spree. His alibi of betting at an Atlantic City casino while his wife and her children were murdered didn't save him. Under interrogation, Blackhorse had admitted that his greed was exponentially greater than his love for Lacey and his stepchildren. Learning of Lacey's plans to divorce him, and take half of everything he owned, he'd promised Harper and others in his employment rich reward should one of them do away with his problem for him. It came with the caveat that they would probably have to flee the country afterwards, but that wasn't a deterrent to people like Harper, Monk, Lyman or Carson – all of whom he named as person's intent on claiming the prize he'd subsequently placed on Joanne Mason's head – but oddly enough he hadn't named Siobhan Doyle in that category of scum. He said she was a lowly driver that Harper had pressed into his service and most likely against her will. Hearing this about Siobhan did change Tess's feelings towards the woman who'd almost murdered her child, but only by a tiny degree.

Joanne was totally exonerated, the hateful Angel of Death tag finally struck from her name.

So too was her sister, Ratcliffe, who first faced charges for harboring and assisting a felon. Those accusations couldn't stand after Joanne was named a victim and star witness in the trial that sent hedge fund billionaire Carl Blackhorse to jail for the remainder of his life, and also earned Lyman and Carson jail sentences for their part in the conspiracy to murder, and in their part in the failed ambush on the convoy in Portland. John Corbett Monk and Siobhan Doyle were posthumously named as conspirators. Harper was named the undeniable killer, and footage discovered on a computer hard drive snatched from a gas station in northern Maine also identified him as the murderer of an innocent war veteran and his son: unbeknown to all, Siobhan had not gotten rid of the evidence as instructed by Harper and had left it in her SUV when abandoning it at the quarry in the hope it would be found and Harper punished. Had she known this Tess might have forgiven the woman one more iota.

Perhaps Harper suspected that Siobhan intended fingering him for the crime, and it could go some way to explaining why he'd treated her so awfully in the last moments of her life. Locking her inside the burning vehicle was unnecessarily cruel but by then it was assumed that the maniac was drunk on murder and violence and enjoyed the creativity of it after stealing the car from the arsonists he'd beaten to death. Somewhere along the line, somebody let slip that Harper prided himself on functioning on logic, but there was absolutely no logic in his subsequent assault on the police station. He intended forcing Joanne outside, and his plan worked, putting her in his sights but how could he ever logically believe that he could defeat the numbers of cops and civilians prepared to defend her. He must not only have been drunk on murder, he had to have been plastered.

Jake Wolsey was jailed for his part in the arson attacks on Tess and Po's property. He was the youngest of the trio of brothers, and had been given the tasks of getaway driver or watcher by the older siblings. He had not lit any fire and despite discharging a weapon at Pinky Leclerc had caused no actual harm: he got off lightly compared to what his brothers suffered at Harper's hands and feet. Both Jake and his mother Carol had been shown leniency, given allowance to attend the funerals of Aaron and James – both brothers' remains were cremated during a private ceremony – before they were returned to prison, in Carol's case to the prison infirmary where further skin grafts were scheduled. Despite the severity of her burns her surgeons had saved her hands from amputation.

After months bunking in with Tess and Po at the ranch, Pinky moved to a loft conversion above a warehouse on the waterfront overlooking the Fore River. His closest neighbors were chain hotels and the Casco Bay ferry terminal. Tess's old apartment on Cumberland Avenue had been comfortable but admittedly his new place enjoyed better views. He had only left the ranch because Tess wanted the spare room ready for their baby girl and who was he to deny her. Anne Ridgeway finally retired: she intimated to Tess that she only kept the curios shop as it was never too busy and allowed her plenty of reading time. She decided she could actually read her novels anywhere she wished to.

Bar-Lesque had been badly singed, but was up and running again in no time, under management of Jazz Reed and Chris Mitchell as before. As for Charley's, Po invested in a new purpose-built autoshop and of course named the old man head mechanic. He was able to re-employ all his former workers, plus specialists able to restore vintage and classic model vehicles to their former glory and beyond. Po drove the Kia Telluride, but it wasn't to say he didn't love a muscle car, and despite what he'd said to Pinky and Tess about the Mustang being unsuitable as a family car, he soon purchased and initiated restoration of a gold and black 1970 Chevrolet Chevelle SS L56, with cash from the insurance pay out. Tess couldn't begrudge her man this small pleasure; she'd domesticated him as far as she would and secretly hated the idea of him growing settled, bored and boring. A lasting change she did press him into was getting rid of the knife in his boot.

AUTHOR'S NOTE

To add verisimilitude to the adventures of Tess Grey and Nicolas 'Po' Villere, I have given them a real world setting. I've tried to stay true to Portland, Maine and other localities featured in their adventures, but always in the understanding that the stories and the locations are completely fictitious or used fictitiously. At times I've played loose and free with the law enforcement departments and characters featured in the books, but it is always with full respect and admiration of the tough job that these public servants do. Any mistakes are mine, sometimes accidentally but also occasionally made deliberately to assist the flow of the narrative, and mostly because I'm a storyteller who makes things up for a living. Thank you for reading; I hope it was time well spent.

Matt Hilton